Murder
at an
Irish Castle

Murder
at an
Irish Castle

AN IRISH CASTLE
MYSTERY

Ellie Brannigan

CROOKED
LANE

NEW YORK

Published in the United States by Crooked Lane Books, an imprint of The Quick Brown Fox & Company LLC.

Crooked Lane Books and its logo are trademarks of The Quick Brown Fox & Company LLC.

Library of Congress Catalog-in-Publication data available upon request.

ISBN (trade paperback): 978-1-63910-258-7
ISBN (ebook): 978-1-63910-259-4

Cover illustration by Olivia Holmes

Printed in the United States.

www.crookedlanebooks.com

Crooked Lane Books
34 West 27th St., 10th Floor
New York, NY 10001

First Edition: April 2023

10 9 8 7 6 5 4 3 2 1

This book is dedicated to
my grandmother, Sunny (Elsie) Brannigan,
a strong woman with an amazing sense
of adventure. I love you!

Chapter One

Santa Monica, California
Tuesday, June 1

Rayne McGrath cracked an eye at the intrusive sunshine streaming through the glass of her twentieth-floor condo and immediately regretted the action. Agony started as a tiny pinprick and then pinballed throughout the rest of her head.

"Maybe I shoulda skipped that last birthday shot at midnight." Her stomach churned in agreement. She shoved back her silk sheets and kicked her feet free of the tangled mess.

"You only turn thirty once," she mocked herself, regretting her confidence of the evening before. "If I live to see the rest of the day, it'll be a miracle."

However, remembering what the magical day held in store banished all lingering effects of the top-shelf Irish whiskey.

Rayne cautiously focused on the sway of palm trees outside the windows, catching a glimpse of coconuts at her eye level. The turquoise ocean in the distance was as bright as the azure sky. The soft white of the clouds was the base shade for her wedding gowns, and she dabbled with nature's palette for her satin trims.

Her designs had prompted a power lunch today with a banking firm about Modern Lace Bridal Boutique, the company she owned with her partner and boyfriend, Landon Short. Rayne hoped an investment might be on the menu, right next to dessert. Thirty was the beginning of the rest of her glorious life.

"Good-bye, miserable twenties," Rayne said aloud as she entered the kitchen of her spacious one-bedroom and chose a double espresso for her Keurig. She'd worked around the clock at her sewing machine and design boards to build her elite clientele, one bride at a time, until Landon. "Hello, success and happiness!"

She wandered barefoot to her room and checked her phone charging on her nightstand, expecting a message from Landon. He was handsome, funny, creative, and crazy about her, just like she was crazy for him.

Nothing. Nothing from her mom yet either.

There was a notification from a UK number she didn't recognize. Probably her uncle Nevin, on her father's side, to wish her a happy birthday. Sweet. Her dad had died when she was twelve, and she still missed him terribly. Would Conor McGrath be proud of the woman she'd become? His smile, his approval, was a big part of her internal decision-making process.

Dad would have urged her to enjoy the extra shot of Jameson.

"Today is your birthday," she sang to her image in the mirror, carefully applying makeup after her shower. This lunch had the power to launch their boutique brand to major department stores all over the world. Rayne smoothed her long black hair into a classic chignon, smudged charcoal powder beneath her gray eyes, and pursed her lips in a kiss. A dove-gray sleeveless sheath completed her chic ensemble.

Rather than being freaked out by the death of her twenties, Rayne felt empowered by all that was possible in this next decade. Leaving her condo, she rode the elevator to the marble-tiled lobby.

"Happy birthday, Rayne," Kendra, the receptionist, called.

"Thank you!" Head high, Rayne strode out the glass door—held open by a security guard, who also wished her a happy birthday—to the sunny parking lot, where a valet had brought around her leased Mercedes convertible. She slid behind the wheel and cranked Spotify on the radio as she eased into traffic toward LA and Rodeo Drive.

The second song on her and Landon's playlist had just ended when her cell phone rang, and she answered via Bluetooth. "Jenn!"

Jenn, her best friend since middle school, shouted, "Happy birthday, Rayne!"

"Thanks, hon—but you just saw me last night for drinks." They'd had a lot of fun with her other girlfriends, dancing and partying away the last night of Rayne being twenty-nine.

"I just wanted to wish you luck today. You and Landon deserve this opportunity more than anybody else I know. Each sketch of a Modern Lace gown is done by you. Did you bring your portfolio?"

"You know I did!" Her sketch pad never left her tote bag. "You're the sweetest, Jenn." Rayne couldn't stop grinning. She imagined the bankers in power suits offering her and Landon an astronomical sum as they gushed over the profit potential, then a celebratory dinner later, alone with Landon and a bucket of champagne. She'd kept the evening free for her boo.

She was hopeful that there would be even more to celebrate and glanced at her manicured but naked ring finger. This could be the night!

"This is your year, Rayne McGrath. You know I know these things."

Laughing, Rayne checked the side mirrors, signaled, and exited the freeway. For once the fender-to-bumper traffic didn't bother her. There was too much to be happy about. "You're right about fifty percent of the time, Jenn."

Jenn giggled. "Shoot me a text to let me know how the lunch goes, all right?"

"You got it. Bye!"

She ended the call with a press of a button on the steering wheel. Her car was the latest model. Image was everything in LA, and she and Landon, as marketing experts, lived accordingly.

They'd coordinated outfits to make a confident statement to the bankers. She would be in dove gray, and he'd be in coal with dove-gray piping on his suit. Landon was blond to her dark, and they made a striking pair when they went out together.

She had the niggling feeling that Landon never would have asked her out that night at the club a year ago if she hadn't been a complement to his carefully groomed image. She set that thought aside.

Rayne parked on a side street and walked to Modern Lace Bridal Boutique, their tiny but strategically located shop. Silhouettes of wedding gowns were painted on the front window, utilizing each inch of ad space on this prime shopping street.

She pulled out her glittery gold key fob and put the key in the lock—or tried to. It was jammed with something.

Ugh. Rayne took off her Chanel sunglasses and peered at what seemed to be a screw broken inside the lock. Vandals? She shaded her eyes and stared into the dim shop but couldn't see anything out of place.

The clothing stores on either side didn't open until ten. She and Landon had planned on meeting early, eight sharp, to rehearse last-minute details of the power lunch, and he wasn't here yet. With only a front entrance, they'd need to call a lock-smith to get inside.

She took out her cell phone and dialed his number. It went to voice mail. "Hey, babe. It's Rayne. We have a . . . situation."

Rayne paced the sidewalk, thinking he'd arrive any minute with lattes, ready to brainstorm. She spoke with a locksmith while she waited. Fifteen minutes passed, and she grew even more alarmed. Landon was never late. Half an hour? It was cause to worry.

The highways in LA were notorious for being death traps. Six months ago, Landon had been in an accident that had totaled his car. He'd been all right—a mild concussion—but talk about scary. Driving to work on these roads was like maneuvering through a live minefield.

"Can't just stand here," she muttered, feeling powerless. What if he was broken down somewhere?

She decided to drive to Landon's, taking the route he nor-mally would. Rayne kept dialing his number.

There was an accident on the side of the highway about half-way between Rodeo Drive and his place on the hill. She slowed but breathed out in relief when it was a black Nissan, not Land-on's BMW.

Rayne hurried toward his house, now afraid he'd overslept. He strove for perfection, and any mistake would set the wrong tone for their lunch. She pulled up in front of a modern two-bedroom bungalow with an attached carport. His car wasn't in the driveway.

She swallowed, and the action scratched her dry throat. After a sip from her water bottle, she climbed out of her Mercedes. Had he taken a different route to the boutique?

Knocking loudly on his front door, she said, "Landon? Lan, hon. I'm coming in."

He didn't answer, so she used the spare key from the fake rock by the planter and opened the door.

Her stomach tightened in a painful clench that made her gasp aloud.

Everything was gone. There wasn't even a dust bunny. His cleaner came every other Friday so his bachelor pad would be ready for the weekend. This was Tuesday. June 1. Her birthday.

"Landon?"

Rayne raced to his bedroom—their bedroom most of the time—but all that was left in the closet was hangers. No designer suits or Italian leather shoes. No toiletries in the bathroom. The house had been wiped clean, as if . . . he'd disappeared.

No. He wouldn't.

With a sick feeling, she walked to the kitchen and peered into the fridge. No champagne. No wine. No celebration to be had.

Empty.

Was this a bad dream?

In a fog, Rayne went out to the front stoop of Landon's vacant home and sat down next to the planter. She squeezed the key hard in her palm.

Her mind screeched to a halt.

No.

Rayne got out her cell phone, hoping this was a stupid practical joke—the kind he liked to play but she never found funny.

Her fingers shook as she logged in to their joint bank account for Modern Lace Bridal Boutique.

She wasn't surprised to see the balance was zero.

"Zero!" she shouted to the quiet neighborhood. "Out of a hundred and fifty grand, you didn't even leave a *dollar*?"

Her phone rang, and she gulped over the lump in her throat.

"Hellloo?" She prayed it would be Landon with an explanation and a camera crew, laughing at how he'd pranked her good.

"Happy birthday to you," her mother sang. Lauren McGrath, star of the long-running *Family Forever* sitcom, had a lovely voice and larger-than-life presence even over the phone. "Happy birthday, dear Rayne Claire McGrath, happy birthday to you!"

Rayne burst into sobs.

"What's wrong, love?" Lauren asked.

"Lauren. I . . . I . . . Landon's gone." Rayne had been taught to call her parents by their first names and use *Mom* or *Dad* only for the occasional endearment. It was a Hollywood thing. "He emptied the bank account." Rayne blinked away tears. "We had lunch with the bankers planned!"

"That *rat*!" Lauren exclaimed vehemently. She rarely cursed, as the woman she played on the sitcom was a devout Christian. "I never liked him, Rayne. You did all the work, and he took the credit. Where are you? I'll come right away."

"But you're at the studio." Rayne sucked in a deep breath. The tears, hot and humiliated, wouldn't stop their torrents down her cheeks. "The studio" meant everything else must wait until the day of shooting was over.

"I'll get a cab and drive you home. Let me tell Paul."

The producer would probably fall over at Lauren's unusual request. "Should I call the police?" Her brain couldn't fathom that Landon would treat her like this. Like a sucker. Like a, like a . . . She swiped her tears. Like someone he hated.

"You should, darling, because of the money missing. I'm sorry. I'm on my way. The address in the hills? Have an officer meet you there."

They each hung up.

With trembling fingers, Rayne dialed the police and reported a missing person. And her missing money. She didn't mention her birthday. The miraculous day was turning into a nightmare.

A trim policewoman in her forties arrived to take Rayne's statement. They stood on the stoop of Landon's bungalow. "Landon Short and I have a business together. The door of the boutique has a screw jammed in, and I couldn't get in this morning."

"The address?" Her tag read *Officer M. Peters*.

Rayne told the officer where the shop was located, unable to focus her thoughts. How could Landon do this to her? They were partners. Lovers. A team! They had a lunch planned that was going to take them to the next level and get her gowns in the top bridal stores.

"I'll check it out for you," Officer Peters said, her voice kind.

Within twenty minutes of Rayne's phone call, her mother arrived in a cloud of jasmine perfume, her designer sunglasses balanced perfectly on her slim nose. She was in her fifties and often turned heads.

The officer did a double take, but this was LA, so star sightings were common. Lauren McGrath was a beloved household figure.

"I'll head to the business address on Rodeo Drive and then file this report," Officer Peters said. "And be in touch with any questions, or information, regarding Landon Short."

"Thank you," Rayne said.

"Darling!" Lauren scooted past the policewoman to gather Rayne into a hug. "Can the police get your money back? It's not right that he absconded with it. What about the boutique, and inventory of gowns?"

Rayne easily carried a hundred thousand dollars in wedding dresses. Brides trusted her to have their gowns ready on their special day. She pressed her hand to her rolling stomach.

The officer lifted a groomed brow. "I will look into this right away."

"Should I go with you to the shop?" Rayne asked Officer Peters. "I couldn't get inside because of the vandalized lock. A screw was broken off in it."

"Oh no! I bet Landon stole the dresses too," her mom said.

"I hope not . . . I have three July brides wanting their gowns." Not counting the hours she'd spent working on the gorgeous dresses, they were crafted with silks and pearls. Luxury tailor-made for each woman.

"May I have the key? I'll try to open it for you, but it might be part of a crime scene," the officer said. "It's best to let us handle it."

Rayne gave the officer the shiny gold fob to Modern Lace.

Lauren peered into the vacant house. "Oh my goodness! It's been cleaned out by a professional service, I'd wager. He's probably skipped the country by now." She straightened and gave the policewoman a look of concern. "We did an episode where the criminal was found by his license plate. Landon drives a black BMW, Officer. Do you know the plate number, Rayne?"

"Uh, no." She didn't even know hers. "It's a lease."

Officer Peters made a note on her tablet. "Black BMW. Let's lock up the house and all leave together."

Rayne snorted—what was there to steal?—but did as the policewoman bade. She then returned the key to the fake rock. He'd taken everything. She couldn't make sense of it. Why? He'd said he loved her. They had plans for the future. Her heart was broken.

"I'll drive," Lauren said, after a scan of Rayne's face.

"All right." Rayne was in no condition to argue.

Her mother got behind the wheel of Rayne's car, and they followed the officer out of the neighborhood. Rayne's body quivered as she tried to hold herself together. She and Landon had discussed investment options. Outfits. Dialogue.

"I can't do the lunch with the bankers. I'll have to call it off. Oh God, Landon had their contact information. I . . . we . . . we were supposed to be a team. How could he do this to me, Mom?"

Her mother sniffed and patted Rayne's hand. "Let's get you home, and we can hash everything out. Did you check your personal bank account?"

Rayne, numb, shook her head. "There's not much in it anyway. A few hundred. I was a fool. We put everything into the business to attract the investors."

Her mom made a brief stop at a convenience store on the way to Rayne's condo for supplies. She passed Rayne a heavy cloth bag to set at her feet. Rayne swallowed her tears. "Wine and chocolate, my love, will see us through."

They parked in front of the condo.

"Andros will valet for us." Rayne climbed out and trailed her mom to the sidewalk, carrying the bag on her hip.

"I just love that service," Lauren said, when they entered the security building and lobby. "If I drove every day, I'd use it too."

Rayne greeted Kendra behind the desk but averted her face to avoid conversation. It was obvious that something had gone wrong since her exuberant exit a few hours ago. Her mom passed over the keys to the receptionist. "Thank you," Lauren said.

It took three tries to hit the elevator button, but Rayne at last managed, and they rode up to the twentieth floor in silence.

Everything about her body and mind and heart throbbed. "I just want a shower," she said. How would she survive?

"You got it. I'll pour."

They'd just entered the condo when her cell phone rang. Rayne answered. "Hello?"

"Ms. McGrath? Officer Peters here. I'm sorry to tell you that the dresses are gone and the cash register is empty. Your shop is a crime scene."

Rayne sank to the couch in shock. The thousands of hours in labor spent on the wedding dresses for the brides who'd trusted her with their dreams for a special day. Poof. "Now what?" she asked.

"You'll need to do an inventory for what was stolen," the officer said. "Contact your insurance."

Landon had taken care of the insurance, and she caught a sob in her chest. Did she even have insurance? She doubted everything. "When? Now? I . . . I don't feel well."

Lauren perched on the couch next to her, watching for cues as to what was happening. Rayne put the phone on speaker.

Officer Peters said, "Tomorrow morning is fine. The locksmith you'd called was there when I arrived and fixed the knob. I asked him to bill you. Come to the station and pick up the key. Also, bring your banking information. We can go over everything then."

They ended the call, and Rayne, on autopilot, handed the phone to her mom. "Could you answer it in case it's the police? I don't want to talk to anyone unless it's a freaking emergency." She hated to think what else might go wrong.

"Of course, darling!"

Rayne marched into the bathroom and sobbed. She hadn't cried so hard since her dad had died. This was a worse loss—this was someone she loved *choosing* to leave her, not like her dad.

Conor had gotten sick, but there'd been time for him to let Lauren and Rayne know he loved them and always would before his journey to heaven.

An hour passed before she left the shower, her mirrored bathroom full of steam, and collapsed into her bed, falling straight asleep even though it wasn't quite noon. How dare she dream so high?

When she next opened her eyes, Rayne heard her mother murmuring to someone on the phone. Paul, probably. The producer and her mom were close friends.

"Lauren?" She shifted on her bed and made out her mom's silhouette through the open door to the sitting room where she perched on a chaise longue. "Mama?"

"Oh! I'll call you back, Paul. She's awake. I will." Lauren clasped her cell phone close to her chest. It was dark outside now, and the moon glowed on the water like a pearl. "Sweetheart, Paul says he knows a wonderful lawyer to help you if you'd like. And wishes you well, of course."

Rayne nodded, then shook her head. "I don't know. I'm . . ."

Her mother sat gingerly on the edge of Rayne's plush mattress. "Rayne, I'm afraid there's more bad news."

"Is Landon all right?" Her heart raced with terrible hope that this was all a misunderstanding. That he hadn't deliberately hurt her.

"They haven't caught the scumbag. No, honey, I was talking about your uncle. Nevin." Her mother brought her fingers to her lower lip, and a tear spilled from her eye. "Uncle Nevin has passed. Thursday."

"What?" It was impossible, yet her heart broke apart a little more. The man wasn't even sixty. "And we're just now finding out?"

"It was a tractor accident. He was mowing . . ."

Rayne thought back to the emerald-green grass that covered grounds so big she'd wondered if they were a park. McGrath Castle had risen like a palace to her child's eyes at eleven when she'd visited with her dad.

He'd taken her to Ireland twice before his death. They'd wanted to go back to the Emerald Isle together, but her mother was terrified of airplanes, and she had a full production schedule for the sitcom. They'd exchanged birthday greetings and Christmas cards with the promise of returning one day.

Rayne hadn't gone to Ireland without her dad, and now Uncle Nevin was dead. Regret filled her. "This is awful. When is the funeral?" It was the worst time for her to leave. Her life was in shambles.

"The lawyer, Owen Hughes, has asked that you be there for the reading of the will. He stressed that it was important. I'm not sure about the funeral."

"I don't want to go right now." Rayne rubbed her aching eyes. "Kinda falling apart here."

Her mom got up and returned with two glasses of wine on a tray with an array of dark chocolate squares on the side. "That is precisely why I think you should go."

Rayne sipped from her glass, then nibbled chocolate. It tasted of sawdust and not at all sweet. "I can't."

"Your uncle loved you. He was all you have left of your father." Lauren blinked a droplet from her mink lashes. "Conor would want you to go."

The dad card . . . her mom wasn't playing fair. "You should come with me."

"I can't." Lauren drained her wine, then filled it from the bottle at her feet. "Drink up, love. It's medicinal."

"You *can* come. I need you."

"My show needs me." Lauren patted Rayne's hand. "You will be fine. You're stronger than me."

"You always say that, but I don't believe it." Rayne shifted listlessly on the comforter. Landon had made a fool of her. She'd believed in him. In them.

"It's true." Lauren sipped again. "I wouldn't have gotten through your father's death without you."

Her mother, deeply in love with her husband, had spent a week in bed in a dark room. Rayne had kept out the press and the sitcom family until Lauren was ready to see them, mask in place.

Rayne conjured a mental image of her uncle. Nevin McGrath, the eldest brother, and Conor McGrath, the youngest. There'd been a sister, her aunt Claire, whom Rayne was named after, but she'd died as a child. All the McGrath siblings had ink-black hair and gray eyes.

Gray as the rain in Ireland, her dad would say. *Just like you.*

"Oh, Mom." Rayne shoved her messy hair back from her cheek. "What a rotten day." She'd wanted to believe she and Landon loved each other the way her parents did, but it wasn't true if he could betray her so easily.

She hardened her heart against loving him anymore. Rayne Claire McGrath was no victim. With a last swipe of her sore eyes, she stomped any feelings for him out so that not even an ember of affection remained.

A single tear escaped to the sheet.

Her mother patted her shoulder and then put an envelope on the tray by Rayne's glass. "It's your birthday, my love. I can help a little until you get on your feet."

"What's this?" Rayne examined the envelope. Her brain whirred and sputtered like a caught thread on a sewing machine.

"Open it." Her mother set down her wineglass and smiled at Rayne with encouragement. "It's a first-class ticket to Ireland, one way. You leave tomorrow afternoon, after your stop at the police station."

Chapter Two

Despite her many misgivings, Rayne found herself on an airplane Wednesday afternoon, headed across the Atlantic for the hours-long flight to Dublin, Ireland. A driver would pick her up and deliver her to the small village of Grathton, another hourish. Add in the eight-hour time difference and she'd meet the lawyer at four in the afternoon on Thursday.

She and Lauren had "discussed" for hours, and finally the discussions had transformed into a list of what to pack for a week. Her mother had arranged everything, with the godfatherly help of Paul and the castle's housekeeper, Maeve, an older woman Rayne barely remembered.

The inventory of the boutique that morning hadn't taken long, but the reality that Landon had not only emptied their bank account but stolen wedding gowns from brides who had trusted them had cut her to the quick.

"Don't like flying?"

She turned to the man next to her with a dazed blink. "I'm sorry?"

He gestured with his plastic tumbler to Rayne's death grip on the armrest.

Normally she loved to travel, but this was not normal—from being robbed by her lover to visiting Ireland without her dad. And her uncle's sudden death. "It's not that."

"What, then? Your knuckles are white, and we haven't had a drift of turbulence."

For that she was grateful. "The way my birthday's gone so far, well, I wouldn't be surprised if we had a bumpy ride."

"It's your birthday?" The man waved at the passing flight attendant. "I'd like to buy this young woman a drink."

"Oh!" Rayne shook her head. "You don't have to do that."

"It would be my pleasure." The man winked. "Drinks are included in first class."

"That's right." She and her dad had also traveled first class, but Rayne hadn't been old enough to care about alcohol.

"Champagne?" The flight attendant waited for her order.

Rayne didn't feel like celebrating anything but reaching Ireland in one piece. "Rum and Diet Coke is fine."

Within moments, the flight attendant returned with a tumbler of rum and cola over ice. "Here you are. Happy birthday."

"Thank you, and thank you, sir." Rayne unpeeled her fingers from the right armrest to accept the drink. Maybe it would help her sleep.

"How old are you, if you don't mind my asking?" The man sipped. "I'm Michael, by the way." He was passing the time, she could tell, not being rude or hitting on her. Then again, how could she trust her judgment after Landon had deceived her?

"I'm Rayne. I turned thirty yesterday." She dipped her head toward the gentleman. "I had very high hopes."

"Expectations will get you every time," he intoned sagely.

Expectations and a louse of a business partner and boyfriend. Rayne refused to share her personal story with a stranger and hoped that by the time she returned to Los Angeles next week, things would be on an even keel.

Things being her messed-up life.

Some part of her hoped that Landon had been kidnapped and was even now being tortured limb by limb and held for ransom, which was why he'd emptied their account. The rotten bad guys must have forced him to jam the lock on the door of their shop.

The other part of her remained in denial about what had happened. She hadn't even told Jenn she was leaving. Go to the lawyer, then the funeral, then come home.

She and her mother had finished the first bottle of wine and cracked open another, along with an entire bar of delicious chocolate. By the end of the second bottle and a bag of reduced-fat potato chips, traveling to Ireland had seemed like a great escape.

Why not see her dad's childhood home, McGrath Castle, before its ownership passed to . . . whoever might inherit? Her dad had entertained her with stories of growing up in a castle, and it had seemed magical.

Yet Conor, when pressed about the experience at dinner parties or book-signing events, would wave the story away as if it weren't important. She'd seen a tiny smile hover over his lips as he corrected wonderstruck guests. "McGrath Castle is in reality a fortified manor house with a turret. Hardly a palace."

She'd heard underlying pride in his voice, and the mystery of why he'd moved from Ireland to the States had intrigued her. Seeing the "pile of stones," another deceptively derisive term, had left her in awe. When they'd come back from their trip, Rayne had told her classmates they were royalty.

Was there anything worse than a pretentious preteen?

"Ah, there's a smile," Michael said. "I knew a drink would calm your fears."

She didn't argue, though it was the memory of her beloved father that had calmed her. "I can't place your accent . . . where are you from?"

His eyes twinkled. "I moved to Cardigan from Northern Ireland as a wean but went to school in London. I've an accent all its own. You?"

"I like it." Rayne touched her heart. "Born and raised in Los Angeles. Can't get more American than that."

"Hollywood," Michael said. "Are you an actress?"

"No." Rayne briefly bowed her head. What was she now, besides foolish? "A wedding dress designer."

"Why are you braving these smooth skies on your birthday?"

She lifted her tumbler, her nose stinging with sadness. Would she ever be happy again? "My uncle, Nevin McGrath, passed away."

His teasing smile fled. "Oh, I'm sorry."

"Me too. I wish we'd been closer. I should have traveled to see him while he was alive, but I never expected him to die so young."

Michael clicked his glass to hers. "To your uncle. And to a better year for you."

"I'll drink to that!"

The pair settled into companionable silence. She chose a movie and plugged into mindless entertainment as he drifted off to sleep.

It was awful to her that a total stranger had been kinder than the man she'd loved.

*   *   *

Rayne arrived in Dublin Thursday afternoon. The sky was gray and overcast as she searched the drivers waiting outside the airport for a card with her name on it. She'd already retrieved her luggage, which was full of stylish clothes perfect for LA. Lightweight and bright. Her heaviest garment was a suit jacket she'd brought for the funeral.

Her mom had slipped money inside Rayne's wallet, dismissing Rayne's concerns even as she wished her safe travels. "It's just a few hundred to help," she'd said.

Rayne sent a quick text to Lauren, letting her know she'd landed safely. There were no phone messages. She'd hoped for one from the police, saying they'd caught Landon.

"Rayne McGrath?"

She whirled to the left, toward a pixie-like voice with a definite Irish accent. Her gaze landed on a tall, slender woman with short, bleached-blonde curls and eyes a stormier gray than Rayne's. A bulky sweater encased her.

"Yes?"

"*Fáilte*. I'm Ciara Smith, here to drive you to Grathton Village and the solicitor's office."

Welcome. The greeting and the young woman's stiff body language were at odds. "Oh, I thought . . . well." She'd pictured a driver in black and white but let that image go for the scowling lady in khakis and work boots. "Aren't we going to the castle first? I'd hoped to freshen up."

Ciara crossed her arms and raised her brow, as if daring Rayne to argue. "Mr. Hughes pushed back the meeting from this morning to accommodate your flight. We weren't sure if you were coming or not."

The decision had been made within hours of receiving news of her uncle's death, as Rayne had agreed with her mom that it would be important to her dad. She wanted to pay her respects as well.

"It's a long flight." Lauren had spoken with the housekeeper at the castle, but it was doubtful a hired hand would be in the loop. Rayne was put off by her brisk and borderline rude manner. Then again, perhaps the woman was grieving for Uncle Nevin. "I was very sorry to hear the news about Nevin."

Ciara gave a clipped nod and gestured toward the parking lot, hurrying across the busy road. The driver expected Rayne to follow without getting killed as she towed her leather suitcase behind her in jerks and yanks.

To the racket of honks from angry motorists, she arrived at the white two-door Fiat in one piece. The woman tossed Rayne's suitcase in the trunk while Rayne climbed in on what would have been the driver's side back home.

"Will there be somewhere to fix my makeup?" She was probably a raccoon-eyed wreck after the flight. Rayne, a true Hollywood native, never left home without a fully made-up face. You might run into a director or producer while at the grocery store, or worse, a photographer searching for a story. She'd been caught more than once just because she was Lauren McGrath's daughter.

Ciara glanced at her as she started the car. "What for? You look fine enough for the reading of the will. It'll be you and Mr. Hughes."

Subtext: Nobody to impress.

But that wasn't the point, and not how she was used to operating. Rayne reached inside her massive Coach purse and drew out a mirror, powder, and a rosy gloss that could also be used for blush.

Despite Ciara's seemingly best efforts to hit every pothole and make abrupt turns, they reached the highway without Rayne giving herself a mustache or losing an eye.

Rayne put away the mirror and supplies to sit back in her seat. Her Dior tote was at her feet, the sketch pad inside untouched since Monday. She just couldn't. "Where are we going again?"

"You don't know where your uncle lived?"

Rayne couldn't miss the snide tone in Ciara's voice. "In Grathton Village, yes. Is that where the lawyer is?"

"The *solicitor* has an office on the outskirts of the village."

Solicitor meant lawyer. Got it. Rayne studied Ciara as the young woman drove. Maybe a year or two older than her, without the benefit of creams and lotions to soften the skin and keep those scowl lines at bay.

Serves her right, Rayne thought. Lack of proper skin care did a world of damage, and it was too late to fix it. If Ciara weren't so prickly, Rayne might offer some friendly tips.

She kept her suggestions to herself as they turned off the main road onto a smaller two-way street between large green pastures. There was no GPS in the vehicle, so she was at a loss for their ETA.

Sheep dotted the landscape like dingy yellow cotton balls. Rayne remembered the sheep from her last visit as being cute. Not so much now. They were in the way, and she was in a hurry. She really didn't like making people wait for her, and Ciara had stressed the point.

A flock of sheep wandered across the road, and Ciara stopped the car as if it were no big deal that the puffballs slowed them down. Why not go around? An odor wafted toward Rayne as a sheep did its business right there. They didn't smell cute either.

"Why aren't the fields fenced?" Rayne took a tissue from her purse and brought it to her nose to block the stench. "What if someone ran the sheep over by accident? It's a driving hazard."

"A what?" Ciara asked.

"Hazard. You know, dangerous. What's that guy doing?"

A medium-sized black-and-white dog, followed by an old man in a straw hat, crossed next, the pup yipping at the last sheep to hurry it up. The sheep twitched its tail but minded. Hysterical! She should tell Landon . . .

Rayne's humor faded. She could share it on her social media. Forget Landon.

"Folks around here know sheep have the right of way. That's Ross, a shepherd on Murphy's farm," Ciara said warily as Rayne whipped out her cell phone to snap a photo.

"No kidding?" Rayne had no clue shepherd was a real gig.

"No." Ciara sniffed and raised her chin, waving at the shepherd. The dog watched them with interested eyes, once the flock was safely across the road. Ciara stepped on the gas with a lurch.

"Hey!"

"Sorry." Ciara continued driving, her small smile not conveying sincerity.

Rayne took another photo—of her driver's sour face.

"What did ye do that for?"

"I'm going to send this to my mom. You know, to show her how friendly Dad's fellow Irishmen are. Conor always said his folks are known for their hospitality."

Ciara's mouth tightened, as did her grip on the wheel. She didn't say another word. Rayne tried to send the sheep photo to her Modern Lace social media, but there was no signal.

After stopping twice for dawdling sheep, they arrived at a populated part of the village. Summer flowers on the front lawns lined stone paths. The buildings were wood and stone with thatched or dark-gray slate roofs.

It was like stepping back in time. It reminded Rayne of one of her mother's studio sets. She scanned the streets for film crews or a production trailer.

This was the real deal. Narrow paved streets with barely enough space for small cars on either side. A churchyard with old, moss-covered headstones close to the road. A stone fountain that spewed brackish water. Moss grew everywhere. A sign welcomed them to Grathton Village.

Things appeared quiet for a Thursday afternoon. The sun remained hidden in an overcast sky.

Rayne did a quick weather search on her cell phone app. Brr. Sixty degrees. No wonder she was chilly. A low of—she gulped—fifty was expected tonight. How cold did it have to be before it snowed? Not the summer weather she'd packed for.

Ciara pulled into an open space on the narrow road just big enough for her Fiat. "Here we are."

The first words she'd spoken in minutes, alleluia. Rayne had been taught to be polite no matter what, but she'd file a complaint with the driving service later. "Thanks for the ride."

Ciara's lips pursed. "I'm comin' in."

"You don't have to—just point me in the right direction. Oh, I guess I need my suitcase." She'd hoped to never see the woman again.

Rayne climbed out of the car, her leg muscles tight from the day of travel. On the right side of the street were stone and brick single-story businesses, and on the left was a field. It had been almost twenty years since she'd been here, and she had zero memory of it.

Ciara rounded the back of the car, snug in her thick sweater. "You're welcome to leave it in the boot during the meeting."

"You really don't have to wait." Rayne shouldered her purse and tote bag. "Unless Lauren arranged for you to drive me to the castle afterward?"

"Your mum?"

"I call her Lauren, but yes. My mother."

"Let's go inside." The blonde shook her short curls. "Mr. Hughes will explain everything."

Ciara stepped in front of Rayne to lead the way to the business on the corner, where flower boxes overflowed with marigolds, daisies, and ivy on either side of a wooden door. The gold name plate read OWEN HUGHES, SOLICITOR.

The driver opened the door. The lobby of the office was packed with dark wood chairs, a verdant green plant, and a central rectangular table with magazines piled on top. A large cuckoo clock gave the time as quarter past four.

"Hello," a woman behind a long desk said. She had shiny brown hair bobbed at her chin. A coffee mug with *Daisy* printed on the side, her magenta shade of lipstick at the rim, was near her desktop computer.

"Thanks, Daisy," Ciara said.

"Is this Rayne?" Daisy stood and held out her hand. "Nice to meet you. I'm Daisy Hughes, Owen's wife. I answer the phones, do the books, and make the tea," she said with a friendly laugh. "Go on in and I'll bring it."

"Thanks." Rayne hurried down a dim hall. Was the atmosphere meant to be dreary, or was there a bulb somewhere that needed changing? She could never survive in a place so dark. She required light.

Ciara pushed open a door at the end of the hall. The bright contrast made Rayne blink to adjust her vision.

"Ms. McGrath!" A man who had to be twice Daisy's age stood and clasped her hand. "Welcome. Thank you so much for coming on such short notice." He patted his belly, which strained against a too-tight suit jacket. "I've made the trip across the pond once to New York, and it was nearly the death of me."

He gestured toward two vacant high-backed chairs.

Ciara claimed one, so Rayne took the other. She looked around the room, whose shelves were stuffed with books. Other chairs had been stacked against the wall. "Did everyone else have to leave? I'm sorry for being late. I hopped on a plane as soon as I could."

Rayne settled her tote and purse by her feet. Respectful of the lawyer's time, she'd turned the ringer off on her phone.

"It's no bother." Mr. Hughes sat down behind his desk. "You two are the only ones involved in this part of the will."

Rayne glanced at Ciara, then back at Mr. Hughes as he got comfortable in his leather office chair. "I don't understand."

He tilted his head. "The smaller bequeathments have already been disbursed."

Rayne's body went on high alert. Her skin pebbled. Her nape tingled. Her stomach clenched. She'd thought some distant relative would inherit, since Padraig, her cousin, was already dead. What did Ciara have to do with this? "Now I really don't understand."

"Don't be so daft," Ciara pronounced. She perched on the edge of the tall chair, visibly tense. Her fingers curled around her bent knees, the khakis worn.

"Ciara," Mr. Hughes admonished with a chuckle. "Our poor Rayne—may I call you Rayne, *mo leanbh*?"

She nodded. Her dad used to call her *my child*, and she calmed down a little.

"Doesn't know what's going on." The solicitor offered a compassionate smile.

Ciara blew out a hostile breath that ruffled her bangs. "Me either."

Rayne had been played for a fool more this week than in her entire life. She gave another nod. "Will you please enlighten me? Before I just call a cab and get back to the airport. I'm in no mood for games."

Considering how her life had spun out of control over the last few days, this was said with remarkable aplomb, Rayne thought.

Ciara snorted. "Good luck with that. I had to get ye today. Grathton doesn't have a hundred rideshare drivers just waitin' to pick you up."

Mr. Hughes held out his hand. "Now, now, girls."

Rayne gritted her teeth and frowned at the elderly lawyer. Girls?

"Sorry! Women, young women. My wife is after me all the time to remember the world is a-changin'."

Rayne's third nod was her stiffest yet.

"Rayne Claire McGrath, meet Ciara Leah Smith. She is your uncle's natural daughter."

What did that mean? Her confusion must have shown, because Mr. Hughes shifted uncomfortably on his chair.

"What he means is, I'm illegitimate," Ciara said. "My mum didn't tell my da about me, nor me about him. I found out when she was ill and she gave him a ring. Didn't meet him until after she passed."

"How awf—"

"Awful? Shocking?" Ciara spluttered with indignation. "Oh, aye, all of those. I met my father nine years ago. Since his son,

Padraig, was already dead, he let me move into the castle. Like he was doin' me a bleedin' favor."

And here she'd been feeling sorry for herself. Ciara had it worse by far, and Rayne empathized with her cousin. Her cousin! But wait—Aunt Amalie and Uncle Nevin had been a love match. How had Ciara happened?

"I grew up in London," Ciara continued. "Never dreamed me Irish mother would hide such a secret, but there we are." She shrugged, daring Rayne to knock the chip off her slender shoulder.

Rayne would let her keep it. She had to focus on her own drama, so she turned to Mr. Hughes. "Okay. Ciara and I have now met. We're cousins." Rayne would keep her distance from negative Ciara, get through the funeral, and fly home. Her mother would never believe it. "What happens next?"

"Calm yourselves," Mr. Hughes advised. He took his time selecting a sheaf of paper from the middle drawer of his desk.

A knock sounded, and Daisy entered with an old-fashioned tea trolley, the likes of which Rayne hadn't seen since black-and-white movies.

Fragrant steam rose from a ceramic pot with gold leaf along the handle. Three cups, three saucers, lemon slices, sugar, and an ivory pitcher of cream.

Daisy passed out the refreshments and put a square of short-bread on the rim of each saucer.

"Thank you," Rayne said. She was both parched and hungry. Her stomach rumbled and her cheeks heated.

"Ah, have a quick bite," Daisy encouraged. "Traveling all of this way from Los Angeles. The city of stars!"

Suddenly Rayne wanted her bed and to sleep around the clock. The warm office, the kindness of Daisy, the fear that something was wrong. Again? Still?

She sipped the tea and nibbled a cookie. "Delicious. Thank you."

Daisy slipped out of the office. Ciara slammed her cup and saucer to the top of the lawyer's desk.

"I'm on pins and needles," Ciara said to Mr. Hughes. "Can we please find out what my father decreed?"

Mr. Hughes clicked his tongue to his teeth but set aside his cup after a fortifying sip.

He shook out the papers, slid his reading glasses on his nose, and cleared his throat. "This is the will of Nevin Foster McGrath, being of sound mind on May the fifth—"

"May, as in last month?" Rayne interrupted.

"Yes." Mr. Hughes looked down his nose at her.

"Sorry." Rayne set her cup and saucer on his desk and clenched her fingers together over her lap. Her black suit was fitted yet comfortable. Quality. It was Dolce & Gabbana, and probably the most expensive thing in this room. She wanted to go home.

"—bequeath McGrath Castle to my niece, Rayne Claire McGrath."

Both women gasped in horror.

Chapter Three

Rayne's learned composure from etiquette lessons her mother had enrolled her in during middle school kept her from jumping up and kicking over her chair. Not so her unruly and temperamental cousin. Cousin!

Ciara leaped to her feet and smacked her palms on Mr. Hughes's desk, rattling the porcelain cups. "No. That heap o' rock can't go to her. It's mine, by birthright! *I* am the true heir. By blood!"

"Sit. Down. Ms. Smith. You are not *by law* a McGrath, and your biological father didn't feel as if you'd earned your place at the castle."

Ciara plopped to her chair, her face red as she tried but failed to control her anger. "I've worked my fingers to the bone on that property. I've spent years learning the McGrath history!"

Rayne was stunned into silence as she absorbed this news and what it might mean. Gray skies compared to blue. Rain rather than sunshine. Sheep. Ghosts, according to her cousin Padraig. A California girl, through and through, she had sunshine in her veins. "I don't want the castle. Give it to Ciara if she does." She swiped her hands together. Problem solved.

Mr. Hughes shook the thick sheaf of paper. "It's not that simple, Ms. McGrath."

She noticed that the lawyer was now referring to each of them a bit more formally, as if to make sure they both understood the importance of the will.

Or perhaps to stifle any more outbursts.

"I own a bridal boutique," Rayne said in a calm tone. That fact remained true, even if the shop was currently part of a crime scene. "In LA. An impossible commute." The hefty lease was up for renewal in September. Landon had driven her by a bigger property closer to the name brands, sure they'd snag the investment to take Modern Lace to the next level. Location mattered. Trusting your partner mattered. *How could he have lied to me?*

She practiced deep breaths and forced herself to stay relaxed. It hurt. Would the pain ever fade?

"Your uncle followed the progress of your wedding business," Mr. Hughes informed her. "Your success on Rodeo Drive. He was quite proud of you."

"A *very* small shop!" Rayne interlaced her fingers over her knee. *Calm, calm.*

Ciara rolled her eyes. "Silk and satin. Right down to the undies."

Rayne arched her brow at the blonde. Her cousin, illegitimate or not, was still family. Why was she being so rude? She probably wore flannel boy shorts beneath those awful khakis.

Just as she was about to launch into a biting observation, Rayne acknowledged to herself that she really wasn't that fabulous. Her boyfriend and business partner had robbed her blind, and she'd been too caught up with her head in the clouds to notice. Had there even been a banking firm?

31

Rayne bit her lip to keep from revealing that she was a fraud. Landon Short had stolen everything—including her pride. She was broke. Her mom had bought her the ticket to get here and would buy her ticket back.

"Well?" Ciara demanded, itching for a fight.

Neutral expression in place, Rayne organized her thoughts. "I don't want to box with you, Ciara. I'm sorry that Uncle Nevin didn't give the castle to you. I have no clue why he chose me! Mr. Hughes, you see that this is impossible to accept."

She needed to return to LA and deal with Landon's theft of her gowns and the money. The only things left in the boutique were trims and lace. Her deluxe sewing machine. He hadn't taken that. Why had he done this? Her chest ached as memories of the two of them laughing and loving popped up. She stuck an imaginary pin into the bubble. He didn't deserve her grief.

Honestly, getting on the plane to escape to her dad's magical Ireland had taken precedence over the crime, but she couldn't stay more than a week. She'd assumed she'd go right after the funeral.

Modern Lace had wedding gown orders to fulfill. She couldn't let down the dozen brides who'd placed deposits for dresses in the upcoming year. Antsy, Rayne squirmed on her chair. The police had to have answers by now.

She glanced at her phone, tucked in the side pocket of her purse. Would there be a message from Officer Peters?

"I realize this is a shock," Mr. Hughes said.

Ciara jabbed a finger toward Rayne. "She's not affected. Probably has ice in her veins."

"I don't, I promise you." She'd been sent to deportment classes held by Mrs. Westinghouse to help with her temper until she'd learned to control it. Her mom had blamed the Celtic blood in her ancestry. "Mr. Hughes, I can't accept a castle. I have no time or experience." Was she letting her father down?

The lawyer raised a single finger, a signal for her to listen close. "Nevin chose you, Rayne, to be the head of McGrath Castle, with Ciara's assistance. Ciara must manage things for a full year. At the end of that year, Ciara is to receive a hundred thousand euro." Ciara sucked in a breath. "After that, she may stay on, or she may leave to seek her fortune with Nevin's blessing."

"That bastard," Ciara whispered, tears shining on her red face.

That was a familiar refrain. She reached for her cousin's shoulder, then pulled back the offer of sympathy when Ciara curled her upper lip at Rayne in clear *don't touch* language.

"I don't want the castle," Rayne repeated coolly. Her life was in Hollywood. "Just because Uncle Nevin gave it to me doesn't mean I have to accept it."

"You're an idiot," Ciara announced.

"Hey!" Rayne crossed her ankles. "I resent your name-calling." She faced Mr. Hughes. "I don't have to accept, do I?"

With an air of immense disapproval, the lawyer lowered the pages of the will. "You do not have to accept." He smoothed the sheets out on the desktop. "But there are consequences if you don't."

Rayne didn't like the sound of that.

Hiding her trepidation behind modulated tones that would do her deportment teacher proud, she asked, "What consequences?"

"If you do not accept this will as is, then the property will be sold immediately. Neither you nor Ciara will get anything. The money will be donated to the church in Cotter Village. The McGrath line will end there."

Blood drained from her cheeks. "You're kidding."

"I do not joke about things like this," Mr. Hughes assured her.

Rayne glanced at Ciara, who was shaking her head in disbelief. "The old man was not in his bleedin' right mind," her cousin said. "I'll tell ye that right now."

"Tsk, tsk." Mr. Hughes sipped his tea and returned his focus to Rayne. He slipped his glasses off to study her with steady brown eyes. "Well?"

Her thirtieth birthday had been an utter disaster. She couldn't top it off with destroying the family line. Her dad would come back to haunt her for sure. "I . . . what happens if I agree to try?" Rayne didn't do mud or dirt or sheep or farms. Horses hated her. She could work round the clock at the sewing machine or drawing board on one of her wedding gown designs, but this? She didn't know where to begin. Maybe she could manage the place from LA?

Ciara stared at her, her short, bleached curls on end from where she'd yanked them. "The castle is not a fancy dress you try on and then return. This is people's lives."

Rayne couldn't send hardworking people to the poorhouse. "I . . ."

"If the castle doesn't thrive, Grathton Village will disappear. There are less than five hundred folks who live here." Mr. Hughes tapped his glasses to the will. "Our young people are moving out to find jobs in the cities. Your uncle thought you were progressive, Rayne."

"I run a bridal boutique," Rayne said. "I am not experienced enough to manage a castle." Her dad's voice in her mind said, *Glorified manor house with a turret.*

"That is why your uncle has made the provision for Ciara and her expertise. He believed that with her assistance, you can change things not only for the castle but the village. Their success is tied together."

Ciara. She'd earn a hundred thousand euro teaching Rayne. If Rayne guessed correctly, the young woman could use it.

Her cousin was justifiably furious and thought that the castle should have gone to her. Rayne agreed. But Uncle Nevin was dead, and there was nobody to argue with. The cold pages of the will didn't allow for back-and-forth discussion. The decree was in print. Stamped. Initialed. Dated.

As of last month. Why?

Rayne shifted forward on the chair. "How did my uncle die?"

"Tractor accident," Mr. Hughes said in a sad voice.

"That's what Lauren told me." Rayne smoothed her slacks. "It seems odd that he would change his will like that, a month before he died. My dad passed away from tumors, and I wondered if maybe Uncle Nevin had something wrong too."

"No," Mr. Hughes explained kindly. "It was a tragedy. The tractor flipped and rolled down the ravine."

Ciara's body vibrated with anger. "It's being investigated."

"Why?" Rayne turned to her cousin.

"Ciara is distraught," Mr. Hughes said, his tone dismissive.

"I see." But nothing was clear. Her cousin deserved the castle, yet her uncle had given it to Rayne instead. He'd pay Ciara a large lump sum if she stayed to help Rayne for a year. Rayne had only a couple hundred bucks in her bank account; Landon had convinced her to bolster their business account and lure the investors. She couldn't afford to be away from LA and her bridal boutique. She had to build the business back up. Where was Landon?

Ciara lowered her stormy gaze to the Coach purse and Dior tote bag at Rayne's feet. "What are you going to do?"

"You're sure that I can't just sell the place, Mr. Hughes? I'd split the profits with Ciara." Rayne could use an influx of money right about now.

"As if there'd be anything left." Her cousin sprawled her long legs before her.

What did that mean? Was the castle not on good financial footing?

"No, you can't just sell, Ms. McGrath." Mr. Hughes placed his elbow on the desktop. "And there is more to consider."

"More?" Rayne pressed her fingers to the jumping vein at her jugular. Thirty was too young for a heart attack, wasn't it?

"If you do accept your *responsibility* as the last McGrath heir, you will have one year." Mr. Hughes put his other elbow on the desk and leaned toward her.

"One year?" Rayne squeaked. What was with her uncle? "To do what?"

"One year," Mr. Hughes continued, "to show increased property value in the castle *and* surrounding village."

"Or what?" She clutched the armrests and braced herself. "The apocalypse will begin?"

Ciara snorted and covered her mouth.

"No . . ." Mr. Hughes's tone softened. "At the end of that year, if you fail, then the castle can be sold, and if there is any profit, you may split it equally between you."

"Not fair," Ciara said.

"And if I succeed?" Rayne had trained her brain to think successfully. To find solutions. To win. "After the year is over. Can I go?"

Mr. Hughes sighed. "Yes. You will receive one hundred thousand euro as well."

Her cousin had no clue that she was desperate for the money. Rayne couldn't live in Ireland. Maybe she could hire Ciara and keep her apartment in Santa Monica . . .

"But you must work at the castle and be in residence for the entire year to receive the stipend," Mr. Hughes intoned, bursting her plan at the first stage. "Once the twelve months have been completed, you and Ciara will be allowed to jointly decide what to do moving forward in the best interests of the castle and the village."

"And what if I don't agree to stay on?" Ciara demanded.

Mr. Hughes turned toward the blonde with a shrug. "Your father felt that you had nowhere else to go, Ciara. The castle's been your home since your mother died. Nevin wagered you'd be logical about helping Rayne, if only to get the money to start over." He steepled his fingers. "He had no way of knowing that he'd die so soon. We were friends, and he planned on grooming you, Ciara. I believe he would have come around to giving you his name."

It seemed Uncle Nevin knew his daughter well. Rayne murmured, "Diabolical."

"That's one word for 'im," Ciara said through gritted teeth.

If the castle was failing financially, Uncle Nevin had been trying to save a sinking ship. Sometimes it was best to get the sailors off to safety and let it sink. In marketing terms? You had to cut the fat. It couldn't be an emotional decision.

Rayne had to save her own company. There was no denying that she could use a hundred grand, thanks to Landon's deceit. She would lose Modern Lace Bridal Boutique's momentum if she wasn't on Rodeo Drive with quality product to sell.

She had to speak with her mom about it all. Lauren would know what to do.

"I need to consider everything," Rayne said, "before I decide."

"You would let the castle go?" Ciara stood, her eyes flashing. "Ice in your veins."

Mr. Hughes drummed the documents with his pen. "You have twenty-four hours to decide."

"Is that legal?" Rayne demanded. "Surely I deserve a little more time."

"Your uncle made these provisions, Rayne, not I," Mr. Hughes said. "You could hire a solicitor and argue the terms, but it would cost money, and put you over the twenty-four hours allotted. The castle was his property to do with as he saw fit."

Rayne looked at Ciara in dismay. "I have a life in America. What was Uncle Nevin thinking—that I would give up everything for Ireland? I can't do that!"

"My father obviously wasn't plannin' on dying," Ciara said. "Let's go. I'll give you a ride to the castle."

"All right. Thanks." Rayne's head clamored. She wanted to rest and let her thoughts settle. It made sense that Ciara probably still lived on the property, since she'd expected to inherit it.

"Wonderful," Mr. Hughes said with a fatherly smile. "Let's meet tomorrow at four for a proper tea with sandwiches, and you can give me your answer then. Come to the cottage."

Rayne shook his hand good-bye—as did Ciara—and followed her cousin down the dim hall to the lobby. There was no sign of Daisy.

"What cottage?" Rayne asked.

"They live in a house behind the office." Ciara sounded bemused. "I can't believe that will."

"I'm stunned, honestly," Rayne said.

They got into the Fiat. The sky remained gray. Shadows filtered to the street through leafy trees—so different from the palm trees Rayne was used to seeing at home. Ciara drove, her body exuding tension. "We need to talk."

"I agree." But first Rayne needed to think. She got out her phone and saw three missed calls from the police station in LA.

Her phone rang. It was her mother. She'd told the police at the station that they could contact her mother with news if she was unavailable.

"Hi, Lauren."

"Darling, how are you doing?"

"All right." She glanced at Ciara. "Can I call you from the castle? I have a cousin I need to tell you about."

"A cousin? How wonderful! But don't forget—I've been worried sick. The police called, and Officer Peters said they found Landon's BMW at the airport. No record of him getting on any plane, though."

The news was a punch to the stomach. He'd abandoned his car. Like he'd abandoned her and their life together. Just gone. Once she could draw a breath, Rayne said, "I'll call, I promise. I have some ideas I need to run by you." She hung up and closed her eyes against the onslaught of betrayal and pain. Her uncle's bequest had just added to her misery.

"Everythin' all right?" Ciara asked. "You look awful."

"Peachy." Rayne kept her eyes closed, not trusting Ciara's softer tone. "I could sleep for a month." The long trip hadn't helped her mental exhaustion from what Landon had done.

"You only have twenty-four hours. To come up with an answer."

Rayne opened one eye to laser it at her cousin. It was kind of nice to have family. She'd thought she was alone. Why hadn't Uncle Nevin mentioned a daughter? Why hadn't Ciara told her they were related? The blonde had secrets. Well, so did Rayne.

39

She wouldn't be sharing her lack of fortune with anybody at the castle. Let them believe what they wanted to. "Did you know about the will and what was in it?"

"No." Ciara lifted a shoulder and slowed around a curve of the hilly road. "As you heard from my outburst. I thought the castle would be left to me."

"Yeah." But it hadn't. Why not? Did it really have to do with a surname? Nevin could have adopted his own daughter and given her his last name.

Her eye closed again, heavy. Sleep beckoned.

"No time for a nap—this is the turn from the village," Ciara announced. "To home."

Rayne forced both eyes wide. This wasn't her home. It had been her dad's as a child. Uncle Nevin's. Aunt Amalie's. Padraig's. The weight of loss and expectation settled on her.

"You've been here before?" Ciara guided the small car around a hole in the pavement. Thick trees grew on either side.

"Twice. As a girl. I was eleven the last time I was here with my dad. He got sick after that and died. Lauren and I never came back."

"I'm sorry about your father. My da talked about him all the time. Said they were quite close as youngsters. They had the rule of the grounds. Knights and warriors fighting off the English." Ciara sent a sad smile toward Rayne.

"I also heard the stories." They had their ancestors in common. What else might they share?

"Why did your dad move ta LA?"

"Conor fell in love with my mother. Lauren loved him too. His poet's soul." Their story was for another time, if she decided it was safe to let this cousin close. Right now, all she knew was that she was hungry. And tired. And hungry.

40

"Should we order dinner in? My treat." Rayne had a credit card with a little room on it.

Ciara laughed as the pavement turned to stone. Trees created an arch over the road leading to the castle. It was imposing in the evening light, with the round tower to the left, the wide stone steps. The double wood doors. Sconces would provide illumination in the dark.

"What's funny?" Rayne snapped, tired of being mistreated by her cousin.

"We don't order in." Ciara glanced at Rayne. "If you want somethin' special, you have to pick it up at the pub or café."

"No delivery?" She was shocked. Certainly everyone in the world had heard of Uber Eats.

Ciara parked in front of a five-car garage. "No. However, Maeve is cooking a special meal in your honor. She has fond memories of when you visited."

"How nice." Maeve. That was the housekeeper her mother had spoken with and she vaguely recalled. It had been a long time ago. "What I remember most is my cousin Padraig scaring the daylights out of me, jumping from behind statues in the hall. He told me the castle was haunted by my—our—aunt Claire, who died as a little girl."

"I never met Padraig." Ciara tucked a short blonde lock behind her ear. "He'd been gone a few years before I showed up on Da's doorstep."

They each got out of the Fiat. Rayne looked at the trunk. Maybe she'd come back later for her suitcase.

"Cormac will get your bags from the boot," Ciara said. "What was our cousin like?"

"Padraig was tall and terrifying at fourteen. Dark hair and eyes. I used to be so jealous of him, living in a castle. He was so lucky! And then . . ."

"He drowned." Ciara sighed.

"Yeah. And Aunt Amalie died of a broken heart. My dad was already gone by then." So much tragedy.

They each quieted and climbed the stone steps to the manor house. The stone walls were overgrown with ivy. It felt familiar and welcoming.

McGraths had lived here since the 1700s. Rayne acknowledged a pang of sorrow at the memory of her dad. What would he want her to do? She'd have to meditate and think on it.

Ciara stopped at the door, her hand on the knob.

"We need to talk," she said again. Her voice was urgent.

"I know. But not now. Food, and rest, please." Rayne braved a touch to Ciara's stiff shoulder.

"It's important that ye understand . . . my da, Nevin, died in a tractor accident while mowing on this property." Ciara held Rayne's gaze with steely-eyed strength. "Under suspicious circumstances."

"Wait. Hold on a minute!" Rayne wasn't sure she'd heard properly. It had been a long trip, and she'd had a lot happen in a short time. The lawyer had clearly said accident. Tragedy.

Ciara gave a slight nod. "I told you, it's under investigation, even though everyone thinks I'm overreacting."

Rayne put her hand to her galloping chest, wanting to go home. Her home in LA. "You're saying Uncle Nevin may have been *murdered*?"

Chapter Four

"Murdered! When ye say it like that, it sounds a wee bit dramatic," Ciara said, her mouth tight. "But aye, I believe so."

"Why?" Rayne rolled the motives for murder through her mental index. Her mom's series, *Family Forever*, sometimes dealt with suspicious deaths in a lighthearted kind of way. *Killed for an inheritance* was right up there at the top of the list.

Which would shine the spotlight on her illegitimate cousin. She'd wanted the castle, and it had gone to Rayne.

But this wasn't a show; this was real life.

The door opened. A man in black slacks, a white shirt, and a black jacket—quite dapper—greeted them. She was a product of Hollywood in that she calculated age and income bracket as second nature. The butler, Cormac?

Midfifties. The suit quality but off-the-rack. Dark graying hair and bushy eyebrows that feathered over his sad brown eyes. A comfortable living.

"Welcome, Ms. McGrath, Ciara. Maeve's set the table in the grand dining room."

Ciara snorted. "Oh, the grand dining room? Breaking out all the stops! What's the matter with the regular dining room, where Maeve doesn't have to walk so far from the kitchen?"

"Ms. McGrath is a guest."

"Maeve said she's family. Which is it, Cormac?"

Cormac drew himself up, shoulders tight.

Rayne shifted awkwardly on the stoop. Ciara seemed to grate on everyone's nerves.

"Both," Cormac said.

"Please, call me Rayne," she interjected. "And the regular dining room is fine with me. I don't want to put anyone to trouble."

"Maybe Cormac here knew that Da would screw me over and give you the castle." Ciara jerked her chin at the butler.

Cormac sucked in a breath—but he seemed more angry at Ciara than surprised at Rayne's inheritance. "You were not raised in this house, or you would understand that this sort of scene is something Lord Nevin would not approve of."

Ciara paled at the rebuke.

He shifted to Rayne with a bow of his head. "My condolences on the loss of your uncle, Lady McGrath."

Lady? "I remember you, Cormac," Rayne said. "You gave me an apple right from the tree. Rayne is fine!"

Cormac smiled at Rayne and bobbed his head, then stepped past her to the car. "I did. I'll get your luggage. I've put you in your dad's childhood bedroom."

Rayne's stomach twirled, and she pressed her hand to her belly. With all the problems of late, she hadn't factored in how being here would bring her closer to her beloved father. Another emotion to add to the stack. "Okay. Can I help?"

Cormac descended the stairs to the Fiat. "No, Rayne. Ciara, please take your cousin to the grand dining room."

Ciara gave Rayne a nudge with her elbow to go inside.

The interior was not as mammoth as Rayne recalled from her visit as a kid, but still plenty big. Slate tiles made up the floor, covered with deep plush rugs. A circular wooden table held an antique warrior carved from bog oak. A round Irish shield once used by a McGrath ancestor hung on the wall. In a bin by the door were umbrellas for rain and a variety of shillelaghs for walking. She and her cousin Padraig had used them as clubs, pretending to be warriors.

A central staircase led to the bedrooms upstairs. To the right were the kitchen, several parlors, a library, and a sun-room. To the left on the main floor were offices and the staff's suites. In the basement was a fruit cellar with shelves of canned goods. Potatoes too. According to Padraig, dead Aunt Claire haunted the castle.

The second floor had bedrooms and two offices, and the third was full of storage—and more ghosts, if she believed Padraig, who might be haunting the castle now himself.

It was getting crowded, with Uncle Nevin the latest.

Though she'd never encountered a ghost, she absolutely believed in the possibility. Rayne shivered and followed Ciara, her heels sinking into the thick carpet runner in the hall, lured by savory scents. Her stomach rumbled, and she realized that the last thing she'd had to eat—other than that half a cookie at the lawyer's office—was the cheese and fruit plate on the plane.

What would Lauren say to this? Her mom offered sound advice, but Rayne had also been very close to her dad. Kindred Celtic spirits. She felt him here, even though his ashes were back home with her mother.

Ciara opened a dark wood door, and Rayne was swept back to the 1800s. A long table covered with an emerald-green cloth and adorned by silver candelabras was the focus of the space. Fresh flowers in crystal vases offered color and fragrance. Silver chafing dishes with covers took up a buffet table along the wall.

A woman with faded red hair and bright green eyes, a gap between her teeth, gave a fork a polish on her apron, then set it down by a white porcelain plate.

"Maeve, we're here," Ciara said.

The woman looked up, grinned, and rushed toward Rayne with outstretched hands. "Rayne McGrath! The spitting image of your da, Conor. Oh, love, welcome home, welcome home. After all these years."

The housekeeper enfolded her in a hug, and Rayne felt like an eleven-year-old—not in a bad way. If Cormac had given her fresh, juicy apples, this woman had bandaged skinned knees and sneaked her cookies. Or as Maeve called them, biscuits.

"Maeve! So nice to see you again." Her heart was full of memories, and her dad was front and center. Being here made her miss him, too, with a fresh sting of grief. He and Nevin had cracked jokes and laughed, her uncle teasing his brother for his poet's soul while Nevin was the caretaker of the castle. So different, yet each allowed the other to be himself and loved him for it.

She blinked away tears.

Maeve placed a worn, soft hand on Rayne's cheek. Ciara stiffened beside her, but Rayne didn't question why.

Bristling seemed to be her cousin's second nature.

"I've made shepherd's pie and roasted veg from our garden," Maeve said. "I hope you don't mind a rustic meal?"

Before Rayne could answer, Ciara sniffed. "Probably expecting filet mignon and caviar. Champagne."

"I wasn't expecting anything," she said to Ciara, then smiled at Maeve. "I'm looking forward to dinner." She realized that only two places were set. "Did you already eat?"

"Oh no," Ciara said. "They want to put on airs, as if our own garden vegetables don't see us through. We normally all eat together."

Maeve's cheeks flushed. "Ciara. You're being rude."

"I would love it if we all ate together," Rayne said. "I insist."

Maeve's mouth quirked. "It's not proper your first night here. Lord Nevin would want to make you welcome."

Another woman, much younger, bustled in, her hair bright red, with Maeve's gap in her teeth. "Mum, nobody cares about that these days. You hang on to the old ways."

"Aine, mind your manners. Come meet—"

"Rayne McGrath," Rayne said, holding out her hand to Aine to make sure they were on the same page. No *ma'am* or formality needed.

"Howareye, Rayne! Aine Lloyd. I'm maid of the house and help cook in the kitchen when Neddy needs someone to chop for him. Mum, I think we should all eat together to find out what's what with the solicitor."

Ciara gave a thumbs-up.

Rayne glared at her cousin to keep quiet. There was so much to consider. What would happen to these sweet people if the castle sold?

It didn't stop Ciara from blurting, "Da left the property to Rayne, who needs to *think on it* before deciding whether or not to accept this pile of stone."

"What?" Maeve brought quivering fingers to her lips.

"If she doesn't, we all get the boot." Ciara crossed her arms over her chest. Her khakis and bulky sweater were out of place in this room, while Rayne's designer suit fit the part. She doubted her cousin cared.

The Lloyd ladies stared at her with identical expressions of shock. "I can't just pick up my life in California for a year to move here," Rayne said, her tone defensive. Surely the family would have places to go.

Cormac joined them, his manner smooth and even-tempered, though his face was pale. His eyes were red rimmed.

"Did ye hear that, Da?" Aine asked. "Lord McGrath left the castle—"

The butler raised his hand. "I heard. We don't know the full story yet, so don't make a fuss—mind your manners. I'm sure there's an explanation."

"I can tell you. My father lost his bleedin' head," Ciara interjected.

Rayne wondered what the staff thought of Uncle Nevin's passing—were they suspicious too? From what she knew of Hollywood plots, if Ciara, as the one to inherit, was first on a list of suspects, the servants would be second.

This room was formal and dated. Well cared for but still old, used. She remembered this space, but also a different dining area with a warmer feel.

"We normally sit in the dining room closest to the kitchen, where you don't need fancy silver dishes to keep things hot. Who has the time?" Ciara flung her arm to the side. "It's ridiculous, trying to impress Miss Posh Rodeo Drive."

"I don't need to be impressed." Rayne's stomach ached with suppressed tension.

Ciara's chin jutted. "We have two full-time hands that join us for meals, three when Richard shows up, if real hardworking folk won't offend your senses."

At this jab, Rayne stiffened. "I work very hard. I didn't ask for the castle or all of the crazy stipulations to your dad's will. I can't be responsible for a village! I have a business to run. In LA."

"I knew you'd turn your back on us," Ciara said, brewing for a fight. "You're the kind of woman who'd leave a babe in the street rather than slow down to save the wean. You're colder than ice. Heartless."

Aine's eyes rounded.

Rayne had had enough of Ciara's insults. "I am not a cold person. And you are no babe in the street!"

"Ladies," Maeve interjected, her arms to her sides. "Why don't you both sit at the table? I'd hate for the food to go to waste. Cormac?"

The butler gave a grave nod. "I believe that the cousins should discuss the will and the ramifications between them, without us."

"She has to decide by four tomorrow!" Ciara's voice cracked.

Cormac's nostrils flared the slightest bit. "If you would like our opinion on the matter, let us have a staff meeting tomorrow at one."

Rayne couldn't stay here, so there was nothing to discuss. "Fine." She exhaled and sat down. Ciara took the chair opposite.

Maeve and Aine served the cousins, and Cormac quietly left the room.

Maeve sighed and wrung her hands in her apron. "It's best you get to know one another. You only have family in this world. I don't understand what happened, and it sounds like Cormac thinks we should butt out for now. I'll respect me husband's wishes, but it's hard to do so when I'm burning with curiosity." She pointed to a panel on the wall with three buttons. "If you need anything, just ring."

"It's grand to meet you in person, Rayne. Enjoy your meal." Aine left with her mother.

Rayne had no choice but to face her cousin. Family. Were they anything at all alike? They were both around five eight, with slim frames. Naturally dark hair, stormy eyes. Inside, where it counted, they were night and day.

Ciara's bleached curls quivered, and she glowered across the table, not bothering to pick up her fork. "You aren't going to stay, are you? Selfish!"

Rayne willed herself to be silent a moment as she admired the golden crust on the mashed potatoes of her shepherd's pie. Then she said calmly, "It's preposterous to think that anybody in their right mind would give up their lives in a different country at the drop of a hat."

"That hat was my father." Ciara flung out her cloth napkin with a snap. "Who is now dead."

Rayne lowered her shoulders. "I'm very sorry." She understood that problem all too well. "Mine died when I was twelve."

Ciara's lower lip trembled. "It's not fair."

Life was not fair. If it were, their fathers would both be alive and perhaps sitting at this table with them. Landon wouldn't have stolen from Rayne. Ciara would have gotten the castle.

Rayne took a bite of the fluffy mashed potatoes and spiced ground meat with soft vegetables. It was delicious. Rustic. Homey, something she normally stayed away from. Gravy? Yum.

She generally ate the bare essentials to get by, usually too busy sewing or sketching to remember to eat. Food was a necessary evil, not something she really enjoyed. This helped to keep her trim, a must in Hollywood. That and twice-daily workouts. She was thin but strong.

While she ate, she wondered if Ciara was serious about her dad having been murdered, or if she'd been exaggerating. The Lloyds hadn't mentioned anything nefarious.

After a few minutes, Rayne put her fork down, stuffed to the gills. Ciara had polished her plate clean. "What do the police say about Uncle Nevin being killed?"

"Garda Williams is an eejit and slow as dirt. Da used that tractor three times a week practically his whole life with no accidents. Why now?"

Rayne sipped from a crystal goblet of water. No ice. Her dad had said that Europeans didn't really use it, and he hadn't put it in his beverages either. "Who"—besides Ciara—"might want him . . . dead?" And surely she'd heard wrong. *Garda*.

"I don't know." Ciara fisted her hand and placed it on the table, next to her silverware. "Grathton is *his* village. There was nothing he wouldn't do for the people in it. Nothing. He's given Richard so many chances to get the mill operating. Mooch lives on the property practically for free. Dafydd lives here, and Amos—he's the grounds manager. They at least have jobs."

"Who else is on the property?"

"Neddy—the cook. He's got a wee room by the kitchen. The Lloyds." Ciara sipped her water. "That's all."

"I wish I'd had a chance to see Uncle Nevin one last time," Rayne mused. "Was he acting differently?"

"His temper was shorter than usual, I suppose. He complained about rising prices over his nightly whiskey."

"Hmm."

"That's it?" Ciara exclaimed.

"What?"

Ciara tossed her cloth napkin over her empty plate. "You don't know what it's like to live on an estate with a village attached.

We grow food the villagers sell and provide meat at a discount for them. It's a responsibility that can't be taken lightly. You need to think of everyone, not just your posh designer bridal shop."

Rayne's chest tightened with her Celtic temper—she counted to five, rooted her reactions to the earth, and calmed down. She wouldn't accept Ciara's guilt trip.

"Those are valid concerns," Rayne said. "But what about my life?"

Ciara stared at her.

"I have a business." Rayne sipped her water. "I have wedding gown orders that must be completed, or several brides won't have a happy-ever-after kind of day, which is what I provide for people." She didn't expect Ciara to understand. No engagement ring on her cousin's finger either.

"Expensive silk dresses," Ciara sniffed. "You wouldn't last a day on this land." She reached across the table for Rayne's hand and rubbed her thumb over the skin. "Soft. Just like you."

Rayne yanked her hand back. She used quality lotion to make sure her skin was taken care of, had her calluses buffed out at the spa. Her cousin could use a full week to get her supple skin smooth.

It made her mad that Ciara had her playing defense again when she prided herself on keeping her emotions in check. Her cousin could do what she liked.

"I would *never* be able to work with you. You're impossible." A year in the same castle was too much to contemplate.

Ciara's jaw clenched. "I dare you to see the grounds in the morning."

"No promises." Rayne was beat—besides, what was the point? Her life was LA.

The cousins glared at each other. Behind the anger was grief, but Rayne couldn't help her cousin. The cost was too high. She cared, of course she did—she didn't have a heart of stone—but she couldn't stay in Ireland.

Ciara rocketed out of the grand dining room, sucking the air with her.

Rayne, exhausted, scanned the paintings on the walls. She'd last been in this room with her dad, Aunt Amalie and Uncle Nevin, and Padraig. Now all four were dead.

Shivering, Rayne hurried from the dining table to the hall.

Chapter Five

Rayne took stock of her position in the hall to get her bearings. She turned left toward the foyer, remembering sliding down the thick wooden rails of the central staircase, her and Padraig laughing like hyenas. Aunt Amalie had warned them not to get hurt, but she'd said it with a warm smile.

Old candle sconces had been replaced with electric bulbs over a hundred years ago, around the end of the Victorian era. Rich velvet wallpaper in maroon and ivory stripes now appeared faded. The suits of armor, shields, and swords had been magical when she was a kid.

There was no sign of the Lloyd family, but she remembered where her dad's room had been, so she climbed the staircase, admiring the open gallery, which led to suites on the left and more bedrooms and offices on the right. Uncle Nevin's chamber was in the farthest corner—right above the main-floor sun-room.

A door slammed on the third floor, which had been used for storage. Padraig had dared her to go inside the cobwebbed attics, and it had terrified her. Was that Ciara or the staff?

Rayne paused to admire the landscapes and portraits hanging on the wall. There was her dad as a young man of twenty-five, before he'd met her mother. He had a brooding gaze and dark-as-night hair. Very handsome.

Uncle Nevin was next to him, and beside his portrait was a professional photo of Ciara, with the same black hair before she'd bleached it white. Gray eyes.

There was no picture of Rayne. She acknowledged that she wished she had one too. It made her feel empty, as if she were lacking something she hadn't realized she was missing.

Five doors down at the end of the hall was her dad's room. The door was partially open, a soft lamp glowing on the nightstand. Her suitcase was on the luggage rack at the foot of the bed. A fireplace took up one wall, and plenty of candlesticks sat on the mantel. During bad weather, it wasn't uncommon for the power to go out. It had scared her as a child until her dad had made a game of it. Now she loved storms.

Several silver-framed photos of her dad also crowded the mantel. There was one of the two of them together down by the lake—she'd been eleven and believed her father would live forever. She felt him here, in his space.

"Conor, what should I do?" She lifted the picture and studied it. "I miss you, Dad. You understand why I can't stay, don't you?"

His dark eyes glinted at her with love, a smile on his face. He was a poet and a rogue. An adventurer who had fallen head over heels with an American actress. Her parents had laughed a lot. Sadness overwhelmed her, and she put the picture back.

Her phone rang, jolting her from the past. Her heart raced, and she reached for her purse on the nightstand. The designer leather, feminine pink and silver, didn't match the deep-blue-and-wood decor.

"Hello?"

"Rayne! Darling, are you all right? What's going on?"

The battery light bleeped five percent. Shoot. Where was her charger? "Gimme a sec, Lauren. There's so much to tell you, but I'm out of batt—" The phone went black.

"Battery." She sighed and searched her Dior tote bag for the charger. Then she spent the next ten minutes looking for a free outlet. The TV and the lamp took both sockets.

So she could sit on the toilet in the en suite with her phone plugged in next to her, or wait until morning. Rayne pulled back the covers, sensing her dad's energy around her, and fell into a deep sleep.

She didn't know what time it was when she was awakened by clanks in the hall right outside her door. They continued sporadically throughout the night. Her cousin Padraig had told her that their dead aunt Claire, a little girl, haunted the castle. At eleven, she'd believed her older cousin.

Rayne was too scared to get up and check. She wasn't the heroine too stupid to live, investigating noises in a house where her uncle might have been killed. Had Ciara done it? The loving Lloyds? Landon appeared in her dreams as well, laughing at her as he showered himself in her cash.

At last, she woke up and stretched, not the least refreshed. Rayne shoved the comforter aside, her stomach rumbling. She took a shower in the en suite bathroom her dad had installed after moving to America. It was only twenty years old, with plenty of outlets.

She rushed with her makeup, charging her phone. It was nine in the morning. Her mother, eight hours behind, was sleeping, so Rayne texted that she was well. She sent a long message about the problem she faced. Could she leave Hollywood for Grathton Village for a year?

It was ludicrous to even consider, and she was certain her mother would provide reason and logic.

Rayne made her way to the homey kitchen, where Maeve and the cook were talking over what to make for dinner. The family chef wore black-and-white-checked pants and a white oxford shirt—no apron. Short iron-gray hair, trimmed dark brows, and a goatee.

"Morning!" Rayne said.

Maeve greeted her with a welcoming smile. "*Maidin mhaith*, Rayne. This is Neddy Plackett, our cook."

It sounded like Maeve said *mah-jongg* or something. Rayne would need a translator before this trip was over. In the past, her dad had explained what she didn't catch in context.

"Morning, milady." Neddy put his paper and pen aside. "Can I get you some porridge left over from breakfast?"

Rayne controlled a nose scrunch. "No, thank you. Fruit is fine. I don't usually eat a heavy breakfast." Or any meal. A protein shake in the car on the way to work was her normal.

"Aye, sure. How about some toast? The soda bread is still warm from the oven," Neddy said, cutting thick slices from a loaf on the counter with a serrated knife, then popping it into the antique toaster. "Apples and oranges are on the counter."

Rayne didn't have the heart to tell him that bread was not on her approved-foods list, and when he set the crock of fresh butter and strawberry preserves next to her plate, she didn't balk. It would be a treat to remember after she was home. Irish butter was delish.

"I'll look for a gym in the village," she said.

Maeve bestowed a confused smile on Rayne, pulled a note from her pants pocket, and handed it to her. "From Ciara. A gym?"

"Like, twenty-four-hour fitness?" What would she do without a gym? Or yoga on the beach? Sea air was her Xanax.

"I don't think we have those." Maeve shrugged.

"In the city, they will," Neddy said.

"Dublin?" That had been an hour and a half in the car. Not convenient.

"Kilkenny is closer, and only forty-five minutes," Neddy said. "How long are you here for?"

"I'm not sure. I'd planned on a week, till after the funeral, but my ticket is open-ended." Well, she could take long walks around the manor before it was sold off. Find the apple tree she used to climb.

"Have you thought more about what you'll do this afternoon?" Maeve asked, her tone hesitant.

Rayne swallowed the best bite of bread and jam she'd ever had. "Mm. Uh, well. I honestly crashed last night. Hoped today I'd wake up to find it all a bad dream. Yet here I am." She wiped her mouth with a soft cloth napkin. "Do you think there's any way the lawyer was mistaken? I mean, it's insane to think Uncle Nevin would destroy everything just because I won't take it on."

"Destroy?" Maeve gasped.

"Sorry! Not literally. Sold," Rayne amended. "I need to hear the will read again, because no freaking way would a sane man threaten to sell the castle just to keep me here for a year. Right?"

"Oh, dear. Not that his lordship ever talked to me of finances, but it's been losing money in a slow trickle." Dots of red colored Maeve's cheeks. "If you stay, we'd help you how we could."

"You could sell this jam," Rayne said, only partly kidding. She opened the note from her cousin. Ciara, in neat penmanship, remarked on how manor life didn't start at noon with a champagne brunch. When Rayne was awake, would she please meet them at the barn to see how the property worked before she let it be sold off to strangers.

"Has Ciara always been so hostile?"

Neddy wisely busied himself with rinsing the knife in the sink.

Maeve glanced at the note. "She had a hard lot with her single mum in London, an Irish lass from Cork. It was a shock to come to the country and suddenly have a da that wasn't always . . . warm." She dabbed her knuckle to her nose and sniffed. "This family has suffered so much loss."

Rayne lowered her voice. "Do you think something happened to Uncle Nevin?"

The cook dropped the knife on the strainer to dry. "What on earth do ye mean?"

Maeve gripped the chairback. "Ciara believes someone killed Lord McGrath. Told the garda, so it's under investigation."

"And why didn't you tell me that?" Neddy demanded.

"You were with your sick mother when the accident happened. Over a week it's been, and we can't make funeral arrangements." Maeve bowed her head as if in prayer, then raised it again. "I simply don't want to believe it. Who would do such an awful thing?"

Rayne gave Neddy the side-eye. He'd been gone, huh? "How long have you worked here, Neddy?"

"Four years." Neddy glanced at her. "I'd like to stay on."

She pushed the plate from her and checked the time on her phone. Ten. "I guess I better get out to the barn to meet Ciara. I really wish Uncle Nevin had given this castle to her. She was sure expecting it yesterday at the lawyer's office. It was a blow for her."

"Is there any way you can stay?" Maeve asked. It was difficult to ignore the pleading tone.

"No. I'm sorry. I have wedding gown orders to make in LA— ladies come to the boutique for fittings." God, she needed to get home right away and find out what had happened with Landon and Modern Lace. She'd poured her heart and soul into her business, and the last year with Landon's partnership had propelled her up the ladder in the design world.

"What are we to do, then?" Neddy asked, shifting so that his back was to the sink.

"I don't know." Guilt turned the sweet strawberry in her mouth to bitter.

"Will you give us a letter of reference?" Neddy wore an expression of disbelief. "I thought I'd have this job for life."

Rayne stood, her knees wobbly. She couldn't think of what might happen to the staff. Surely there was enough of a pension for the Lloyds and Neddy. She didn't know the first thing about running a manor like this. "Of course. If not me, then Ciara." She wanted to distance herself but felt trapped in the kitchen. "I should go."

Aine appeared in khaki slacks, rubber clogs, and a light-blue floral-print long-sleeved shirt.

"Will you take Rayne to the barn, *mo leanbh*?" Maeve asked. "Ciara wants to show Rayne the property. Don't forget our staff meeting at one."

To try and entice Rayne to stay, no doubt. Well, she would harden her heart for everyone's own good. The same one her cousin accused her of not having hurt like crazy. "I remember the way. Thank you!"

Maeve cleared her throat as Rayne headed to the hall, pointing toward the cellar door. "This is a shortcut, dear. Mind your shoes! It's quite muddy by the paddocks. Maybe you should change into something less . . ."

"White?" Aine filled in. The young woman exuded happy energy, her red hair in braids. Her green eyes twinkled as if she were always on the verge of a joke.

"Oh!" Rayne had paired a short-sleeved cream cashmere mock turtleneck with denim capris, covered in silk floral patches, and ivory Converse. "This should be fine. I'm just looking at the property."

"Well, if you come to your senses, there are wellies by the kitchen door here in many sizes." Maeve's disapproval was clear in her folded arms and tapping heel.

Other people's shoes? Uh, that would be a hard no.

"At least take your uncle's flannel to put over your gorgeous jumper," Aine said. "It's cool weather compared to where you're from." She pressed a soft gray button-up shirt into her hand.

"Thanks." Rayne scooted by the trio in the kitchen to the door leading to the cellar and all that wonderful jam. Canned goods, too, which Maeve made apple tarts with. Another door led outside.

Sixty degrees was still cold, despite the sun peaking like a beacon over the barn in the distance, and she was grateful for the flannel shirt. There was a path cleared with river rock to keep her shoes clean, and she followed it as if she were Dorothy on the yellow brick road. She shrugged on the flannel, catching the faintest hint of lavender. Fabric softener?

Rayne rounded a bend and slowed as she made out a couple of figures. Ciara's bleached hair sat like a cotton puff on her head, and next to her was a man a few inches taller than her, wearing a brimmed cap, jeans, and shirt. His chest and biceps stretched the fabric in an attractive way.

Which of the three men on the property was he?

The barn was old and made of stone, with a patched thatch roof. Three horses were in the paddock to the right of the structure. Rayne's pulse hummed in alarm, but they were safe on the other side of the fence. In another pen were dozens of ivory sheep with black faces. Maybe more—she didn't care to count them.

She plugged her nose, wishing she'd brought her silk scarf. Just as stinky as the other sheep from yesterday. Funny how her childhood memories didn't come with the pew factor.

A gray dog with white markings paced the fence line, next to a larger black one with white ears and a white muzzle. She recognized the sheepdog breed from when she'd visited here as a child.

They were working dogs, her da had explained when she'd wanted to play with them. There were cats and her aunt's indoor terriers that the kids could cuddle, but she'd always been drawn to Rua, a large Irish setter with soft fur, and would sneak to the barn in search of the old dog.

"Hello," she called, when she was about ten feet away from where Ciara and the hottie stood in front of the barn.

The man whistled to keep the dogs at the paddock, though their ears lifted with interest in the stranger.

"About time you joined us," Ciara snarked, her gaze snagging on Rayne's borrowed shirt. "I need to leave, or I'll miss my appointment. Dafydd Norman, meet my American cousin, Rayne McGrath." She tilted her nose and told Rayne, "He's my fiancé—resident shepherd, mechanic, and doer of whatever else needs doing."

"How are ye," Dafydd said, not offering a hand but raising both of them to show the dirty gloves. "I guess I am a jack-of-all-trades." He gestured toward the barn. "I'm sticking close to the sheep pen, since we had an injured lamb. Amos is inside now."

"Oh. Will it be all right?" Lambs were cute. Much cuter than grown sheep.

"Aye." Dafydd adjusted his cap. "It's too late now for Ciara to drive you around the place."

More guilt. Rayne was just fine not shaking hands. She was amazed that her bristly cousin had a fiancé. It made her feel better about allowing the manor to be sold off—until her next thought was that Dafydd would be out of a job as well. What would happen to the sheep?

Ciara stuck her chin out. "If I'm late, Richard will disappear on me again. You'll have to wander on your own, princess. Morning around here starts at dawn."

"I didn't agree to a time," Rayne said. "Let's blame jet lag."

"Excuses to avoid work." Ciara pecked Dafydd on the cheek and pulled keys from her pocket that Rayne assumed belonged to the old pickup near the paddock.

"I can take you on a tour," a man said, coming from the barn. He was gorgeous, with wavy dark blond-hair and blue eyes, broad shoulders, and snug jeans. His thighs were muscled. If Vikings wore leather work boots, this man would fit the bill. Dafydd paled in comparison.

"Hey. I'm Rayne McGrath." She smiled.

The Viking swiped his hand on his hip and offered it to her, giving a firm shake. "Amos Lowell, grounds manager. I have a cottage on the property."

Another man who would lose his position once Rayne left. He would hate her as much as Ciara. Great.

From the corner of her eye, she saw an Irish setter bolting through the sheep like an amber-furred wrecking ball heading straight for them.

They all turned when one of the sheep bleeped in alarm.

Deep-red fur, a high tail, and four paws leaped over the top rail of the fence and skidded to a stop before Dafydd.

"Blarney!" Dafydd reprimanded, his tone impatient.

The dog turned golden-brown eyes on Rayne, and her heart melted. "Blarney? What a sweet pup." She didn't have a pet in LA. No time.

Dafydd whistled and Blarney sat, his long tail sweeping the mud. Another whistle, then Dafydd gestured toward the barn, where both the older sheepdogs waited in the shade as if it were hot.

Blarney's body wriggled, and she could tell he was young, a puppy really, wanting to play and make friends.

Mud flicked side to side. He stared at her, then the other dogs, not wanting to obey Dafydd.

Just to be safe, Rayne backed up a few steps, conscious of her ivory sneakers. She slipped in some mud but maintained her balance thanks to Amos's hand on her elbow. The man was solid.

Ciara palmed the keys. "You need boots, Rayne, to wash the muck off, not fancy trainers. There are several pairs in the kitchen. Where you got Da's flannel."

A warm shirt was one thing, another person's enclosed shoes another. "I'll be careful."

Dafydd gave another whistle, and the next thing she knew, Blarney had forgotten his order to join the other dogs and was darting right for her.

Rayne braced her body as the dog jumped joyfully against her. She stepped back—into Amos—and Blarney dropped to all fours with a playful bark. Looking down in horror, she saw two paw prints, muck and all, marking her cashmere sweater. It would be ruined. She needed a dry cleaner quick. It didn't help that Maeve and Aine had warned her.

"Bad dog!" Dafydd said, hiding a smirk.

Had he whistled that command on purpose?

Chapter Six

All the mindfulness training in the world couldn't prevent Rayne from whirling toward her cousin as Ciara burst out laughing.

"What is the matter with you?" Rayne asked. She turned on Dafydd. "Did you make the dog do that?"

"I wish," Dafydd started to say, but then at her furious expression, he explained, "Meaning, lass, that Blarney has a mind of his own. I told Nevin the pup had a willful temperament. Your uncle spoiled him."

As if realizing he was the subject of discussion, Blarney lowered his head and whined.

"Makes him hard to train is all," Amos said. His blue eyes sparkled. "Time and patience will be needed."

"What's Blarney supposed to do around here?" Rayne pointed to the sheep pen, recalling how he'd knocked them all over as if they were pins and he were a bowling ball. She hoped his job wasn't to be a sheepdog.

Amos backed up from her, and she realized he'd let his hand linger on her hip. "Gundog."

Rayne shook her sweater so the loose mud fell, knowing better than to wipe the cashmere or it would truly be ruined. Too bad she hadn't buttoned her uncle's flannel shirt. "I don't like guns."

"Your uncle enjoyed hunting. Blarney's job is to fetch birds on the property after we hunt them, for food," Dafydd said. His accent was different from Amos and Ciara's. "So far, he's been a bad investment."

"Uh, he can hear you," Rayne said, as the dog lowered his head.

Blarney peeked up at her with those golden-brown eyes, and she melted once more. He scooted closer to her.

"As amusing as this has been, I'm late, and Richard is already a pain in the arse. Just wait till he finds out that he's booted from his home as well as a job. Lunch at one," Ciara told them all, "in the usual dining room. We must discuss what's going on. What to do." Her voice caught. "Amos, show my cousin around the gardens and the lake? You should be there too, since this affects you."

Rayne held up her palm. "I need to go change before the stain sets." She lifted the hem and shook more mud loose.

"Waste time, then." Ciara glared at Rayne. "What do you care?" She turned on her heel and ran off, behind the old truck.

"Ciara, *annwyl*," Dafydd said, stepping after her.

Within seconds, the car Ciara had picked Rayne up in had zoomed into sight, moving past where they stood to the driveway at the front of the house. Must have been on the other side of the pickup. Dafydd shook his head.

"Stubborn." Dafydd stared at Rayne, then Amos, then Blarney. "Just like Nevin." *And you* was implied. He strode into the barn, followed by the older dogs, and allowed the door to bang shut behind him.

Blarney perked up, and Amos blew out a breath. "You resemble your uncle," he said. "With the hair and eyes. Stubborn too?"

"Maybe just a little. Between you and me, I had to take deportment classes for my wild Celtic temper." She sighed. "My mom insisted it was for my own good."

Amos smacked his leg and laughed. "A true McGrath." He gestured toward the old pickup. "Your chariot, ma'am."

Blarney leaped into the open bed in the back.

"I guess he wants to join us." Rayne was torn between going inside and touring the property with a stained shirt. The truth was, it would take a miracle to get the mud out. She had only a few things with her, none of them fitting for outdoorsy activities.

"We'll be in the truck the whole time, and you can change clothes when we return before lunch." Amos studied her with frank curiosity. "Nobody to see your shirt, if that's what's bothering you."

"All right." He probably categorized her as a diva too. How could he know the hours she put in at her sewing machine? Building a business from the bottom up hadn't been easy. Nothing had been handed to her. If anything, she'd felt the need to work harder because her mom was famous.

Oh well. Rayne opened the door of the truck, which was so ancient it creaked. There was a long bench seat with a blanket tossed over it as a cover. The truck was probably older than she was, and looked it. "This yours?" She patted the cracked dash.

"No." Amos chuckled. "Nevin let everyone use it to drive around the property. I have a motorcycle."

Rayne imagined Amos riding a Harley and swallowed, her mouth dry.

Amos started the engine and it ground, then revved. "It's got some life in her. It helps that Dafydd is a whiz with engines."

She sat gingerly, half expecting to be poked in the butt with a spring. Before she could close the door, Blarney squirmed in next to her.

Laughing, she petted the pup. "Sure is friendly."

"He misses Nevin." Amos glanced at her with a smile. "I think Blarney recognized that flannel shirt and hoped you were him."

"Ah!" Rayne nodded with understanding. "That's why he was in a hurry and knocked the sheep over. That's sad."

"Aye."

She searched but didn't see any seat belts. "Is there . . . ?"

"No." Amos grinned. "But we don't go that fast in this truck. God knows what would happen if it went over thirty."

"Okay." Rayne settled back to be in the moment and banished all the statistics drummed into her head about seat belt safety. She rolled the window down and enjoyed the breeze on her skin. Nature was good for the soul.

"Maeve said that you were here as a child, twice. What do you remember about the property?" He drove away from the barn.

Blarney somehow finagled his way between them and lay with his head on her thigh, shoving her against the door. She pushed down on the manual lock and prayed for the best.

"I was eight, and then eleven. I remember the lake and the sheep. The creek. Hiking. The turret—it was magical." Rayne eyed Amos's strong profile and put his age at around midthirties, but outdoor living might have her guessing wrong. His income? Hard to tell. A property manager in the States might make more than one in rural Ireland. "How long have you been here?"

"I moved to Grathton Village as a teen, when my mum married a guy with big dreams and bigger schemes."

Like Landon. Snake. "What happened?"

"Mum died when I was at university. He sold off her things and left no forwarding address. I needed a job, and home, and Nevin gave me both."

And now here was Rayne, about to take it all away. *Oh, Uncle Nevin. What were you thinking?*

"Were you close to my uncle?"

"Friendly, but not mates. Nevin wanted to take care of this castle for the next generations to come," Amos said. "It was everything to him."

They continued along a dirt road. To her left were several cottages about the size of your average tiny home. "Who lives there?"

"I have one, Dafydd has one. Richard, who runs the mill when it's working. There used to be more staff, but we've made do, pitching in when it's time to harvest or shear sheep for wool. It's a family."

She cringed inside. Amos wasn't making an overt case for staying but showing her the truth.

"Are you sure my uncle wasn't drinking or something?"

Amos laughed. "He liked his whiskey as well as the next Irishman, but no, he wasn't drowning his sorrows. Early to bed, early to rise, that was him."

"He and my dad were night and day," she said. "My father was a poet and artist. Nevin was king of the castle. Literally. Lord McGrath."

"Conor did well in America?"

"Yes." Rayne ran her hand down Blarney's soft fur. "He missed Ireland, but he loved my mother more. His poetry connected with people."

Amos chuckled. "Nevin was quite proud that Conor was a published author, married to an actress."

Rayne smiled at the way Amos said it, with the emphasis on *actress*. "My mother is one of the kindest people I know. I strive to be like her, but, well . . . deportment classes."

They shared a laugh.

The truck bounced along the dirt road. To the right was a lush garden with vegetables. Fruit trees. They turned a curve, and she sucked in a breath when she saw the lake. "Oh, wow! I forgot how amazing this is! Like, spectacular."

Amos's chest rumbled with his laughter. Blarney sat up to catch the view as well. Ducks swam on the still water. Geese. Branches from a flowering tree provided shade. The contrast of the blue sky against the greenish-gray water and the pink of the flowers, the yellow of whatever bloomed at the water's edge, made her fingers itch to capture the scene.

Rayne reached for her sketchbook to create a memory she could fill in later. Her bridal designs at Modern Lace weren't just whites and soft hues but bright colors too. A bride these days could defy tradition. "My bag!"

"What's wrong?" Amos's grip tightened on the wheel in response to her alarm.

"I forgot my sketchbook. I never leave without it and my pencils." It was nice to have the urge to draw. She hadn't felt it since Monday, the longest time in years that she hadn't drawn something.

"You're an artist, like your dad? I thought you made fancy dresses."

"I guess so." She looked at him with a wry smile. "Design is about color and texture and so many other things combined. The finished gown is a work of art."

"You have a beautiful smile, Rayne McGrath."

She blushed at his sincere compliment. She made an effort to have the right clothes, the right makeup, because you never knew when you might be photographed.

Hollywood was a pool of folks hoping to be noticed. She was no different. She wanted her designs to be in high-end department stores all over the world. For her, that would be success.

Blarney licked her hand.

What was she doing here, in Grathton Village? She needed to get home. To pick up the pieces of her life. She didn't have the credentials to save anyone else.

Not even this lovely property her dad had grown up on. The McGrath legacy. Nerves caused her skin to itch.

Amos pulled over to the side of the road and pointed to an expanse of green lawn. "There's the maze your uncle uncovered, from the early 1800s. Nevin found a survey map while going through boxes that had been damaged in storage from the roof leak. He couldn't believe it when he was able to locate it."

"A maze?"

"Yes. Now you have to use your imagination." Amos's sexy smile invited her to play along.

No problem. "Okay."

"He was going to rebuild it with hedgerows after harvest this October, but you can see, if you squint, the oval lines from before."

They'd parked at the top of the hill, overlooking a valley. Rayne noticed mounds of earth and stone in the distance, as if there had been buildings once upon a time that the land had reclaimed. She couldn't discern a pattern for a maze. Missing her sunglasses, she shaded her eyes.

"See?"

She shook her head. "No. Sorry."

"Let's get out."

They did, Blarney stretching and chasing butterflies in the grass. Amos stood next to her and raised his hand over her forehead in a very close move that made her forget all about Landon.

Almost. She'd been a fool and wouldn't soon forget that.

"Now do you see it?"

Rayne squinted. The pasture was beautiful and green, surrounded by oak trees. Just barely she could make out the oval pattern of a maze. And beyond that, more bungalows. "Yes! Is that a creek?"

"Aye."

"I think my dad might have painted this. It's familiar."

"A poet and a painter?" Amos said. "Talent runs in your veins, Rayne." He pointed out sheep along the rolling hills, the windmill off in the distance. "And if we turn around, the castle is behind us." They shifted, side by side, and there was the tall turret of the castle above the trees. "This hilltop is my favorite place on the castle grounds."

Rayne sighed heavily. "I can see why. It's so beautiful." And she would surely put an end to the McGrath heritage. "I wish . . ."

Amos turned to look at her with compassion in his blue gaze. Tempted to confess all about Landon and the theft of her business, she just couldn't. She was going home to LA, and she'd rather these people think her a diva than know she was a failure. Broke. The truth was that she needed the money as much as Ciara.

Blarney nudged her leg, and she shook free of the spell. Rayne pulled her phone from her pocket. No bars. No texts from her mother. No call from Officer Peters. "It's a little after twelve. We should go."

"The lush trees around here make it hard to get a signal," Amos said.

They were beautiful. The whole property was. Rayne cleared her throat. "Amos, I'm sure that everyone will want me to stay here in Ireland, but I can't. Uncle Nevin's will decreed that I have to live here without going back to LA for a full year or he will sell off the property, ruin the village, invite the plague."

Amos's lips twitched.

"I'm no messiah. It's not a reasonable request." Rayne searched his face and found understanding.

"It's not," he agreed.

They got back in the truck, Blarney choosing to stay in the bed this time for the bumpy ride to the castle. They reached a green stretch of steep hill and a red tractor on its side toward the bottom of a ditch. A raven perched on a large black wheel. Amos slowed.

Her heart hammered. "Is that where it happened? It's a sharp incline!"

"Aye. Nevin mowed that three times a week. Knew the terrain like the back of his hand," Amos said, his voice sad. Scars in the green from the wheels in the grass marred the lawn.

"Do you think it was an accident?"

Amos stepped on the gas, and the truck jolted forward. "Yes."

He didn't sound certain. The tractor appeared to have tipped, and she could see it happening. Tragic. Was Ciara so riddled with grief that she imagined murder? What was taking the police so long?

A few minutes later, Amos slowed to a stop in front of the manor. She hadn't come up with a way to question him further. Her gut told her he was a good man, but she couldn't trust her instincts.

She unlocked the door from where she sat. "I'm going to change my shirt, and I guess I'll see you in the dining room."

A breeze blew Amos's blond waves as he nodded. "You have to make a choice that suits you, Rayne. Nevin's a right bastard for putting you in this position."

She climbed out of the truck, one hundred percent in agreement. "Thanks."

Amos drove to the barn, Blarney watching her from the bed with somber golden-brown eyes.

Why did she feel so guilty? This wasn't her problem! She had so many of her own right now.

Rayne raced to her room and called her mom, quickly changing from her ruined cashmere sweater to a leopard-print T-shirt with satin ribbing around the collar and sleeves. She placed the flannel shirt on the dresser.

Her mom answered. "Honey! Are you okay?"

She put the phone on speaker and touched up her foundation and lipstick. "You read my texts? This is such a mess. What can I do?"

"It's outrageous! What was Nevin thinking? Scratch that. He must not have been. I talked with Paul. He said in the States, an owner can do what he wants with his own property. He's not sure about Ireland."

Rayne dabbed powder on her nose and smoothed the frown line between her brows, her stomach clenched tight. "If I don't agree to his terms, people will lose their jobs. The castle will be sold." She choked on the words. The sheep, the horses. Sweet Blarney. What would happen to them all?

"I'm sure they can find something else," Lauren assured her. "Don't take that on. Darn that Nevin anyway."

"The lawyer said that the village doesn't have a lot of opportunity for growth. The kids are moving away to the closest big city for jobs. They're tied together somehow." She pursed her lips and added a layer of gloss. Who could she ask? She didn't know any of these people enough to trust them. They would all want her to stay here.

"Your dad truly missed Ireland. I didn't realize how much until after his death, when I found poetry he hadn't shared with me." Lauren's voice deepened. "He loved me, but he also loved his home and his history. That's your history too."

Rayne left the bathroom and put on clean black jeans and black leather boots. Silver earring . . . where was the other one? There! Next to the picture of her and her dad that she loved, taken at this castle. She averted her gaze and piled her hair into a loose ponytail.

"Any word about Landon?"

"Not yet, hon."

As if things could get worse. "I'll be home as soon as I can. I'll have more details after the meeting with the lawyer and his wife for tea today."

Her mom deep-sighed.

Her nape tingled. "What?"

"Well. I just wonder, Rayne, if this isn't a sign of some kind."

She plopped on the edge of the mattress. It dipped. Her mom was something of a mystic in her real life, unlike the Christian character she portrayed on *Family Forever*. "Like?"

"You had big plans, and the universe really changed direction. Fate, whatever you want to call it."

"Yeah." Rayne twirled the silver earring. "Landon Short screwed me over. Twelve women paid me to make their dream wedding dresses, and I don't have time to veer from my dead-lines." Panic rose in her belly.

"I read the tarot cards before I called you. Change. Chal-lenges. But those challenges will lead to great opportunity."

Her skin chilled. "What are you suggesting?"

"You will need to buy new fabric anyway. What would hap-pen if you agreed to stay there for a year?"

Rayne couldn't catch a breath. She'd thought her mother would be sensible. Logical. Born and raised in California, her mother was a mix of hippie and pragmatist. "I can't do that!"

"Think past the no, darling. What if? I'd help you put your things in storage. I just replaced the siding on this place, or I'd give you whatever you needed. I can offer a chunk to get you seed money for the wedding dresses, so you can complete your orders. You can sew there, can't you? Your dad said it was huge. Aren't castles big?"

Ginormous. She nibbled her thumbnail, her mind tumbling. "Yeah."

"Rayne. This will give you a chance to be close to your dad. And you're forgetting a bonus—if you stay for a year, you get a hundred grand. Ciara does too."

And everyone would have their jobs. If she could make this a success.

Her mom said softly, "Twelve months will pass, no matter what."

Rayne threw herself back on the bed and stared at the ceiling in her dad's room. "I thought you were going to tell me to come home."

"I think you should look at all of the options. You have the chance to do something really great. And yes, I would help you here too. Whatever you decide."

They said good-bye, and Rayne accidentally fell asleep, missing the meeting with the staff.

This didn't endear her to Ciara, and even Aine seemed to give her the cold shoulder when she came downstairs. When they left for the Hugheses' house for tea, Rayne still didn't know what to do.

Chapter Seven

"Stop giving me the death glare, would ya?" Rayne said to her cousin. Ciara was so mad that she drove the car like a robot, with abrupt moves. "I didn't mean to fall asleep."

"You think you're so special—spoiled, rich, American. Making everyone wait on you. Well, we ate without you. I hope you're hungry." Her cousin wore slacks and a shirt in funeral black, her hair mussed. God forbid she put on lipstick.

"That's silly!" And mean. And it was good they were having tea with sandwiches at the Hugheses'. She grabbed the door handle as Ciara made a sharp turn. "I've apologized a zillion times."

"A zillion. You are so dramatic!"

"Me? Ha! You could be a queen of the screen!" Rayne brought her fingers to her chest. Her heart beat crazily at the outburst. She'd supposedly learned to control her temper a long time ago, yet two days with Ciara and all of that *om* was out the pickle-peppered window.

Her phone rang, and her best friend Jenn's picture popped up on the screen. Here was a friend who knew how to be one. The two of them were inseparable in their free time. Rayne realized that it wasn't just her business and her apartment that were in jeopardy; her social life was on the line too.

She texted. *Can't talk now.*

Jenn replied right away. *I know. Landon's a jerk. Come live with me. Lauren told me everything. Major suckage.*

You live in a studio. No room.

The truth was, Rayne needed space to make her dresses. Her apartment cost thousands a month, and the lease on Rodeo Drive was astronomical. It was now a police scene with only the remains of her supplies. Trims and fabrics. No dresses.

Her stomach rolled, and she felt sick.

This was June, and thankfully her June bride dresses had been sent already, which meant that three were due in July, three in August, two in September, and she could worry about the rest later. She had the sketches and measurements for her ladies. She'd have to get the materials she didn't have and find a place to create. And her state-of-the-art sewing machine! It had been worth more than this Fiat.

"Your skin is green. Are you going to hurl?" Ciara asked. "Should I pull over?"

The two-lane country road dipped and curved, and an incessant parade of sheep crossed to one side or the other in front of them. Big trucks with hay took up more than their share of the street. She would rather drive in LA than here, which was actually more dangerous.

"I'm fine." Rayne clutched her phone in misery.

Jenn texted again. *Call me when you can! I'll pick you up from the airport and we can get drinks.*

Last time they'd had something to celebrate, but what a joke that had turned out to be. While she'd been drinking whiskey with her friends, her lover had cleared out their bank account, their business, and his house, leaving his car at the airport with no forwarding address.

Ciara parked behind the solicitor's office in front of a white cottage with a red door, red-framed windows, and a new roof. Flower boxes in front of the windows were filled with Daisy's namesake in a variety of colors. On any other day? Adorable.

"Can you tell me what you're going to do?" Ciara removed the key. "I think I deserve to know."

Rayne's shoulders bowed. "I can't stay in Ireland, Ciara."

Her cousin got out and slammed the door so hard the car shook. Rayne also exited but made a point of closing hers quietly.

She tried to understand Ciara's predicament, which was as farfetched as a Hollywood plot.

Grow up in London with a single Irish mom. Mom dies. Find out you have a dad and a village, then dad dies and you don't get a cent. Brutal.

If Ciara were nicer, Rayne would invite her cousin to the States. Once she got her own life sorted.

Daisy opened the door to the cottage, just as cute as she'd been yesterday. Bright sundress, her brunette bob curled softly at her chin, red lipstick. "Welcome! Come on in, ladies. I've got the tea brewing. Scones just out of the oven."

Rayne's stomach growled at the sugary scents.

Ciara refused to look at Rayne as they entered the home. It was small, hardly bigger than Lauren's three-car garage, and crammed with interesting knickknacks. Clocks, figurines—every surface was covered. At another time, Rayne would have loved to admire the items on display.

"Hello!" Owen Hughes greeted them, stepping from a hall. "Why don't you come into the parlor?"

The parlor was the size of Rayne's bedroom growing up and stuffed with furniture. The tea service sat on a round table surrounded by four chairs. A clock on the wall cuckooed three and a half times, the last cuckoo drawing out like a broken toy.

At Rayne's concerned expression, Owen chuckled. "A gift from Daisy's father. She refuses to toss it in the bin."

"Just needs the wire reconnected, Owen." Daisy blushed. "Da wished for a boy and got me instead." The very feminine woman shrugged. "Sit, please."

"Is this a social call?" Ciara asked in a tart tone.

Owen held out the chair for Ciara, but his bushy brow rose in disapproval. "Could be. Depending on Rayne's decision." He eyed Rayne hopefully.

She didn't budge from the threshold of the room, suddenly feeling as if she committed to tea, it would mean more than that. "I can't stay."

Owen sighed. "Let's have tea. There are some things you should know, Rayne, before you make your final decision."

Rayne waited, praying that the kindly lawyer would admit it was all a mistake. A joke. Between Landon and Owen, the most complicated practical joke ever. She'd take it over the current reality.

Owen held out the second chair. Rayne reluctantly sat. He scooted her in, then did the same for Daisy.

He took the fourth chair.

"Well?" Rayne asked. "I hope you're going to tell me that Nevin was not in his right mind."

"He was," Owen said, dropping his napkin over his lap. "He didn't think he would die for some time."

"Why the changing of the will?" Ciara asked. "I think it's suspicious."

Daisy poured tea and handed them each a white cup with yellow daisies on the side.

"Thank you, lamb." Owen glanced at Rayne, then Ciara. "You and he were much alike and butted heads over different ideas."

"He butted heads with everyone!" Ciara said. "Not just me."

"Aye, your da loved to argue." Owen wore a fond expression, as if the trait was endearing. "Nevin wasn't sure you were the right one to inherit. He wanted to train you himself." Sipping, the lawyer studied Ciara. "He discussed adopting you."

Ciara gasped, and tea sloshed from her cup—she set it down before she could drink. "That's cruel."

Owen patted her shoulder. "Don't doubt that he loved you, Ciara. Nevin wanted more than anything to save McGrath Castle and the village." He turned to Rayne. "Our youth have moved away for proper jobs and careers. Driving back and forth on old roads isn't easy. Spotty service for phones. Unreliable internet." He added sugar to his tea and stirred it with a small silver spoon.

Ciara scowled, but Rayne could see her cousin was on the verge of tears.

Daisy offered small plates to everyone with sandwiches cut in professional squares. Scones. "These are gorgeous country hills, but they're too young to appreciate it."

Rayne agreed with the kids. What quality of life could there be with no gym? No fast food. No Uber Eats.

"This way of life needs to be preserved," Ciara said, leaning forward. Her knee bumped the table leg. "It's dying."

"A slow death. On that, you and your father agreed." Owen focused on Rayne. "Your uncle followed your progress on Rodeo Drive. Your bridal boutique. Your mother was very proud of your success. Nevin wanted you, Rayne, to bring Grathton Village into the twenty-first century. He planned to ask your advice."

"Me?" Rayne quickly swallowed a small corner of her scone.

Ciara snorted and added honey to her tea.

"Why not?" Owen asked. "You have a business marketing degree. You have your finger on the pulse of the latest trends. You're financially successful."

It was true that she'd studied fashion and had made friends with several social media influencers. No longer true that she had thousands in the bank. She cursed Landon Short beneath her breath.

Daisy nodded encouragingly. "Your website is top-notch. I can see why you were named as an up-and-coming entrepreneur. Nothing but luxury."

"I don't have my sewing machine here," Rayne said, grasping for an excuse. "According to the rules, I can't go back home. Is there a way around that? Can I work from LA and from here? It would be a lot of travel, but we could manage."

"No." Owen's tone was final.

She shook her head. "There's no compromise?"

"Your uncle made this plan thinking he'd live a good thirty years more. He was in the prime of health. This was the worst-case scenario." Owen dabbed his lips after a sip of tea. "And it happened."

"It's not realistic." Rayne chose a chicken salad square and ate the savory bite.

"I understand." Owen looked at the clock. Twenty-four hours was up. "I need your answer, Rayne."

Ciara stared at her, pain and sorrow, grief and anger in her gaze. She'd crumbled her scone rather than eaten it.

Her cousin could stuff the anger. It wasn't fair that Rayne would need to give up everything. Was her mother right? Had she lost because of fate? Was she meant to be here?

"Tell me the stipulations one more time."

"You're drawing this out!" Ciara whispered, stricken.

Owen stood and pulled the will from his pocket. He cleared his throat and read the rules again.

Rayne sat forward and listened hard. Bottom line? No new revelation to save the day. If she stayed for a year and Ciara stayed, they'd each get a hundred grand. *If* the castle showed a profit. That would get her back on Rodeo Drive, if she could handle the dress orders from here. The things she'd need to do, like buy a sewing machine, brought that tingle of creativity combined with necessity that had seen her through many long nights of sewing.

Because the Hugheses and the folks at the manor thought she was such a success, they were giving her respect that she would lose right away if she shared that she'd been duped by Landon Short. It was pathetic that she cared, but she owned her feelings.

Rayne lifted her chin and prayed that she wouldn't screw it all up. God, was she a total fool? If so, she wasn't going down alone. She lasered a gaze on Ciara.

"*If* Ciara agrees to the one-year plan, if she manages the property, and if I have rooms made available for my sewing studio, then I will stay. One year."

The plan gave her a home for the next twelve months.

Plenty of space to sew and meet her obligations.

Ciara smiled in relief but then braced herself, as if waiting for the other shoe to drop.

"What?" Rayne couldn't believe the nerve of this woman.

"Why? I know it's not your big heart." Ciara shifted.

Owen dropped the pages of the will to the table, shocked into cursing. "Ciara Smith! She just saved your arse!"

"And you think I won't be under obligation?" Ciara huffed. "I should say no."

Nothing was signed yet. Rayne leaned forward, tapping the table. "But you won't."

The cousins glared at one another.

After a full minute, Rayne picked up her tea and sipped, helping herself to a delicious scone. "What flavor is this?"

"Oh, currant," Daisy said. "Thank you." She glanced at her husband. "Congratulations?"

That was how Rayne felt exactly.

After the paperwork was signed, the *t*'s crossed and *i*'s dotted, Daisy pulled her aside with a wink. "Any chance I can order something silky for the boudoir?"

Chapter Eight

As they left the cottage, Rayne wanted desperately to call her mother and tell her the news—it was Lauren's fault that Rayne had wavered in her determination to get back home. And now? A year in Ireland! She was terrified. If she failed, the castle would be sold off. Was she simply buying time?

"I have so much to say, yet I can't form a coherent sentence," Ciara said, her tone begrudging as they drove back to the castle.

Rayne held on to the passenger door as her cousin zipped around curves, dips, and peaks in the five minutes it took to reach the manor house. "I totally understand."

"We need a staff meeting. Think you can manage to stay awake this time?"

"Rude!" Rayne clicked her tongue to her teeth. "You try being in my shoes, traveling from LA."

"Don't wear heels. Never have, never will." Ciara glanced at Rayne. "While you were getting your beauty rest, we agreed to reschedule the meeting over dinner. Everyone will be curious."

"With so many people, we'll need the grand dining room." Rayne's finger tapped her knee, and she wished she had her sketchbook—this time to make a list and sort her priorities. "Think you can handle more than one fork two nights in a row?"

Ciara snorted and lobbied, "How's the white cashmere sweater?"

And her cousin scored a direct hit. "Ready for the trash."

"Guess you have so much money that you can toss expensive clothes into the bin." The teasing tone of the sweater comment was gone in this sentence.

Rayne glimpsed Ciara across the console. Would it take a full year for them to understand each other? "It's not that at all! I know my fabric, and it's ruined."

"Give Maeve a chance before you throw it out. She's a wonder."

Ciara pulled into the driveway and parked. Night two, and Rayne had committed to twelve months. She stayed frozen in her seat. How had things changed so fast?

What would her best friend, Jenn, say? And the police, with Landon? Rayne might need to sneak away if she had to sign something or fill out more reports. But that could probably all be done online or by fax.

It was surreal. And yet, strangely, possibly doable. She got out of the car, and Blarney met her with a tail wag. She patted the dog's head.

"Hi, Blarney boy. It's such a cute name. What does it mean?"

"*Charm* or *flatter*," Ciara said. "Sometimes to a fault, as with this one. Had Da wrapped around his paw." She sent a sad look to the pup. "Probably wonders where he is. I still wait to hear Da's voice too."

Rayne nodded, recalling how it had been the first year or two after her dad died. Waiting to hear his laugh as he came through the door, singing off-key. Disappointed when it didn't happen.

They walked to the bottom step. "I hope Dafydd isn't too hard on Blarney."

Ciara stiffened at the possible critique of her fiancé. "You know nothin' about rural living. Blarney needs to pull his weight."

Rayne flipped her ponytail. "And just how should he do that? He's a dog."

"He's a tracker. He hunts pheasant, grouse, ducks. Geese." Ciara pointed to the barn. "Go on now, Blarney."

"Is he not welcome in the house? I remember Aunt Amalie's dogs were when I was here before."

"Dafydd wants to train him and take over dominance. Setters can be willful, as you saw earlier today."

Blarney whined at her with imploring eyes. Rayne patted him again. "Just be good," she said.

Cormac opened the door. Blarney barked and raced off— his path leading after a squirrel rather than to the barn. Maeve popped her head around her husband's body to see them, her gaze full of curiosity and fear.

"Are we out?" Aine asked from Cormac's other side. Her nose was red and her voice thick. "To the street with only the clothes on our backs?"

Rayne felt awful that the young woman had been afraid. "No! I've agreed to stay for the year." Somehow they'd make it work, but she would need so much help she didn't even know where to begin.

"Oh, praise heaven!" Maeve called.

"Thank ye, Jaysus!" Aine sagged against her father.

Cormac gently shoved both his wife and his daughter back into the foyer. "Lloyd family. Remember your places, please." He wore a wide, relieved grin.

"Dafydd and Amos are in the parlor with drinks. Neddy's dishing up ham hocks and colcannon, a family favorite," Maeve said as Rayne and Ciara entered the manor.

Scents of garlic and mustard brought back a memory of her dad and uncle laughing. Padraig. So much tragedy, and yet so much love here too. Aunt Amalie had ruled the roost with a satin glove.

The foyer was filled with light from the afternoon sun, though it was now past six. "When does the sun set here?"

"Between nine thirty and ten," Ciara said.

"Cool! It's normally eight for me, so that's an extra hour or two." Rayne would love a chamber with loads of natural light to work in.

Aine giggled. "Aye. Sun rises at five. I was going to suggest last night that you wear a sleep mask but it wasn't a problem for you."

"No. It wasn't." Rayne had been out cold—mostly. "I hope to acclimate soon."

"Long, soft days in June," Cormac said. "You'll find that the weather is very moderate here. Doesn't get too hot nor too cold."

"A little warmer might be grand," Aine said pertly.

"Let's join the boys in the parlor for a predinner drink," Ciara suggested. "I could use several!"

Maeve shook her head. "Oh no. Neddy's got dinner ready to serve. He'll be pleased as punch that he's not out of a job. We all are. Cause for celebration."

"Let's meet in the dining room," Cormac said. "Five minutes? I'll bring an extra bottle of whiskey for drinks with dinner."

Rayne ran upstairs to refresh herself, leaving her phone on the sink to charge. She'd texted her mom that she'd decided to give it a try but a plan to implement was required ASAP.

It was ten AM in LA, and Rayne suggested they talk at nine her time. Her mother sent an okay emoji, and Rayne hurried downstairs, starving, since she'd been too upset to enjoy the scone or more than one square of chicken salad sandwich.

When she entered the grand dining room, it had a familiar vibe. Not so strange and new anymore. Amos, his shaggy blond hair combed into submission, blue eyes vibrant as he smiled at her, had apparently heard the news.

Dafydd, dark-brown hair and eyes, wasn't as welcoming.

Ciara had met her perfect brooding match in the shepherd.

Rayne silently wished them the best of luck and sat next to Maeve and Amos. Aine and Neddy served ham hock colcannon, a mashed potato dish with ham chunks and cabbage that he'd topped with a fried egg. "Richard isn't answering his mobile," Maeve said, gesturing toward an empty setting at the table. "He normally joins us for dinners but hasn't lately."

Why was that? Cormac supervised the pouring of drinks, and when all had something, he sat down. The head of the table was empty, and Rayne noticed them all glance at the place where Uncle Nevin used to sit.

"I suppose you might want to sit there?" Ciara asked.

Rayne drew back. "Why would I?"

"Well, you own the castle. Should we address you as milady?"

"Can we call a truce through dinner, cous? I'm hungry, this looks great, and I really would like to get to know everyone." Rayne held Ciara's gaze.

Cormac bobbed his head with approval. Maeve patted Rayne's hand. Ciara, across from Rayne and between Neddy and Dafydd, agreed with a stiff nod.

"I'm so relieved," Aine admitted, folding her napkin over her lap. "I broke down like a babe, afraid we'd have to move. This is my home. I was born here!"

"For another year, anyway," Dafydd said. "Then what?"

Ah. That was his issue. "I don't know," Rayne answered, with all honesty. "I guess we take things one day at a time. I'll need your help."

Aine dragged a fork through her potatoes. Maeve glared at Dafydd. Cormac cleared his throat and lifted his glass. He'd given them each two inches of Irish whiskey.

Cormac met each of their gazes. "To Nevin McGrath, and McGrath Castle surviving another day. *Sláinte!*"

Everyone around the table cheered, and pressure to save the castle bowed Rayne's shoulders. "Any word about his . . . accident?"

Cormac shook his head. "These things go slower in the rural areas, but Garda Williams will investigate as he should. I've known the lad since he was a babe christened at church."

Rayne opted not to share her views on organized religion. Her dad had kept his Catholic faith on the down-low at dinner parties. It was a Hollywood thing. "What does *garda* mean?"

"Garda is a constable," Amos explained. "A police officer. The closest garda station is in Kilkenny."

Forty-five minutes away seemed like a lot. "What happens in an emergency?"

"The neighbors pull together," Cormac said. "There's not much crime around here."

Ciara reached for her whiskey. "You'll see I'm right—what happened to Da was no accident."

Awkward silence followed that statement, and Rayne discreetly scanned the occupants of the room. All but Ciara busied themselves with their meal.

Rayne dug into the fluffy potato mash with chunks of ham. A side dish of fresh lettuces had been served with a light dressing. "This is wonderful, Neddy. Michelin star."

91

"Thanks! An egg added to anything feels luxurious." The cook sipped his whiskey.

"Everything tastes better this evening." Maeve swallowed a bite and looked at Rayne with an earnest expression. "Things around the manor are a wee bit run-down, as you might have noticed. After Lady Amalie passed, your uncle, well . . ."

"The fence in the back pasture needs to be mended," Dafydd cut in. "I can hire some locals and knock it out in a week, to corral the sheep."

Rayne nodded to show she was listening but deferred to her cousin. "Ciara is in charge." She had dresses to sew.

"You have final say"—Ciara's jaw clenched—"Lady McGrath."

"None of that is necessary." The title sounded like a part to play. After a sip of warm peaty whiskey, Rayne said, "I have no clue what I'm doing, which is why Uncle Nevin named you as manager. That's like putting the set designer in the producer's chair."

"Eh?" Neddy asked.

"My mom's an actress—*Family Forever*—it's a long-running sitcom, and I practically grew up on set." Her belly was pleasantly full, her mind settled now that the decision had been made.

"You're pretty enough to be an actress," Aine said shyly.

Rayne smiled at the young woman. "Sweet of you! That was never my passion. I wanted to create beautiful gowns like the costumes for the studios, but the money is in bridalwear."

Or had been. Before Landon stole it. She took a deep drink of her whiskey.

"All about the money with you," Ciara said.

Rayne met her gaze across the table, not engaging in a debate. "Think what you like. I don't have time to run the castle *and* my bridal business, so we've gotta split duties. I'll need to order a sewing machine and find a fabric wholesaler. I have orders to fulfill by contract. Where is the biggest city?"

"Dublin big enough?" Amos asked. "If not, a flight to London is less than two hours."

She'd flown into Dublin, and the drive to Grathton Village had been an hour and a half. Kilkenny was forty-five minutes the other way. Sure to have a gym or fitness center, according to Neddy. Also the garda station, if something popped up with Landon that required her attention.

"If someone could drive me to Dublin to shop . . ."

"When do you need to go?" Amos asked. "I've got to stay close to the village for the next few days to monitor the Simpsons' foal."

"You're a veterinarian too?" Rayne asked, impressed.

"No. I have experience with animals is all," Amos said. "We all pitch in where we can."

"Thanks anyway, Amos." Nobody else volunteered. "Or I could borrow the car? Get a cab?"

"I'll drive you to Dublin," Aine said. "It will be *craic*!"

"How old are you, Aine?"

"Nineteen."

At thirty, Rayne felt ancient. "Let's go on Monday. I'll use the weekend to regroup. I love a plan."

"No surprise there," Ciara said.

Ignoring her cousin, Rayne said, "I'll pick up two white-boards while I'm out—one for the castle and the other for my wedding dress schedule."

"I don't need a whiteboard," Ciara said. She used a slice of soda bread to dab the buttery sauce left on her plate. "Nothing wrong with the calendar in the kitchen."

"I like to be organized," Maeve agreed. "I live by my day planner."

"True!" Aine leaned forward to grin at her mother. "Heaven help us if Mum doesn't get her chores crossed off."

The diners around the table chuckled.

"I'll need to connect to the internet," Rayne said. "I'm burning through my hot spot."

"We don't have internet at the castle." Ciara patted her cell phone. "We use our mobiles for what we need or go to the café to connect to Wi-Fi."

Rayne had no words. Internet was a must. She'd check her phone plan for options.

"Sunday morning is church," Cormac said. "After that, we usually have a full Irish breakfast."

"Oh. I don't really do church."

Maeve raised her brow and made a humming noise. "It's community. The McGraths have always gone to church together on Sunday. This will be the second Sunday without your uncle there."

"Mum, she's a grown woman." Aine shifted on her seat. "Can make her own choices about where she prays."

Rayne concentrated on her potatoes. "I'd like to catch up on my sleep tomorrow, then walk the property."

"Saturday is still a workday for us. Should we give you a list of things that need fixing?" Dafydd asked.

"Yep. Decide which fire to stomp out first. You know, Ciara, Owen never gave us a budget."

She'd built her business up from nothing. She'd saved a hundred and fifty thousand to tempt the investors.

Easy pickings for Landon. Shame on her. Rayne finished her whiskey.

"All right?" Amos asked. "You looked overwhelmed for a moment. Don't blame you."

"I'm fine." Rayne blew out a breath. She needed to build again, that was all. She would make it back if she was able to stick it out here for a year. Oh, and turn a profit.

"The roof on the west wing has been patched with a tarp, but I fear it won't hold through another winter. We moved the furniture we were storing there to the gray room at the east wing," Cormac said.

"Roof." She nodded at the butler. "Okay. Definitely a priority."

"If we don't have a fence, the sheep wander." Dafydd tapped the table next to his plate with agitation. "Nevin should have invested in another sheepdog, not a setter with a bad disposition."

Rayne looked at Dafydd. "Invested?"

"Aye. We have two sheepdogs, but they're getting older. I think his lordship thought it would be a breeze to train Blarney to act as a third, but a tracker is not a herder. It's in the genes. It was his money, he said, in no uncertain terms." Dafydd appeared very put out at this. Had he argued with Nevin?

"How much do they cost?" Rayne asked.

Dafydd sat forward, his forearm on the table. "Fifteen hundred euro."

She turned to Amos, then scanned the other faces around the table. "Is that a lot for a dog? I have friends who easily pay three thousand or more for a pup."

"Designer, like your wedding gowns," Aine said. "I saw your website. The dresses are so nice. Like Cinderella for the ball."

"Thank you, Aine." Maybe taking her along as a shopping companion would be a blessing in disguise. Rayne snapped her fingers. "Is there somewhere I can set up to use as a studio? It would need good light. Room for mannequins, a table for my sewing machine. A cutting table."

"The sun-room is full of light, but there's no door," Aine said.

"I need privacy." Rayne recalled the beautiful space on this floor of the manor that was practically all glass.

Maeve seemed dubious. "There are lots of chambers but not very much light."

"Well." Cormac glanced at Ciara. "There's always the pink parlor."

"Next to Da's suite? No way!"

"Why not?" Maeve asked. "It's got plenty of room. I dust it every week, so it's clean, and mostly windows."

"Da never used it." Ciara lowered her fork.

"He loved his wife," Cormac said kindly. "Now he and the missus are both gone. Rayne inherited the castle. It's her right to use the rooms."

"*Love.*" Ciara jumped up and tossed her napkin to the table. "What about his girlfriend Lourdes?"

Uncle Nevin had a girlfriend? Rayne couldn't have been more shocked by that statement—and yet Ciara's existence proved that he had been with women besides Aunt Amalie.

"They weren't serious," Maeve said. "Sometimes a person needs . . . companionship."

"This is wrong in so many ways! I'm going to bed. Rayne, if you want to learn about your new home, then meet in the kitchen for breakfast at six. Saturday or no, the animals need to be fed."

Ciara left without a good-bye to any of them, even Dafydd. Dafydd reached for another piece of soda bread from the basket in the middle.

Rayne looked around the table at all the faces who were her responsibility. "I'll set my alarm. I think bed's a good idea." It didn't matter that she'd slept the day away; she was tired again. "I have a teensy headache."

"You go on up," Maeve said. "We appreciate the sacrifice you're making to give up your life in LA, Rayne."

She accepted their thanks but felt awkward about it all. "Night."

Amos, Dafydd, Neddy, and Cormac stood politely when Rayne rose from her seat. She smiled at each of them though tiny pinpricks of pain between her brows.

Stress. She needed to sleep before it became a migraine.

Rayne walked upstairs to her dad's room. The door was slightly open. She knew for a fact that she'd closed it.

Chills broke out on her skin, and she poked her head inside. Nobody was there.

Her cell phone had been knocked off the charger on the bathroom sink.

She read the screen and saw a text from her mom saying she'd been called in to the studio to reshoot a scene Paul wasn't happy with. Lauren related that she was proud of Rayne for staying and trying to save the manor.

Lauren closed by texting that she knew Conor would be proud too.

Chapter Nine

The alarm blasted at six AM, and Rayne blearily smacked the off button on her cell phone. Sunday morning. If she were back home in Hollywood, she'd have a leisurely cup of dark roast with vanilla almond milk before meeting Jenn for yoga on the beach, followed by mimosas.

All night she'd been wakened by rattles and scuffles. The castle had been built in seventeen something, so it made sense that there would be ghosts. Heck, she might even know a few of them. It just wasn't cool that the noises had prevented a deep sleep. There were loads of articles in her women's health magazines about proper sleep cycles and the hazards of interrupted REM.

Tempted to stay in bed and pout, Rayne pushed the comforter back and prepared for a morning outside with a tad more caution than she had yesterday. She'd slept through her alarm, angering Ciara, but then spent the day wandering the gardens—in heels, so she'd had to come back for her sneakers. Blarney had been her companion as she'd walked. Today she would maintain her style, as fashion was her thing, but she could make jeans and boots look *cute*.

She missed her walk-in closet and clothes. Her designer accessories from hats to scarves to belts. And her shoe collection? She sighed. Heavenly.

Last night, as she'd put lotion on her skin before bed, she'd also jotted ideas in her sketch pad. The leisurely walk had been a terrific stress reliever. She had to find her uncle's banking information and get the truth of where the castle, the grounds, and the village stood. His office. Maeve or Cormac would have the keys.

Rayne winked at her image in the mirror, channeling Audrey Hepburn with her scarf tied around her ponytail and pearls in her ears. Navy-blue peasant top, thick jeans, brown leather boots, matching brown leather belt.

Audrey was an icon for a reason—classic style and a heart of gold. She'd believed in love and family. Being a humanitarian.

Rayne's parents had also impressed old-fashioned values on her, which in part was why she'd agreed to this crazy scheme. Deep in her core, family mattered. Her relationship with Ciara mattered. Had her uncle really planned on adopting Ciara?

If someone had killed Uncle Nevin, then it was doubly cruel for Ciara to be robbed of her father. It didn't make sense that the culprit would be Ciara.

Rayne exited the room to find Blarney sleeping in front of her door in the hall. "Blarney! Morning, pup! Does Dafydd know you're inside?"

Blarney wagged his tail and licked her hand, his golden-brown eyes pleading with her not to tell.

"It'll be our secret. Come on, boy."

They reached the kitchen, and Aine smiled when she saw the dog but put her fingers to her lips to let Blarney out the side door by the cellar. The young maid was dressed in tan slacks with a white blouse, her red hair styled in waves to her shoulders. Her green eyes were lightly lined and mascaraed. Flowered earrings dangled. A cutie.

The pup went out as Ciara entered from the hall. Her cousin had a freshly scrubbed face, her blonde curls damp. Cocoa canvas work pants, a loose T-shirt. Socks.

Neddy had on his cook's uniform and stood at the stove stirring scrambled eggs. Toasted soda bread waited in a rack on the table next to the jam and butter.

"This is just to tide us over until later. Bacon is coming," Neddy said. "Tea?"

"I would love coffee," Rayne said.

"I like that too," Aine said.

"You don't need to suck up to her, you know," Ciara grumbled.

"Hey!" Rayne protested.

"I wasn't." Aine poured two cups from a pot on the counter and handed one to Rayne. "Cream? Sugar?"

"Both."

Ciara watched Rayne prep her coffee. "You might as well call that dessert."

"I suppose you would take it black?"

Neddy brought Ciara's tea with a side of honey. "Here you are."

"How is honey different?" Rayne demanded.

"It's healthier," Ciara said. "We get the honey from a bee farm down the road. Local bee pollen also helps against allergies."

Rayne had heard that too but was lucky she didn't have allergies. "How many people live in Grathton Village?"

"Four hundred and fifty, give or take," Neddy said.

Rayne gulped. Was she responsible for them all? "Oh. What businesses are there, besides the lawyer?"

Ciara blew on her tea, then sipped. "Three pubs, one B and B, a doctor, a windmill—you remember me telling you about Richard Forrest?"

"The one who keeps missing dinner who lives on the property?"

"Yes. He operates the mill."

"What else?" There wasn't a gym or food delivery, and her hopes dipped for a coffee shop.

"Two cafés and a general store."

"A petrol station," Neddy said, smiling at Rayne. "The church, the orchard, and lots of lovely rolling hills with ruins in them."

"Ruins?"

"Aye," Ciara said. "Ireland was riddled with castles once, not built as sturdily as this one."

"Sounds like a fun hike." Rayne ladled eggs and a slice of meat onto her plate. She'd seen remnants of stone structures everywhere during her walk. "What's this?"

"Bacon." Neddy watched her with a confused expression.

It didn't look like her bacon from home. More like boiled ham, pale and sickly. She preferred her bacon crisp and in strips. "Oh."

"Not good enough?" As usual, her cousin sounded ready to brawl.

"Chill out, Ciara. Yoga is a must to calm your mind and your body." Rayne pinched her fingers together. "You need to *om*. Seriously."

Aine giggled.

Ciara slathered creamy butter on her toast. "I don't have time for yoga. You know why? I work from seven to six every day. If we don't work, the animals aren't cared for. The crops aren't taken care of. The bloody lawn won't get mowed."

Rayne didn't react, understanding from the last sentence that Ciara was angry about her dad. Rightfully so. There were no answers about his death, just like there were no answers about Landon stealing Rayne's money and dresses. Her freaking dreams.

They couldn't commiserate, because no way did Rayne trust Ciara to not poke at her. It didn't help that Uncle Nevin had gone on about how successful Rayne's Modern Lace Bridal Boutique was.

"Maybe you should call that Garda Williams guy," Rayne suggested.

"What for?"

"An update!"

"He'll call when he has news." Ciara bit into her toast.

The woman was impossible. "I'm just trying to help. I can understand why you'd be frustrated by the lack of information. How long has it been?"

"The supposed *accident* happened a week ago Thursday. It was after dinner, about eight?" Ciara looked to Maeve and Aine for verification.

"About that," Maeve agreed.

"The sun doesn't set in June until almost ten, so Da wanted to make use of the daylight hours to catch up on the grass. He'd been behind schedule."

"Why's that?" Rayne blew on her coffee to cool it down.

"He had appointments but didn't explain, and then we had an emergency at the mill, so dinner was late. Broken paddle." Ciara placed her toast on the dish.

"That's right," Maeve said. "I made mutton stew. Not as good as Neddy's, but—"

"I was with my mum." The cook sighed. "I didn't get to see Lord McGrath again."

Ciara bowed her head. Aine patted her arm in empathy.

"I miss him too," Aine said. "He treated me like family. Knew me since I was born."

Ciara raised her head, defensive to her core. "And I wasn't. That doesn't mean I didn't love him, or him me."

Rayne was going to introduce Ciara to yoga before she died of a stroke. "Aine wasn't putting you down, just sharing that she's sad too. I miss Uncle Nevin. It doesn't take away from the grief that you feel, cousin." She softened her tone on the last word. Though it had been nineteen years since she'd last been here, they'd shared holiday cards and birthday greetings. Uncle Nevin had insisted she have an open invitation to the castle and consider it home.

She'd planned on coming and bringing Landon once she was a success. She pinched the bridge of her nose.

Ciara nodded once.

"I pray that you're wrong, Ciara," Maeve said. "That it was an awful accident. Knowing that someone hurt his lordship on purpose is so much worse when we still don't have answers. No body released to the church yet for burial. We need to have a wake; prayers to send his soul to heaven."

Rayne sipped her sweet coffee. "Who all had a beef with him?"

"Beg pardon?" Maeve asked, brow quirked.

"Sorry. An argument. A disagreement."

"Lately? For sure, Freda Bevan." Aine brushed crumbs from the table to her plate.

"Over what?"

"The councilwoman shouted at Lord Nevin during a council meeting," Maeve said.

Ciara lowered her mug to the table with a slam. "I forgot about that. Freda physically threatened Da. She blocked his ideas for modernization at every turn."

Rayne perked up with interest. "How did she threaten him?"

"Punched his arm. Da laughed about it. Freda was so mad because he wouldn't sign her petition to join Grathton with the next village over. We have four hundred and fifty people; they have just over two thousand. The bigger a village is, the more council amenities it gets. I wasn't paying attention. It's a bad idea to combine our populations."

"I'm going to need a crash course in local politics in addition to property management." Rayne smoothed her furrowed brow.

"Freda is fifty and plump. Probably hormonal and lost her temper. It happens to the best of us." Maeve shrugged, her cheeks pink. "She would never plan to hurt Nevin McGrath."

Rayne conjured a picture in her mind of an irate menopausal woman with rage in her eyes. Scary. Rayne's grandmother had gone through the change like a champ, thanks to supplemental hormones and a special diet recommended by Oprah.

Aine reached for the last piece of not-bacon. "Would you like this, Rayne?"

"No, thank you." She started to think of other things she might miss from America. Not only crisp bacon, her shoes, and her best friend, Jenn, but her mother. She and Lauren were very close. Her mom was afraid of flying, so the chances of her coming to visit over the next year were zero.

Was there anything in that will about vacationing in LA? Sweat broke out along her forehead. Her mother gave cool-headed advice and a shoulder to lean on.

"I'd like to talk to Freda," Ciara said. "Find out when she and Da spoke last."

Rayne lightly dabbed her forehead with her napkin so as not to ruin the 50 SPF setting spray she'd applied over her powder.

"Good idea. Who else did he have an argument with? Any more punches?"

"Well," Ciara said slowly. "There wasn't actually a brawl, but Richard called Da a cheap bastard when Da didn't want to fix the broken paddle."

Rayne gasped.

Ciara shook her head. "To be fair, Da told Richard he had to step up and pay his share for the mill. No more delays."

Maeve, Aine, and Neddy all nodded. It seemed they'd agreed with Uncle Nevin's decision about the paddle.

"There are two angry folks right there," Rayne said. "Have you told this to the police officer?"

"Garda Williams hasn't asked," Ciara said with a sniff. "He's still investigating." She studied her fork. "I may have annoyed him with my repeated calls."

So Rayne's cousin had already checked in one too many times.

Maeve clucked her teeth to her tongue. "Poor lamb."

Ciara, a poor lamb? Ha—more like a wolf in sheep's clothing. There must be something in Ciara's past that the housekeeper was referring to, and Rayne wanted to know. She looked from her cousin to Maeve.

"Lord McGrath had a booming presence, but he cared about his people beneath it all. In the heat of the moment, he tended to forget that there were other opinions besides his," Maeve said diplomatically.

Rayne remembered Uncle Nevin and her dad in steamed debates that often ended with the phone being slammed down. In person, the discussions had been more mellow, as Aunt Amalie and Padraig had been around to soften Uncle Nevin's edges.

It seemed that Ciara had inherited her dad's temper. From what Rayne had seen, Dafydd didn't do much to soften it but rather fanned the flames.

"You should go to the village and ask around," Maeve said. "Folks might open up, since they don't know you."

"She looks just like Da and Uncle Conor," Ciara said. "People will guess right away she's the new lady of Grathton. It's all the gossip at the pub, according to Richard. The new American."

Aine shrugged. "Most will think that's brilliant. You can use your accent. It's grand."

Rayne grinned. "That's right. I'm the one with the accent here. I would like to meet everyone. Not sure about today, though. I'd rather prep for the week and get things in order as much as possible. Maeve, where would I find Uncle Nevin's banking information, or the financials?"

"Why?" Ciara rudely interrupted.

Rayne turned toward her cousin, digging deep for patience. "We need to know how much money we can allocate toward fixing the fence and the roof and getting internet. Uncle Nevin likely had a budget, right?"

Ciara settled her shoulders and blinked her lashes. "Da said we were broke. Is that true, Maeve?"

Rayne watched a myriad of expressions cross the housekeeper's face before settling into a blush. "Oh, I couldn't say. His lordship spoke to Cormac about things like that. Lord McGrath's office is on the first floor, to the right of the staircase. Let me get you the key."

Chapter Ten

Maeve patted her pocket, and keys jangled from inside. "Whenever you're ready, just let me know."

The sooner the better, to Rayne's way of thinking. "Ciara, I'd appreciate it if you'd look at the books with me."

"No, I'd rather not. I'm rubbish at math." Ciara shook her head.

"It's just numbers." Rayne smiled encouragingly. "I used to think the same thing, and then I found out how empowering it was to do my own accounting. I also use math for measurements in my business."

Ciara rolled her eyes. "Not surprised you can do math too."

"Practice helps. I made a very expensive mistake once when I needed yards of silk and mistakenly ordered feet, so I didn't have enough. I had to rush and pay extra for the correct amount of fabric." Rayne cringed at the awful memory, but lesson learned: measure twice and cut once. "The last thing you want is a sobbing bride on her wedding day."

"I love weddings," Aine said, eyes dreamy. "Oh! Now that Rayne is here, Ciara, maybe she can help you with your wedding to Dafydd."

Weddings were her jam. Rayne straightened and studied her cousin. Ciara was pretty. Slender. Lean from her physical work. Tall. She could carry off a bold design because of her figure. Something dramatic. Rayne had left her sketchbook upstairs. Would Ciara model for her?

Ciara scowled. "Stop looking at me like I'm a piece of meat at the butcher shop."

Ew. Did people really buy meat that way? Rayne preferred hers USDA approved and wrapped in plastic.

"Sorry. Happy to help. When is the special day?" Please not July, August, or September.

"We haven't decided." Ciara drank the last of her tea and peered at the empty mug with regret.

"You wanted to wait until the fall, right?" Maeve asked. "Samhain is a splendid time of year for a wedding."

Ciara's mouth twisted as she glared at them all. "The wedding is on hold indefinitely. My father is dead. I don't have an inheritance and need to work for my cousin. I'm not feeling so festive."

"We're managing the property together. You're getting a pretty nice payday out of it," Rayne reminded her. "If Dafydd's smart, he ain't going anywhere."

Aine snickered.

"What happens at the end of the year?" Neddy asked.

"Ciara and I decide what to do with the property." Rayne shifted on the hard wooden chair. Her cousin was more interested in her empty mug than in looking at her. Whatever. "We can keep the castle or sell it. Our choice. It has to make a profit, according to the will, and the village too. *If* we both manage to stay for the whole time, we can discuss the particulars then."

At that, Ciara raised her head. "What do you mean *if*?"

If Landon was caught and her money returned. If she could stand being away from America. If she didn't have to return to LA for one reason or another and Owen didn't cut her out of the will for breaking the rules.

"Sorry. Wrong word choice." Rayne shrugged. "*When*. Let's get back to who else might have had a grudge against Uncle Nevin."

"My father and I argued. You think I'm guilty?" Ciara stared at Rayne.

Rayne paused. What would her feisty cousin say next? The girl had to find a way to relax. "Are you?"

"No. I was against modernizing," Ciara admitted. "I love this place the way it is. Who cares about new furnishings when the land is so beautiful?"

Maeve *tsk*ed. "You were raised in London, dear, so you don't see that the last update was in 1950, and that was the bare essentials. Nineteen twenty-five before that."

Rayne scanned the walls and trim. The ceiling. "Paint is cheap. It will add a fresh aesthetic without costing a fortune. I'm very handy with a needle and can create new drapes and cushions."

"Those aren't important things!" Ciara sounded like Dafydd just then—the pair in harmony.

"Beauty is very important for the soul," Rayne countered. Her parents had taught her that.

"It's a waste of money, and I don't know that there is much," Ciara declared.

"It doesn't have to break the bank!" Rayne knew how to stretch a dollar and make a splash.

Ciara rose and splayed her palms to the table. "I'm going to the barn. I have real work to do, not just talk about it."

"I'll gather the eggs," Aine offered.

"Thanks, Aine." Ciara simmered down. "I'm worried about the sheep that was injured. We lose a percentage of the herd each year, but I'd rather not if we can help it. We need that fence. And to hire another man to walk the fields. Dafydd is pulled in many directions. Are you coming?"

How much money would there be to fix everything? "I'm going to your dad's office first about the banking. Then we will know exactly what we can afford and what we can't. No sense in arguing over it until then."

Ciara read the time on her phone. "It's almost seven. Daylight's wasting. Is that your plan? Stay inside and do paperwork while the rest of us perform manual labor? Guess you think your college degree makes you better than us."

Rayne didn't react and gave herself a pat on the back for keeping her cool. "I don't think that at all. I created my business doing something I love. I don't really love sheep." She shrugged. "If I can better serve the castle by finding how much money there is for the estate, what's wrong with that?"

Aine nodded.

Neddy got up and gathered the empty serving bowls—to avoid being drawn into the argument, no doubt.

Rayne stood and also started to help.

Maeve covered Rayne's hand. "We all have jobs to do that make the manor and the property run smoothly. Lord Nevin's death has cast a stone in the cog, but we will find our rhythm again."

"What?" Ciara scooped a curl behind her ear. "Like Da was never here?"

"No, my sweet!" Maeve cried, turning toward Ciara. "That's not what I meant. Your father is everywhere around us. He'll be buried on the property with the rest of his ancestors. With Padraig, with his sister, Claire, and with his beloved wife, Amalie."

"Wait a minute—there's a cemetery on this property?" Rayne had never seen it. Her dad had asked to be cremated and buried beneath the tree in back of her mother's house. No wonder there were ghosts.

"Aye," Maeve said. "Rayne, as Lady McGrath, your task is to keep the family property intact for the next generation."

"That will be up to Ciara." Rayne planned on a career. "No kids for me, thanks. I don't even have a fiancé." It still hurt, but she knew she was better off. *Good riddance, Landon.*

"After church, go to the village and see what the folks are like," Maeve suggested. "We might not have a gym, but the mile walk there and back will do you good. There are bicycles in the shed if you'd prefer."

"We'll see about church, or the village. I hope to be elbow deep in bank ledgers." *And answers.*

Ciara blew out an annoyed breath.

Rayne stood her ground. "Ciara, if you give me your cell phone number, I'll text you if I find something."

"Maeve can—I'm late." Ciara strode from the kitchen outside through the cellar side door.

It slammed shut.

"I rub her the wrong way," Rayne said.

"Seems so," Maeve agreed. "For now. But it's not just you. She hasn't had an easy time of it. His lordship didn't know how to handle having a grown daughter all of a sudden."

"Never a mention to us that he had a daughter," Rayne said. Which was strange.

"At first, I don't think he knew how, and then as time went on, it seemed too late," Maeve said. "Lord Nevin grew to love

Ciara very much. Aine, will you show Rayne to his lordship's office?" She handed over a key on a fob. "Return this to me, please."

"Are all the doors locked with a key?" Rayne asked. Her dad's room had a twist lock on the knob from the inside.

"No, no. But the office has one. We all have our private rooms." Maeve scribbled a phone number on a scrap of paper after checking in her day planner by the landline. "Ciara's mobile number. Aine can also show you the pink parlor, to see if that will suit for your sewing."

"Thank you."

"Let's go there first, eh?" Aine led the way out of the kitchen to the central staircase and upstairs. Turning right rather than left, they followed the emerald-green, brass-trimmed carpet runner on the polished wood floor down at least five doors. There were small tables every so often with vases or figurines. Paintings on the walls. There was an entire suit of armor, and Rayne recalled Padraig scaring her when he hid behind it.

"There are some lovely things here. Like, they could be in a museum."

"I know. I'm so lucky to live here. Almost there. Lord Nevin's suite is at the very end. Here we are!" Aine stopped and twisted a brass knob on a shiny polished wood door. "The pink parlor. Lady Amalie's suite. It's connected to his lordship's."

Aine opened the door, and Rayne followed. Cormac had been right on target in thinking this room would work as a sewing studio. "This is perfect. Natural light. All of this space. Wow." She'd never been at this end of the hall in her aunt and uncle's private rooms. The lord of the manor had the best of the best.

"You like it?" Aine asked.

"Adore it. Holy cow."

Aine giggled. "Holy cow?"

"Sorry. My mom doesn't curse because of her sitcom, so I learned to not really swear either."

"My mum doesn't believe in it. Washed my mouth out with a bar of soap, and I never did it within her earshot again. Now, when she's not around, I can hold my own at the pubs. We Irish do like a good curse." Aine gave her a smile. "You might hear *feckin* a lot."

"Feckin?"

"Aye." Aine tucked a hand in her pocket. "It's like swearing, but not really."

"I'll have to share that one with Lauren. She'll get a kick out of it."

Aine gestured to the room. "Is there enough space?"

"Yep. This is the size of my apartment living area back home. The walls are huge. The windows perfect. And hardwood floors, thank goodness. Easier to clean than carpet for fabric scraps."

"Brilliant!" Aine whirled toward the door on her brown loafer. "I can help you set up after we buy the things you need in Dublin tomorrow."

Rayne sank back against a pink brocade armchair. "Aine, I have so much to do in order to meet my deadline. I also want to help with the castle and bring it into the twenty-first century. How do you feel about the changes?"

Aine scrunched her freckled nose. "Me? I guess . . . I like the old, and the new."

"I do too. It's why I named my boutique Modern Lace. Lace is old and dainty and exquisite, but with a modern twist, lace is back in style."

Aine clapped. "Modern Lace Bridal Boutique. It's a grand name. Well, besides helping Neddy in the kitchen to slice and chop, I do the mending at the castle. If you need assistance."

Rayne reached for Aine's hand and squeezed, the pair in perfect accord. There was enough room for a third table. "I might take you up on that!"

"Let's go to Lord Nevin's office. Mum is in a hurry to get ready for church, or she wouldn't have given me the key. She doesn't like to lose sight of her keys ever—takes her responsibilities very seriously."

"All right. I'm glad we came here first. I hope the office search will be just as simple." Rayne stepped toward the door. "Do the men ever have breakfast in the house?"

Aine tilted her head. "They have small kitchens in their cottages. Dinner is shared most days, for the company. Oh, on Sundays sometimes Neddy will prepare a full Irish breakfast after church. Depends on who's around."

"A full Irish breakfast? What is that?"

"Two kinds of sausage, beans, tomatoes, mushrooms, eggs . . . oh, just wait. You'll love it." Aine rubbed her tummy when they reached the hall. She shut the door to the pink parlor that Rayne couldn't wait to revamp.

They went down the stairs and over to a large wooden door with a gold knob. Aine unlocked the door and pressed the button to turn on the switch. The panel was old-fashioned, just like the rest of the castle.

Rayne laughed to herself. *As a castle should be.*

The light came on, and Rayne admired the room while circling the mammoth desk. Ivory and blue swirls patterned the walls. There was one medium-sized window with dark-blue drapes, which were shut. A mirror hung over the fireplace.

"It's huge." She gestured toward the desktop, which held a pen and paper. A landline. "There's really no computer?"

"No. Lord Nevin didn't have one. Joked that he was too old to learn." Aine shrugged a narrow shoulder. "You might have noticed that the connection here is spotty at best."

"Yeah. Darn it." Well, she couldn't do business online unless that changed. It was perhaps more important than a fence. Didn't the sheep have the run of the place anyway? "Thank you, Aine. I'll make sure the door is locked behind me on my way out."

The maid left with a smile.

Rayne's phone dinged a text message. She opened the drapes and stood next to the window, pulling her cell from her pocket. She had two whole bars! Her mom wanted to chat.

The office was to the left of the property, below her dad's bedroom, give or take a few chambers. She had a view of the vegetable garden, where Blarney was chasing dragonflies. What a cute pup!

She dialed her mother, who answered at once, pleasure in her warm voice. "Rayne! How are you?"

"I'm all right." She forced a calm tone so her mom wouldn't worry. "Fine, considering the task ahead."

"I have such good feelings about this, hon. How can I help?"

"I need to return my car—it's a lease, so not a big deal. I'll call the dealership from here and explain that I'm out of the country for the foreseeable future."

"No problem. Next?"

The call dropped. Frustrated, Rayne dialed her mother back. "Sorry about that. Where was I? Oh yeah. My apartment. I hate to break the yearly contract, but it's foolish to pay for a place I'm not going to be in."

"That might cost a fortune. Hmm. Let me talk to them and see what I can do from here. If we can get you out of it, what should I do with your stuff?"

"I have my laptop and sketchbook, but I'd like my clothes. Do you mind sending them?"

"I can hire people who are pros," her mom assured her. "Do you need anything in storage?"

"The furniture all belonged to the rental." Rayne's life had been more transient than she'd ever realized. "I really don't have that much, other than clothes and makeup."

"And a divine shoe collection."

Rayne chuckled. "It's very muddy here, Mom. My amazing shoes are not that practical."

"I guess not."

Embracing her practical side would need to happen sooner than later. "Any word about Landon?"

"No. I phoned the station earlier, and Officer Peters said the chances of finding the money are slim to none. Landon will have spent it or put it in a new bank account."

"I'll call her to let her know about my address change." Her chest ached. "I really could use the cash right now. I don't think the castle was making money. Losing, more like it."

"Really? Huh. Your dad bragged that Nevin was a fab money manager and could squeeze profit from a stone. Nevin was determined to save the castle for future generations."

"I've heard that he felt that way from multiple sources, but making a profit?" Rayne wandered from the window toward the desk. A framed photo of Uncle Nevin, Aunt Amalie, and Padraig sat on the corner. On the other side was a candid picture of Nevin and Ciara, both smiling, in front of the barn.

"Maybe not millions, but not in the hole. Lemon drops! Remember, Rayne—that was eighteen years ago. Where does the time go?"

"A lot could happen, you're right. Like, he had a daughter show up out of the blue that he never mentioned to us." Rayne opened the top drawer of the desk. Pens, paper clips. The usual detritus.

"If Conor was still alive, we would have known." Her mother blew out a breath. "I should have made more of an effort to stay in touch rather than the occasional call or holiday card. What's in the bank?"

"I don't know yet. He doesn't have a computer!"

"That doesn't sound very modern to me. I thought he was all about the future?"

Her uncle had been a complicated man. Rayne gritted her teeth. "Lauren . . . I'd like to take you up on your offer of money—but just until I get on my feet. I need enough to buy fabric for the wedding gowns in July and August. Those brides will pay the other portion of their gowns on delivery, and I'll have enough for September and October."

"I'll send a few thousand. I wish I could return the siding on this sugar-blasted house to give you more. Who knew?"

There was no way to plan for this kind of double tragedy. "It's okay. Thank you. I will pay you back. The biggest joke is they all think I'm loaded."

She opened the two side drawers. Phone books. Coupons. Advertisements. No budget.

"You're not telling them what happened with Landon and the boutique?"

"No. I would lose all respect from Ciara. She really has a grudge against me about this castle. And I don't blame her, that's the problem. Uncle Nevin. Ugh."

"I'm sorry. Secrets are better out than in."

"I usually agree, but I'm going to wait. Nobody seems to think Uncle Nevin's death was suspicious except Ciara. I feel bad for her, but she's got a chip the size of Texas on her shoulder."

"What do you think? Could it be murder? If so, ten days is a long time for it to go unsolved. Forty-eight hours on any of the shows I've done."

"You're right. At least in the States. Cormac said things operate at a slower pace here." Also, in real life.

She turned to the tall cabinet, which held six drawers, but it was locked.

"Do they have a sewing machine you can borrow?"

"I'll need to buy one, Lauren. I can't skimp on the machine or the fabric. Aine is driving me to Dublin tomorrow." If she couldn't find a machine, she would have to sew each entire dress by hand. She flexed her fingers at the thought as they cramped in sympathy.

"I'm very proud of you—" And like that, the call dropped. Oh well.

Rayne's heart was lighter after the talk with her mom, despite the drops. While she wouldn't make money from returning her car or wiggling out of the contract for the furnished apartment, at least she wasn't bleeding cash—if her mom could sweet-talk the rental office.

Her mom was pretty amazing that way.

Hours later, Rayne was dusty and out of luck. She'd rummaged through all the shelves and peered behind the cabinet. She'd pulled the books from the shelves. There was nothing in the desk about banking information. No key either. She'd even gotten on her back to check under the desk like she'd seen once in a movie. Desperate, she called Owen Hughes from the office landline.

"Owen Hughes here."

"Hello. This is Rayne McGrath. I'm wondering if you could tell me where the banking information is for the castle?"

"Just diving right in, eh?"

She glared at the phone, glad it wasn't a video call. "In addition to reliable internet, we need a fence and a roof, according to Ciara. I'd like to know how to make that happen."

"Hmm. Well, I s'pose she would know best."

"What's the property worth?" Rayne tapped the desk. "Maybe we should just let it go now and not waste a year."

"A castle near Cork sold last August for seven hundred and fifty thousand euro. Of course, it was in excellent shape, and bigger than what you have." Owen cleared his throat. "I believe Nevin banked with Bank of Ireland."

That was a lot of money and worth trying for. "Was the property in the black?"

"We didn't discuss his finances, Rayne. Nevin was a private man." Owen gave a little cough. "We didn't see you at church this morning. Your uncle never missed the nine o'clock service."

She rolled her eyes. How did anyone stand this kind of scrutiny? She didn't blame the kids for moving away. "And how was it?"

Owen chuckled. "Father Patrick led a prayer for Nevin, that his soul would finally be at peace. Even cracked a joke—heaven knows that man loved nothing more than a good argument."

Chapter Eleven

Frustrated, Rayne left the office and went to the kitchen. At half past twelve, Neddy was making bread, probably a daily task at the manor. There was no sign of sausages or eggs.

"Did I miss the full Irish breakfast?"

Neddy grinned and pounded the dough. "Not everyone would be around this morning, Maeve said. Next Sunday for sure. You want something to eat?"

"No. I'm fine. I've eaten more here than I normally do in a month. Is Maeve around?" She hoped Maeve would have a key for the locked cabinet.

"Maeve and Aine will be doing laundry, since they've both returned from church already. Nine to ten, followed by an hour of chitchat," Neddy informed her.

"Do you go?"

"Of course!" Neddy rounded the dough and gave it a pat. "Father Patrick will call you out by name the following Sunday if you don't. And people love to gossip!"

She'd probably been the subject this morning, since Owen had pointed out that she hadn't been there. How to get around the church situation? "Everyone goes at nine?"

120

"The Catholics of this parish, aye. Unless you're ill or house-bound, in which case Father Patrick will bring the sacrament to you." Neddy laughed. "There is also an eleven o'clock service. There are as many churches as sheep in Ireland."

"That's a lot," Rayne said. "Where is the laundry room?"

Neddy gestured with an elbow. "Follow the corridor behind the staircase leading to the back. You'll smell the bleach." He wrinkled his nose.

"Thank you!"

The hall was dim behind the stairs, but she pushed through her nerves, the scent of cleaning supplies covered with lavender fragrance a surefire trail to the laundry room.

She knocked on a door to her right and opened it. Inside was a large area so basic it had concrete flooring, drying racks, a washing machine, and a separate dryer. Shelves had been built to hold various tubs and jars. Rags and sponges. Mops.

Maeve had a kerchief over her hair and sweat on her brow from the steam in the room. No wonder the Lloyd ladies had such amazing skin. This spa treatment would cost a couple hundred in Hollywood. "Hey!"

Maeve turned from the pile of towels she was folding. Aine lifted her head and smiled. "Hello. Welcome to the steam room of McGrath Castle."

A door was propped open leading to a back area with a clothesline laden with sheets drying in the air.

"Is the dryer broken?" Rayne asked.

"I prefer the crispness of sheets on the line to the dryer," Maeve said. "It's extra work but worth it."

Rayne had been too tired the past few nights to think of her sheets but would compare tonight. "It smells like lavender."

"We grow it on the property, and add lemon too," Aine said. "For brighter whites."

Rayne sent her clothes to the dry cleaner. Her parents had as well. Her dad had been a published poet and an artist, with an office overlooking a fountain at her family home. He'd favored designer jeans and button-up shirts in luxurious fabrics. He'd loathed shoes. Her mom had her studio clothes, her red-carpet clothes, sundresses, and workout wear.

McGrath Castle was night and day to her LA home.

"Can we help you?" Aine asked.

"Oh, yes, but I hate to interrupt."

Maeve looked at her watch and squeaked. "I lost track of time. Amos has to run to the village, and I thought you should go with him. He'll show you around."

Rayne peered down at the jeans she was wearing to work in. "Um, should I change clothes?"

"No! No. Things are very casual around here," Maeve said.

"You look glamorous," Aine said. "With your pearls."

"Thank you, but . . . I was wondering if I could get the key to the cabinet in Uncle Nevin's office? I can't find it, and I think the bank statements must be inside."

"Oh." Maeve seemed doubtful. "I'll need to check. I don't know where it is. Could be on his personal key ring."

"Makes sense. Where is that?"

"He woulda had it on . . ." Maeve bowed her head.

Rayne deflated. His body when he'd died. The coroner or police might have it. "I see. Well, if you could help me find it, or an extra, that would be great—when you have a chance. I can't move forward with the finances until we know what they are."

"I will, I will. Now, I told Amos half past twelve to pick you up. You should probably get out there. I know you'll love our village."

Dismissed, Rayne had no choice really but to leave and wait for Amos. She was curious about the village, so no harm done.

"See you later. Should I pick up something for lunch?"

"Great idea!" Maeve said. "You and Amos should get lunch at the pub. Don't worry about us here." The housekeeper returned to work. "Six o'clock for Sunday roast."

Was Aine hiding a smirk?

Rayne left the steamy laundry room wearing lavender like a fragrance mist.

She strode down the hall the way she'd come, around the base of the staircase to the foyer. Now that she was looking for things to repair or upgrade, she saw faded wallpaper, tired paint, and outdated pictures on the wall. Like, fifties old, not classic old. There might be something in storage she could rummage through to make the place more authentic to its historic roots.

She went out the front door, where Blarney lounged in the shade on the landing. He greeted her with a body wag and bounced toward her.

"Sit!" Rayne said, before Blarney imprinted his paws on another shirt. Despite what Ciara thought, she was not made of money.

To her surprise, Blarney sat.

"Good boy," she said, patting the silky soft fur around his ears.

While she waited, Rayne took stock of the landing—made to be impressive. At least twenty feet wide and six steps down. Planters sat on each wide step, yellows and purples exploding in color. Green ivy. Moss.

Sculpted stone lions bracketed the seven-foot double front doors. Her eye for detail, honed by growing up on set, cataloged height and width. With her back to the entrance, the gorgeous property spread before her.

The stone barn in the distance with a thatch roof. The paddocks with sheep and horses. To her left was a long, crushed-stone driveway. Like in *Gone with the Wind*, trees had grown into an arch for a hundred yards or more. The driveway, big enough for two horse-drawn carriages side by side, led to the main street of the village after a curve. The driveway and the street were probably the same width.

Amos slowly drove toward her from the barn in the pickup, his long, shaggy Viking hair flowing out the rolled-down window. The truck had nothing so fancy as electric buttons, just old-fashioned manual handles. It suited Amos, actually, but wasn't as sexy as the motorcycle.

She couldn't imagine him in LA unless it was on a movie set for a period film.

Amos pulled over, and she descended the six wide stairs to the ground. Blarney whined to join them, but Amos said, "To the barn, Blarney. Find Dafydd."

Blarney raced off but got distracted by a butterfly and went to the lawn to the right of the manor. Beyond that were fields that she and the dog had walked yesterday.

Amos chuckled. "I hate to agree with Dafydd on principle, but I don't know what Nevin saw in that pup besides companionship."

Rayne smiled and got into the pickup. "How old is he?"

"Almost a year," Amos said. "Still a decent age to sell him in exchange for a sheepdog."

"What? You can't sell Blarney. He belongs to the family."

Amos glanced at her. His bright blue eyes held no humor. "Nevin mentioned that things were not as profitable as they used to be. If that's true, then we might need to downsize in order to get out of the red."

"Oh, I know all the marketing terms for that. I had my degree in business."

"I heard." Amos's lips twitched with amusement.

She blushed. "Sorry. I'm sure Ciara blasted me from here to New York. London, at least."

"Your uncle was very proud of your accomplishments, Rayne. Don't let Ciara get to you. She's grieving for her da, underneath it all."

"I know." Rayne cleared her throat, admiring the shade and shadow the cover of trees provided. "How's the injured sheep?"

"On the mend." Amos spoke reassuringly. "It will be returned to the flock tomorrow."

"How many sheep are on the grounds?"

"A hundred and twenty. We aren't a sheep farm per se but keep the flock for sustainability. We sell the babies, sell the wool, and eat the meat."

"That sounds so clinical," Rayne said.

"I'm the manager of the property, so it is to me." Amos reached across the bench seat to pat her leg. "Too much?"

"No. I need to learn how things are done here, and I could use your help for sure." Amos didn't treat her like an interloper.

"Happy to." Amos brushed back his wavy hair. They stopped at the end of the road, then he turned left rather than right. "Hundreds of years past this was a main thoroughfare. About seventy-five years ago the planners moved the road. That was the beginning of the end for Grathton. Nobody had a reason to come by here."

"Now that might be a bit too much." Rayne leaned against the passenger door and shook her head. "Are you always so blunt?"

"I'll make an effort." Amos laughed. "I usually talk to sheep or horses, and they don't mind my lack of polish."

Businesses were on the right side. The left was green fields and hedges on the McGrath property. Stone and brick buildings practically leaned against one another. "I'm fine with you being who you are."

"Thanks." Amos sent her a quick smile. "You might notice that things on this side of the village aren't as landscaped as the area by Owen Hughes's office. Dr. Ruebens's is there, and the town services building. The church. A general store. On this end of the five-k stretch will be food. Three pubs, two cafés, and a bed-and-breakfast. The petrol station is down this way as well."

"Five kilometers is about three miles." Rayne ran five miles every day on her treadmill. "I was worried about not having a car, but I guess I can walk everywhere."

Amos nodded. "There's a bicycle with a basket in the shed. A horse if you'd like to ride." He patted the dash. "You can always bring this old girl if you need to."

Horse? Uh, no way. Rayne slumped against her seat as Amos pulled into a parking lot. Of five spaces, three were already filled. "There are an inordinate number of pubs, it seems."

"Ireland is a pub culture, don't you know? This one is the Sheep's Head. The other is down a ways, called The Pub. It's older than Sheep's Head, but for meat pie and chips, this is my favorite. The Pub has better fish and chips, so I'll go there on a Friday. Mary's is the third. It's your basic watering hole if you can't get into the other two."

Rayne wasn't sure what to make of it all, especially the old sign with a sheep's head painted on it over the entrance. The hinges creaked like they'd never been oiled, and she feared it might land on her.

The building appeared to have been made of the same stone as the castle. Amos opened the door for her, and Rayne shivered. Dim lights flickered in the interior. Amos nudged her in.

Hops and curry spice overpowered her senses, and she missed the light lavender of the laundry room. Noise blasted her eardrums. She realized that she'd frozen in the threshold, and the light behind her was likely blinding the customers.

Snickers sounded around her. Great, Rayne thought. Just the impression I hoped to make. *Not.*

Amos walked her toward the bar. An old slab of tree trunk served as the counter. Rings of glasses and bottles had stained it into an interesting kaleidoscope design. The whole place was no bigger than a shoe box.

"Rayne McGrath, this is Beetle Doyle, manager of the Sheep's Head Pub."

Beetle? She kept a straight face. The man's eyes were near black. Tattoos covered every inch of skin. She, a modern woman, was grateful for the hulking Viking at her back.

"Nice to meet you." Rayne started to offer her hand, but the bartender was glaring into the crowded space over her shoulder.

"I'd like two meat pies with chips. Cheese and curry sauce." Amos withdrew his wallet and put cash on the counter. "Two Beamish stouts."

Rayne hadn't brought her purse, only her phone. "Thank you," she said. "I'll need to find an ATM."

"No worries," Amos said.

Beetle slid over the drafts, and Rayne accepted hers without arguing that she didn't drink beer. She didn't ask for the calorie count, as she realized Ireland probably had different rules than California.

A whisper from behind her reached her. "Spoiled feckin American."

Hey!

Amos steered her away from that corner to the other, but it wasn't like they could get far. Ten tables were eight too many, never mind the barstools crammed up to the tree trunk counter.

Beetle whipped around the side and dropped off their food.

French fries she recognized, smothered with shredded cheese and some kind of sauce. Brown gravy oozed from a golden-crusted pastry. Dare she ask what was inside a meat pie?

"Silk undies, I heard," the voice said, louder. "What a waste. Nevin lost his bleedin' mind. It'll be the ruin of us."

Rayne turned to peer into the shadows, making out a man with red hair so copper bright it shone in the dim interior. "Who is that? He doesn't like me, and I've never met him."

"Richard Forrest, the miller with the broken paddle." Amos drank his beer. "Ignore him."

"Why is he so upset with me?" Rayne remembered that Ciara'd had a meeting with him, which her cousin had missed or hadn't gone well. *Note to self—ask Ciara about the meeting with Richard.*

"I need help with the mill, and will the McGraths lend a bloody hand? A loyal tenant on their property?"

"Sit down, Richard," Beetle called. "Or I'll cut you off."

Whoever Richard was sitting with cheered.

"I don't understand," she murmured to Amos.

"Nevin did help Richard with the broken paddle at the mill, but he wasn't going to forgive late rent or excuses."

"So Uncle Nevin owns the land, and people rent from him?"

"Aye."

Rayne nibbled the corner of a fry, trying not to touch the foreign sauce.

"What's the matter?" Amos asked, calling her out. "Shredded cheese and curry sauce is the best way to eat your chips. No need to dip the pie."

Amos bit into the pastry with strong white teeth.

Chips were french fries, that she knew. "I prefer ketchup."

"Trust me," Amos said. "Just a wee bite."

Rayne slid a fry through the sauce and touched her tongue to it. It was surprisingly sweet with a kick of spice. Like the Thai curry at home. She tried a full bite this time. "Wow."

"Right?"

Rayne had several more fries, her mouth stinging pleasantly.

"Now the pie, Rayne. Onion, beef, celery. I thought all Americans were foodies. You have a permanent look of fear for anything new."

She shook her head. "I am an order-out kind of girl who eats less than fifteen hundred calories per day, with two workouts."

"What kind of life is that?" Amos asked, his hand to his chest in exaggerated horror.

"I need to look good in my gowns to model them. Just starting a business means cutting costs where you can." Landon had been her mannequin as well. Forget Landon.

"And now you're a success."

Rayne lowered her gaze, feeling like a fraud. "I'm not a millionaire."

"Yet." Amos smiled at her. "Eat your pie!"

Rayne took a bite and swallowed a groan of happiness with the crust and gravy. She'd never had anything like it in her life. "This is great."

"I know." Amos jerked his thumb over his shoulder at something the miller was mumbling. "Forget about Richard. He and your uncle went at it because the whole town knows Richard lost his money at the horse tracks. Nevin drew a line in the sand, that's all."

"They argued?"

Amos chuckled. "Nevin McGrath was not a quiet man when it came to sharing his opinions. Of course they did!"

Chapter Twelve

Rayne sipped her draft, the dark stout the perfect accompaniment to the spicy curry and gravy. The din in the pub wasn't as jarring as it had been when they'd first entered. How fast could hearing loss occur?

"So Uncle Nevin argued with Richard, and with Freda, who punched him. Owen mentioned that he loved to argue. I guess Father Patrick said a prayer this morning that my uncle would find peace at last in heaven."

"Freda smacked him in the arm," Amos clarified. "No need to report to Garda Williams. Freda and Dominic—that's the police officer—grew up in the same town over, so it might not matter."

Interesting. "In the States, an officer of the law is supposed to differentiate between job and friends."

Amos tilted his head and laughed. "Oh, yes, same here. And just like where you are, it more than likely doesn't always work."

He had a point. "Ciara thinks that something happened to her dad."

Wiping his mouth with a paper napkin, Amos shook his head. "It's grief talking."

"How can you be so sure?" Rayne recalled how oddly he'd acted when she'd asked him about it as they'd passed the tractor.

"I was the one who found him that evening," Amos said. "Me and Blarney."

Her eyes widened, and she sat back in the chair. That might explain his reaction. "What did you do? What did you see?"

"It was around eight. Still lightish. Sun don't set until late. When you work the land, that means more hours to get things done. Like mow."

She drank her beer. "I get it. When I'm against the clock with a gown, I'll work until I start to make mistakes."

"Exactly. I think your uncle was tired. He complained of a headache and took some medicine. Said he wanted to get that section done and then he'd come in."

"And then?"

"I'd stopped to check on one of the horses who had a stone in his hoof on my way to the bungalow after our meal when I heard the tractor grind somethin' awful. A shout, and then it slid down the hill on its side, marking up the grass. It's got a hydraulic system to assist with maneuverability on the inclines. It's to help prevent tipping, but no guarantee."

Her stomach tightened as she recalled the brown scars in the lawn.

"Blarney barked and ran for me. Crazy as it sounds, I think he was asking for help."

Rayne wiped her fingers on a paper napkin, wishing for some hand sanitizer. "That might seem strange to most, but I live in Hollywood and grew up in the same neighborhood as that famous pet psychic. Not Tyler Henry but the other one. A lady."

"There's more than one famous pet psychic?" Amos's brow rose toward his hairline.

"Hollywood," she said with a shrug. "What happened next?"

Amos lifted his glass and swirled the inch of liquid left inside. "We called the garda station, and Garda Williams arrived within forty-five minutes. Blarney never left Nevin's side."

"Poor pup!"

"Nevin was dead, it was obvious. His eyes were open, no pulse. I didn't dare try to move the tractor for fear of hurting him worse. Now that is crazy when I say it. He was already gone." Shadows filled his gaze. "For all of his bluster, Nevin was a good man."

"No foul play that you noticed?"

"The tractor had tipped over on him. Just an awful accident. He wasn't feeling well and should have stayed inside."

Amos sounded sincere. And it made sense that Ciara's judgment might be clouded with sorrow. Her dad's death was tragic, and the aftermath, the will, even more so.

"I see your point," Rayne said, finishing her beer.

"This is a small, close-knit village. I can't imagine one of our community getting so angry as to plan to kill their lord. The McGraths aren't technically nobility, but they've been the head of this village since the 1700s. The original Andrew Conor McGrath was a warrior for his king and was presented this land as a gift."

Rayne felt a silly spurt of pride in her DNA for something her ancestors had done. Made her glad she'd agreed to try for a year. Then she'd take her money, pay Ciara, and get back to where she belonged.

LA.

Beetle hustled toward them—his presence not so startling after the first shock. He could be the cadaverous survivor of a punk rock band from the seventies. "Another round?"

Amos looked at Rayne questioningly.

She couldn't eat another bite. "Not for me, thanks."

"No thank you, Beetle." Amos smiled at Rayne as the bartender rushed away.

"I need a nap." She pressed her hand to her tummy. "I don't eat this heavy on a regular basis."

"How about a walk, then, to let it settle?" Amos suggested. "As I said, the entire village street is around five kilometers."

"Great. Let me dash into the ladies' real quick."

"Over on the other side. No separate jacks for men and women."

Jacks? How bad did she have to go? Not only would the facilities probably be icky by American standards, she'd have to pass by Richard. Would he say anything?

"Your face is easy to read, Rayne." Amos covered a chuckle with his napkin to his lips. "Richard is trying to get your pity and your money."

Well, she didn't have any cash, so that part was easy. He hadn't earned her sympathy. She slid off the chair and dropped her napkin to the plate. "Right."

Rayne crossed the old wooden floor, the soles of her shoes sticking from who knew what after all this time.

She kept her focus on the door with a sign that read TOILET. Richard stared into a large stein of beer as his friends finished up their meal. Safe.

Inside, she flicked on the light. Though just a single stall, the room was clean. *Jacks* meant restroom. Another funny word to add to her vocab. She should keep a journal to remember this experience when she went home.

On her way back to the table, she wasn't as lucky. Richard stared at her. This close she could see that his nose was red, with drinker's veins. Brown eyes hardened as he gave her an imperious look.

He stumbled off his stool as if he was going to talk to her up close, but Amos intervened.

"Have a seat, Richard," Amos said. "We're just leaving."

Richard shoved Amos . . . Amos didn't budge. A wall of muscle.

"I want my paddle fixed, Lady McGrath. I will take you to court if you don't get it mended. I can't work without it."

Rayne trembled at his use of *lady* and wished she could toss it aside like a snagged bolt of satin.

"You hardly ever grind grain to flour anymore," Amos said. "It's obsolete, which is exactly what Nevin told you. He asked you to look into wind power, and what happened?"

"Wind power!" Richard said. "Makes up over thirty-six percent of our power usage. I *did* check, Amos."

"And what did Nevin say?" Amos subtly inched Richard toward his table.

"He wasn't willing to mark up the countryside for a wind farm." Richard scowled at Rayne and Amos both, blaming her in particular.

She nodded, in agreement with her uncle. Windmills were not attractive, even if energetically sound. She was all about the beauty too.

"What am I supposed to do?" Richard pounded his chest. "He offered a place as field hand, like that lowlife Dafydd. My family were millers."

You had to change with the times. What else could someone with that skill set do? "Do you grow the wheat?" Rayne asked.

"No." Richard returned to his table, bowed over as if exhausted by all that standing up. "Not anymore."

She would need to discuss this with Ciara to get her cousin's opinion. Maybe there was a school Richard could attend or a trade he could learn to begin again. Fifty wasn't that old. "Think of some different careers you might like. See me next week, Richard. Sober, please."

"Aye, milady."

The hair on her nape rose at the title. Amos escorted her from the pub into the daylight, the door standing ajar. Though cloudy outside, it was bright compared to the interior of the bar. "What are you thinking?"

She tucked her hand in her pocket. "Richard must know how to use a hammer and nails. A paintbrush? We need some improvements around the castle, and why not use local people?"

"American!" Richard called after her just as the door closed, as if to have the last word.

Rayne lifted her face as the sun briefly escaped a cloud. It was June; there was a lovely breeze and, so far, no rain. She'd trained herself to default to positive thinking. It was the West Coast way to be chill and relaxed.

Her hot Celtic blood had been tamed but not washed out, and it flared at Richard's taunts. She tamped it down. "Let's go. Hard to take offense at what is true. I am American."

Amos chuckled. "He left out *feckin* or *spoiled* this time. Progress?"

She laughed. "I guess."

"Nevin tried to work with Richard, but he had no patience for a man who wouldn't help himself."

Rayne had Richard's measure, and he would no longer bother her. She and Amos ambled down the old sidewalk. After a long block, businesses rose on both sides of the street—two narrow lanes with the occasional car. They walked companionably.

"Tell me about Dafydd, Ciara's fiancé."

"He's from Wales," Amos said. "Nevin hired him a few years ago when his other shepherd passed on at seventy-five."

"Is that his official title? Shepherd? No wonder Ciara was so annoyed with me." Rayne sighed. "I didn't realize that following the sheep around was a for-real career."

"There's a wee bit more to it than that . . . and Dafydd fills in many other jobs. He's brought that old truck engine back to life I can't count how many times, and he's the only one Nevin trusted with the tractor engine."

"Mechanic slash sheep watcher. Can't imagine it pays much. But totally not my biz if he makes Ciara happy."

Amos folded his arms behind his back as he observed, "You and your cousin are very different."

"Did you ever read the story, I forget the name, but it's about a city mouse and the country mouse?"

"No." Amos made sure his steps were in sync with hers, his body between her and the road. A gentleman. Of course she compared him to Landon in her mind. Landon the rat. The snake.

Amos cleared his throat to capture her wandering attention.

"Well, it's me and Ciara. I'm obviously the city mouse, even though she grew up in London with her mom, right?"

"Aye." He agreed to be polite, Rayne could tell.

"There's nothing wrong with making money, wearing beautiful things, and appreciating a good happy hour."

Amos nodded. "Money is part of life. I don't see the barter system coming back anytime soon. What's happy hour?"

"It's when a bar or restaurant has a special on drinks, like buy one, get one free, and tapas. It's popular in the city after work to stop before going home for dinner."

"Huh. Reducing prices for drinks would be illegal in Ireland. One of the many amendments to the Intoxicating Liquor Act."

"No way." Rayne couldn't imagine the Irish having such a law. "Anyway, I usually skipped the dinner part and would go back to the boutique with Landon."

"Who is Landon?"

Rayne never should have let down her guard. "Nobody important. No happy hour?" He'd told her that they were a pub culture! She had a lot to understand.

Just then they reached Sinead's Coco Bean Café, which had a picture window that let in lots of light. Though the place was small, the ten tables inside didn't seem as crowded as the pub.

"Is that a bakery?"

"Sinead opened this café with her husband ten years ago now. She's famous around here for her Guinness chocolate layer cake with Baileys Irish cream frosting."

Rayne reached for the door handle and opened it, letting the sweet goodness escape. Rich coffee scent tickled her nose, followed by a wallop of caramel. Cheese and fruit platters were on the menu along with salads.

"I think this could be my home away from home." She imagined sitting at the back table with her sketch pad and coffee, nibbling on a toffee square advertised on the counter.

"Howareye!" A petite brown-haired woman came around the counter and the glass case showcasing the treats inside. "I'm Sinead Walsh, and my husband is going to be so disappointed that he missed meeting you, Lady McGrath."

"I'm fine, thank you. Call me Rayne! I plan on being back so often you'll both get tired of me." She laughed and looked up at Amos. "Do you have money to buy some of those toffee squares to bring back to the . . ." Not castle. It seemed too over-the-top.

She suddenly understood her dad's deprecating *glorified manor* comments. ". . . mm . . . kitchen? I'll pay you back as soon as I get to a bank."

"There are three in Kilkenny, for sure," Sinead said. "The petrol station will have an ATM. Hate to pay the fee, though."

"That's right." Amos pulled his wallet from his pocket. "Let's have a dozen boxed to go. I don't mind."

Sinead wrapped them and put them in a bag. "So nice to meet you, L-Rayne. Bye now."

"And you."

"Bye! Bye-bye," the woman's voice trailed as she continued with another good-bye.

Rayne and Amos left the bakery, and she put her fingers on Amos's wrist. "I'm so sorry that I didn't think to grab my purse when we left. Maeve sprung this outing on me when I dropped in the laundry room to ask about Uncle Nevin's keys."

"She did? Hmm." Amos chuckled. "I think we're being tossed together by a matchmaker."

Rayne felt ridiculous for not seeing it sooner. It hadn't been Amos's idea either. "Snickerdoodle."

"Huh?"

She peeked up at him. "My mom isn't allowed to swear on set, so we used different ways to curse."

Amos laughed. "It's cute. So are you. I'm not mad about Maeve."

"You're not?" Rayne kept walking toward the next shop on the row. The buildings weren't attached but super close, with maybe a foot separating them.

This area was not quite as nice as the other end of the village where Owen Hughes had his office. Maybe that was something else she and Ciara could tackle—sprucing up the whole village visible from the road.

She didn't want to think about any attraction to her Viking. Not hers, per se. She had no business being attracted to anyone. Tuesday she'd been in love with Landon. Maybe she was still numb over it. She refused to acknowledge any residual affection whatsoever for the man who had treated her so poorly.

"I'm leaving at the end of the year," she said. "Twelve months is a long time to be away from Rodeo Drive, and I'll need to go back."

Amos gave an easygoing shrug. "Who knows what tomorrow brings."

Truer words had never been spoken. Her cell phone rang, and she pulled it from her pocket. Three bars! "Hello?"

"Rayne, this is Ciara. Garda Williams has news about Da."

Her body tensed. Good or bad? The way her luck had been lately, she mentally prepped for the worst. "Like?"

"The garda will be here in fifteen minutes. He's asked to speak to the family. That's you and me."

"Okay. I'm on my way from the village."

Before Rayne could mention the toffee squares, Ciara said, "Yeah. I heard. We're all working, and you're out on a date with Amos." Her cousin hung up—the landline really made a wonderful racket when it was slammed down that the cell phone couldn't compete with.

Rayne pocketed the device before she threw it. "Why is Ciara so bell-pepper mean?"

"Trouble?" Amos stopped to look at her.

"Yes. Maybe. We need to speak with the police officer, that guardian person, in fifteen minutes."

Amos switched the handle of the bag to his other hand. "The actual translation of *An Garda Síochána* is Guardian of Peace."

"That's nice," Rayne said. She hoped the man would have answers for them. The police officers at the station she was dealing with back home, even Officer Peters, didn't denote peace or harmony. Their guns meant business.

"Let's go, then, Rayne." Amos turned them around to head back.

They reached the truck in the lot of the Sheep's Head Pub, and Blarney barked from the pickup's bed.

"How did he get here?" Rayne patted his red-furred head and crooned hello, peering into golden-brown eyes. The dog was happy to see her, and it brought her joy. No lie.

"He's attached to you," Amos said.

"It's cute, though." The dog wagged his tail.

"It will be a problem for Dafydd."

Rayne needed to sit down with the Welsh shepherd and have a heart-to-heart. No way on this green earth was he going to sell Blarney.

Chapter Thirteen

Amos dropped her off, giving her the toffee squares. "I had a wonderful time. I'll see you at dinner later for Neddy's roast lamb and Irish stew. He's bringing out all the classics to impress you."

"How sweet!" Rayne laughed. "What would you call it if I wasn't here?"

"Stew." Amos gave her a two-finger salute.

Rayne slipped out of the car and gently closed the passenger side door. "Very funny, Amos." She patted Blarney on the head. "Stay with Amos."

The grounds manager drove at a crawling pace toward the barn, and she bounded up the stairs. She'd reached the top when she heard a vehicle in the drive behind her and turned.

The police car was a white Hyundai with blue and yellow markings. It parked to the side of the path, and a man in a hat, blue polo shirt, and blue pants got out. There was a yellow crest on the chest and arm of his uniform. No holster or gun that Rayne could see. He appeared to be in his early thirties, with pale strawberry-blond hair and a smattering of freckles. Bright green eyes.

He gave her a friendly smile.

"Hi," she said.

The officer climbed the steps. "Hello, ma'am. Garda Williams." They shook hands on the landing.

Cormac opened the door as she was introducing herself. "I'm Rayne McGrath."

"The new lady," Cormac said.

"Call me Rayne, please," she insisted.

They went into the foyer.

"Maeve has set tea up in the blue parlor." Cormac led the way, his posture rigid and correct. Did he know something already?

Her shoulder blades itched. She remembered deportment school classes and the book on her head as she crossed the room with eagle-eyed Mrs. Westinghouse watching for any mistake.

"It's a shame the circumstances of you being here," the garda said. He was very polite. Likable. She could also see that he might not strike fear in a criminal and wondered if that was part of Ciara's dismissal.

She was about to find out.

Rayne followed Cormac into the parlor and took a seat in a padded armchair in front of the unlit fireplace. Dafydd was next to Ciara. She didn't recall ever being in this room before. The walls were papered in blue.

"Before you complain, Dafydd is my fiancé, and I want him with me." Ciara tilted her nose in the air. Dafydd braced his feet on the ground from his spot on a navy-blue sofa, not budging.

Rayne shrugged. She didn't care. Amos didn't believe there was foul play, and she saw why he wasn't on the same wavelength as Ciara. She hoped murder would be ruled out and they could lay her uncle to rest.

Maeve had brought tea and poured out cups. Rayne passed her the toffee squares for later. Cormac cleared his throat, and the dawdling housekeeper slowly left the room. She'd admitted to being curious, and this news affected her as well.

The garda sat in a wooden chair but didn't drink the tea. "Ciara, you had mentioned concerns about your father's death."

"Aye," Ciara said. "What is taking so bleedin' long?"

Garda Williams pulled a tablet from his pocket. "The toxicology report came back with nothing unusual found in his system."

Ciara bowed her head, and Dafydd patted her shoulder. She blurted, "It's not right!"

"I agree with you, Ciara," Garda Williams said. "Something isn't right. I'm no mechanic, but I asked my team to look at the pictures of the tractor. Where the body was found in relation to the fall down the ravine."

Rayne sucked in a breath at that—the garda was doing his job. "And?"

"I want to take more pictures. We're lucky it hasn't rained, but the dry spell won't last forever." Garda Williams touched the brim of his cap. "This is the Emerald Isle."

She supposed that a thousand-pound tractor might be too big to bring to the station.

"Let's go," Ciara said, half rising to her feet.

"Actually, my partner is out there now."

Tricky. Did that mean the policeman suspected one of them? Lauren would appreciate the plot thread.

Rayne's cousin sank down to the couch again.

"We didn't give you permission," Dafydd protested.

"It's a crime scene." Garda Williams tapped a pen on the tablet. "We don't need permission."

Ciara gave Dafydd a strange look and inched away from him on the couch.

Hmm. Had Dafydd known about the change in the will before Ciara?

Rayne needed to get into the locked cabinet, where she was certain they'd find answers. "Garda Williams. I was searching for my uncle Nevin's keys, but they aren't here at the house."

"Oh." For all his boy-faced innocence, the officer knew how to play it cool. "Why is that?"

"I'd like to read the household accounts but couldn't find them in the desk. He has a locked cabinet they might be in."

"I'll see what I can do. You've inherited the castle?"

"Yes."

Garda Williams studied Dafydd and Ciara. "You thought you would inherit, I imagine, Ciara."

"What are you saying?" Dafydd jumped up, stepping in front of his fiancée.

"Nothing." The officer rested his pen on his tablet. "Yet. Where were you Thursday afternoon, the day of the accident?"

"Ciara and I were walking around the lake." Dafydd drummed his thumb nervously to his knee.

The garda turned to Ciara. "Is that true?"

"Aye." Ciara jutted her chin. "Amos saw us. Then we all had dinner together at the house."

Garda Williams shifted his gaze back to Dafydd. "What exactly is your job title on the property?"

"Shepherd," Dafydd said, his tone short. "Is that all?"

The garda watched the shepherd and drew out the moment before finally saying, "Aye."

The Welshman crossed the parlor in a rush. He looked back, expecting Ciara to be with him. He made a noise of disgust when she wasn't. He slammed out of the room, the door closing behind him.

"What's going on?" Ciara asked in a quiet voice. "Do you suspect Dafydd?"

Garda Williams leaned forward and squinted toward Ciara. "The only person I don't suspect is Rayne, because she was in the States when this happened. I think your da was a victim of foul play, and I won't rest until I find out."

"We should be on the same side, then!" Ciara cried.

Rayne mostly agreed. She was ninety percent sure Ciara was innocent. But what about that ten percent?

"I heard the will was . . . unusual. Unfair to you, Ciara."

"From who? Gossips!"

"Part of understanding a case is talking to people. Not gossip," the garda said. "Information pertaining to a supposed crime."

Rayne liked that. She should send that phrase to her mom to share with Paul, the producer.

"I was taken by surprise," Ciara admitted. "Dealing with my da's death, and then finding out that the home I thought would always be mine somehow might be sold, didn't seem like something he'd do."

"Why did you think something was amiss?" Garda Williams asked. "What tipped you off?"

Ciara's face turned crimson.

"Well?" Garda Williams pressed.

"Just a feeling in my gut," Ciara murmured.

Oh, well. That didn't make her cousin look at *all* guilty. Rayne refrained from tossing her hands in the air.

The garda guy pressed his lips together. "A feeling." After a long pause, he asked, "Did you know Nevin was taking heart medication?"

"No. He was as healthy as a horse!" Ciara sniffed. "Fifty-seven years old, never a problem."

"Well," Garda Williams said, "according to Dr. Ruebens, Nevin developed heart palpitations a few months back."

That was why he'd changed his will, Rayne thought. Sensing one's mortality could alter a person's outlook. She shifted toward her cousin. "Mr. Hughes said Uncle Nevin wanted to adopt you, Ciara. Could be why."

Her cousin sat back with a shocked expression.

"He said that?" The garda jotted something down on his tablet.

When her dad had gotten sick, they'd had time to go over his last wishes. "Conor had tumors," Rayne said. "He switched from being this dreamer to all of sudden wanting everything in black and white. The house, his ashes."

Ciara scrubbed her cheeks with her palms. "Da never told me he wanted to, or that he was even thinking of it."

Rayne shrugged, but her heart was filled with empathy. "Maybe he ran out of time."

Garda Williams rubbed his smooth-shaven jaw. "Death isn't easy. I'm so sorry, Ciara."

"No." Rayne agreed one hundred percent. "It isn't. A suspicious death is worse. When will you have answers?"

"These things take time." The garda glanced at Ciara, who studied her unpainted fingernails, then faced Rayne. "The medicine in his system was the heart medication. Not unusual. What concerns me is that it wasn't the prescribed amount."

Rayne straightened.

The garda said, "I will need a list of who was at the castle that day."

"Could he have accidentally taken more? Would it have killed him?" Rayne's body was on fire with nerves.

"I can't say." Garda Williams pursed his lips.

Ciara hadn't been wrong at all regarding her dad's demise.

"No strangers that day," Ciara said. "I remember it vividly. I'll sit down with Maeve and make a list. You know folks drop in at the manor for food pickup or to talk with Amos about their animals. To get Da's signature. He had an open-door policy."

"I know that. A list will be great. Thanks." Garda Williams stood. "I'm sorry, again, for your loss. Both of you. I'll be in touch about Lord McGrath's key ring. If I can drop it by for you, I will."

"I appreciate it," Rayne said.

The police officer left. The cousins got up and stared at one another. Rayne, in shock—her uncle had been murdered. Ciara, in sorrow. Grief that her dad had been *killed*.

"Dominic is smarter than he looks," Ciara said on a sob. She pressed her knuckles to her mouth. "I thought he wasn't even trying."

Rayne hugged Ciara—from the side and cautiously, just in case her cousin brushed her off.

To her surprise, Ciara leaned against Rayne. "I didn't even know Da was sick. Why wouldn't he tell me?"

"I'm sorry."

"Heart problems. I can't even imagine . . ."

"We can ask his doctor for details," Rayne said. "Doctor Ruebens."

"Good idea." Ciara exhaled, one hand to her waist. "I hope he wasn't in pain."

Rayne gave her shoulder an extra squeeze. The garda's information explained so much.

"That would be the worst." Ciara shifted to face Rayne, her mouth drawn. "Help me go through his bedroom? I don't want to do it alone, but I think we need to search for answers. Talk to Cormac and Maeve."

Rayne nodded. The butler and housekeeper would know things. Why hadn't they mentioned it?

"Of course. Whatever you need! That had to be why he changed the will, Ciara. The heart problems."

Her cousin gave a slow nod, as if trying to absorb the new reality.

"When would you like to go through his room?"

"No better time than now," Ciara said. "But first!"

Ciara strode toward the wall. She pressed a button on a wooden panel, revealing a drinks cabinet. She poured whiskey from a decanter into their tea mugs.

"Here's to Nevin McGrath," Ciara said. Her large gray eyes were damp with tears, her cheeks ruddy.

"To Uncle Nevin and finding out who murdered him."

"I'll kill them," Ciara promised, the air around her bristling with what Rayne's mother referred to as wild Celtic energy.

Rayne believed her cousin meant it.

Chapter Fourteen

Rayne and Ciara left their empty teacups in the blue parlor on the tray and went up the back staircase to the wing where Uncle Nevin's bedroom was. "Padraig showed me this," Rayne said, using her cell phone as a flashlight on the narrow steps that opened to a small utility room with a sink.

"I wish I'd known my brother," Ciara said. "I hated being an only child. You?"

"I didn't mind it. My head was always in the clouds." Her parents had both encouraged her imagination, and she'd never felt alone.

They followed a plush-carpeted corridor worn with time and many footsteps, stopping at Aunt Amalie's pink parlor and what would be Rayne's sewing studio after tomorrow.

Ciara opened the door to the pink room full of light, gesturing inside. "Sorry if I overreacted yesterday. It's just that Da made this room seem sacrosanct, you know? Amalie was the love of his life."

Which left Ciara's mother out in the cold, Rayne imagined. She'd been curious about *how* Ciara had happened, but it wasn't the kind of thing you just went and asked, even as a brash American.

Her patience was rewarded.

"Da spent the night in London while separated from Amalie, with my mum, who ended up pregnant. She decided to raise me herself. I mean, she found out that he'd gotten back together with his wife. It was the right thing to do." Ciara nodded as if giving herself an affirmation.

Rayne sensed that her reaction to this information could make or break her relationship with her cousin. "Your mother seems very strong."

"She was. Stubborn too." Ciara's chuckle was self-deprecating. "Like I needed a double dose. Found out who he was when Mum was sick with stupid cancer, and she told me to come here. I wasn't sure about it, you know, but in the end, I couldn't stay away. Made myself mental wondering what he'd be like. I was twenty-two and no wean, you know?"

Rayne nodded, assuming *wean* meant little kid.

"Thirty-one now," Ciara said.

"I just turned thirty."

"I know. And got a castle for your birthday."

Rayne snorted in surprise. She'd been thinking of her losses. "That is one way to look at it. So, how did Uncle Nevin handle your arrival?"

"Da was embarrassed by me, I think, showing up out of the blue after his great love for Amalie. She'd passed away five years prior to my mum. After Padraig. Broken heart, I bet."

"I always thought so."

Ciara slowly closed the door of the parlor. "It's good that you use this space for something nice. It deserves to be used."

They stepped toward Uncle Nevin's bedroom door. "Thanks."

"What was Amalie like?"

"Aunt Amalie was beautiful. Long golden hair—curls. She was so stylish but welcoming too. Like, she would always give hugs. Didn't matter if Padraig and I had just come in from outside, she didn't mind the dirt."

"That's sweet."

"She was kindhearted. Her two dogs—my dad called them little yappers—followed her everywhere. Anyway, she doted on Padraig. Maybe she knew her time with her son would be short?"

Ciara's chin hiked. "Don't tell me you believe in that nonsense. Dead is dead."

"You're Irish, Ciara. You had a *feeling* your dad was killed." Rayne thumped her chest. "You're supposed to believe in ghosts."

Her cousin rolled her eyes.

"I've been hearing rattles outside my door at night." Rayne shivered. "You don't notice any noises?"

"Probably the furnace or mice. We should get another cat. I'll ask around at the pub. There are always free kittens."

Rayne decided to keep to herself that Blarney was sneaking into the house to sleep in front of her door. How did he do it? "I remember a big fluffy cat when I was here as a kid."

"Da loved his animals."

"It's funny. We didn't have pets growing up. Don't know why. Lauren said there wasn't much time, since everyone was so busy."

"It's strange that you call your parents by their names."

"Hollywood is bizarre," Rayne said. "No argument there."

They reached Uncle Nevin's closed bedroom door. Ciara's shoulders trembled. "We were just finding our way. He taught me every detail about this castle and the McGrath family history. I loved those times. Getting to know each other."

Rayne easily pictured them head to head, going over books or pictures, and it warmed her heart. "I believe Mr. Hughes, about the adoption."

"I wouldn't be so sure." Ciara opened the door to her dad's bedroom. "He never once mentioned it to me. I go by Smith."

Rayne went in and scanned the space. Uncle Nevin's spice cologne lingered in the air as a reminder of the man. He'd been the lord of the manor, while Conor, her father, had been the artist. Their styles were polar opposites though the two of them had looked like twins. This room was laid out like her dad's, but done in maroon instead of blue.

"It's like mine."

"Even has a bathroom," Ciara said. "He liked your da's addition so much that he had one installed as well."

A large four-poster bed was placed against a wall, and there was a fireplace on the opposite wall. A wardrobe rather than a closet. Two nightstands. Sage accents. An armchair. Small desk. A bookshelf. "Where's the TV?"

"There isn't one. I have a telly in mine. Da preferred to read before bed." Ciara opened the door to the bathroom. It was small by American standards but had a stand-up shower, toilet, and pedestal sink. Above the sink was a medicine cabinet with a black cloth over it.

"I can't live without a TV in the bedroom." Rayne stopped cold. "What's with the sheet?"

"It's an Irish thing, to cover the mirror and block the spirits. If Da had a window, it would be cracked to let the spirits escape. Cormac told me that in the old days, Da would have been laid out for a viewing before burial. Folks would smoke and drink to his health and toast a safe journey to heaven. He must've done that in here." Ciara rubbed her arms. "It wasn't me."

"May I see what's in there?" Rayne gestured toward the cabinet.

"Go ahead."

Rayne opened the cabinet, careful not to drop the cloth, and revealed a razor, spice cologne, bandages, aspirin, and a prescription bottle.

Bingo. There wasn't much else.

"Did he store things elsewhere? Like, did he take vitamins at all?" Her medicine cabinet was filled with vitamin A to zinc.

"I don't think so." Ciara reached for the heart medication and read the label. "Nevin McGrath. Take one pill daily. Dil . . . ditz . . ." She gave the bottle to Rayne.

"Diltiazem." Rayne scrunched her nose. "I have no idea. Never heard of it before." She reached for her phone, but cell service was awful inside the stone building, especially in an interior room—the most secure if the castle was under attack. She read the fine print. "It may cause dizziness. And yet he was driving the tractor?"

Ciara leaned against the sink. "Poor Da."

"Let's show this to the policeman." Rayne counted the pills inside. Four left of thirty. The date he'd picked up this prescription was two weeks ago.

"All right." Ciara raised her head and pushed away from the sink. "Garda Williams said the dosage was more than it should have been in Da's system. I wonder how long he's been taking this?"

"We can call the doctor and find out." Rayne patted Ciara's shoulder. "He can tell us what we need to know."

"Right." Ciara's gray eyes were filled with pain. And, being Ciara—anger. "Now?"

"Today's Sunday, so he's probably not open." Rayne walked out of the bathroom. "Tomorrow, maybe."

"You're going shopping for fancy dresses." Ciara edged by Rayne. "With Aine."

"Not dresses. Fabric to make wedding dresses that brides have put deposits on." Ciara showed no respect for what Rayne created.

Her cousin went to the mantel above the fireplace and studied the picture of Uncle Nevin and Aunt Amalie on vacation in Paris. "He was happy with her, here. I rarely saw this side of him."

Rayne half smiled. "He was a brooding Irishman."

"Your da was the one who brooded." Ciara winked at Rayne to show she was teasing. "He kept Uncle Conor's books on the shelf with pride."

Rayne turned on her heel, the pill bottle still in her hand. "He did?"

"See?"

Rayne followed the line of Ciara's finger to a special shelf with five thin glossy covers and *Conor McGrath* printed on the spine. "I remember these."

Her father had published five books of Irish poetry with a big publisher. The advance had been minimal but the house prestigious.

By book three, Lauren had said, things in the sales department had gotten better. Her dad had a way of connecting with people's souls. If he hadn't died, he would still be creating magic on the page.

Rayne had the books in a place of honor in her childhood bedroom. It might be nice to read them again while she was here, since it was gonna be a while.

"You should move into this room, Ciara," Rayne said. "It's big!"

"Oh, no. I couldn't." Ciara wrapped her arms around her waist. "It wouldn't be comfortable. It's Da's."

"Funny. That's how I feel about staying in my dad's room." They chuckled. "We should switch, maybe."

"Why bother moving?" Ciara said.

"You could spread out. Change things up. My dad's room has a bathroom too—does yours?"

"No." Ciara tucked her hand in her pocket. "I'm not that spoiled."

"There is nothing wrong with pampering yourself now and again. I think we should put some thought into refurbishing the rooms. You'll see that I am right, cous."

"I feel odd about it. I've lived here for nine years in my room. It's in the middle of the hall next to the library. Da gave me my choice when I arrived. I still like it."

"Okay—suit yourself. It's probably tiny."

Ciara lowered her arms to her sides. "I was gutted after my mum's death. I didn't know Nevin from Adam. He didn't have to let me live here at all."

Rayne clutched the prescription bottle, putting herself in Ciara's shoes. Though she wasn't an actress, she'd been around acting and movie sets her whole life. Her imagination was quite active. "Did you just show up on his doorstep?"

"Practically! Mum had phoned him, so he knew about me, though we'd never met. He picked me up at the airport. It was awful. Horrid. Awkward."

Rayne nodded.

"I was a wreck. And he introduced himself as Nevin. That's why I think I was surprised you call your mother Lauren."

"Well, you call him Da now."

"I do. Did. It took a while, but we got used to it. To each other." She cleared her throat and stepped away from the unlit fireplace. "Then I messed up."

"How?"

"Six months had gone by. My boyfriend back home called and said he missed me. I wasn't fitting in great here. Amalie's presence was overwhelming, and Da, you know, he likes to shout to make his point."

Celtic temperament. "What did you do?"

"I was an idiot and should have given it more time, but, well, I moved back to London. Stayed for a few years. Called Da once a month or so. I think he could tell things weren't going so splendid, because he told me I was welcome *home* anytime."

Rayne put her hand to her heart. "Oh! How old were you then?"

"Twenty-four?" Ciara nodded. "I broke things off and was here within the week. It upset him, I think. Having me choose to leave when Padraig and Amalie were dead."

That really resonated with Rayne. "So you've been proving yourself to him ever since."

"Pretty much. I didn't mind his shouting once I understood it. You might not have noticed," she said wryly, "but I have a wee bit of a temper myself."

Rayne chuckled. "He should have given you the castle."

Ciara's body stiffened, and her walls zipped right back up. "He didn't. Let's find out what happened to him. How did more medicine get in his system? It was a new medication, so we need to consider that he might not have meant to take so many."

"Sure." Her cousin couldn't even say overdose . . . and what was with her *just feeling* as if there was more to it? "One of the side effects is dizziness, and if he suffered that while driving on that very steep ravine, well. It could be an accident. In the States, they would keep this open as a suspicious death while they investigate."

"Like Garda Williams is doing."

"Yep." Rayne admired the four-poster bed in Nevin's bedroom. Ornate scrollwork matched the headboard and dresser.

"This craftsmanship is superb. Conor didn't have these gigantic posters, thank heaven."

Ciara's room was in the middle of the corridor. Could she be playing a prank on Rayne to freak her out by pretending to be a ghost? To what end, though? Ciara needed Rayne to stay here for the full twelve months.

And then what?

Rayne couldn't even imagine what the year would bring.

"Let's finish searching the room. I don't like this. It feels like a violation of Da's privacy." Ciara tugged open the top bureau drawer. "Shirts." She patted them. "Neat fold."

Rayne peered into the drawer. "He could teach Marie Kondo a thing or two. Impressive."

"That's Maeve's handiwork." Ciara pursed her lips. "What are we looking for?"

"Anything informative. A journal. Letters?" Rayne smirked as she checked the shelves near her dad's books. "A confession?"

Ciara shut the first drawer and went to the second of three. Opening it, she moved aside jeans and pants. The third drawer held socks, underwear, and two bulky sweaters.

"I bought him these for his birthday. Guess he didn't like 'em." She lifted them, her voice thick. Cards he'd been saving dropped to the maroon area rug. "Oh. These are from me—he kept them in the sweaters."

"Sweet."

Ciara sat cross-legged on the floor and read the cards, her nose turning pink with emotion. Rayne's did that too when she was upset.

Rayne pocketed the pill bottle and opened the wardrobe. Three suits hung on hangers. Shoes, polished, below. Ties.

"Da's church clothes," Ciara said from her position on the floor. She put the cards back in the envelopes but stayed seated.

The shirts were pressed. "Who does this for Uncle Nevin? Maeve?"

"No, Cormac. He and Da were very close."

The butler had to know about the heart medicine.

"What's with this *church* business?" Rayne closed the wardrobe door. "Do you really go every single Sunday?"

"Aye. It's the McGrath duty."

Rayne scrunched her brow.

"It's not so bad," Ciara said, seeing Rayne's expression. "Nine AM service, with Dafydd and the Lloyds. Neddy too. It's quick, and Father Patrick is so funny. You can stay for tea and a chat after if you like. Get all the church gossip. Just a word to the wise: anything you say to Gerda Meyer will be in the church bulletin."

Rayne had no intention of going to church and would certainly beware of Gerda. "I called Owen Hughes earlier. He commented that I wasn't at church. He also told me that Father Patrick had led a prayer for Uncle Nevin."

"Aye." Ciara fanned the envelopes in her lap. "Father Patrick asked about a burial service, but . . ."

"Hopefully the policeman will know something soon."

"I guess we need to pick his favorite suit for his funeral." Ciara sucked in her breath, bringing the cards her father had saved to her chest. "He liked the navy-blue best."

"I will help you however I can." Rayne patted the prescription bottle in her pocket. "Just let me know, all right?"

"Aye, sure. Not now, though."

"Okay." Rayne moved to the nightstand next to his bed. It had two drawers. "Shall I?"

"You do it," Ciara said. "What if he's got . . . I don't know."

"Porn?" Rayne laughed but sobered, imagining how awful that might be. "I'll do it."

"Ta."

She opened the drawer. Inside was a Bible and letters tied with string. Amalie to Nevin. Nevin to Amalie. "Adorable. You're safe, cousin."

Rayne climbed across the gigantic mattress to the nightstand on the other side, pulled it open, and gasped. These letters were from Lourdes, and Nevin had torn them up. She hurried around the end of the bed to show Ciara. "From the girlfriend and torn in half. I wonder what they said?"

Ciara held up her hand. "Nope. Don't wanna know."

"But Maeve said a man has needs," Rayne teased.

Ciara dropped the cards to her lap and plugged her ears. "Lalalalalala."

Rayne studied the halves of letters. It was good-quality stationery, and Lourdes's penmanship a scrawl. Who wrote letters anymore? Old-school. They could hold clues.

"Ciara. It's strange that they're torn but stuck in a drawer. Why wouldn't Uncle Nevin toss them if he doesn't want anyone to read them?"

Her cousin lowered her arms and rose in a single fluid motion, as graceful as a ballerina. Her expression grew serious. "That's a very good question. Lourdes would know about the heart medicine, perhaps."

"If you're sleeping with someone, you're close. She might."

A knock sounded on the partially open door.

"My dears," Maeve said, opening it as she entered. "Garda Williams is in the blue parlor. He has another question for you."

Chapter Fifteen

"Good timing!" Rayne said. She showed Maeve the prescription bottle. "Did you know Uncle Nevin was taking medication for his heart?"

"I know everything that goes on in this house," the housekeeper said with a sniff.

"He told you?" Ciara asked, standing next to Rayne, her arms crossed.

"Did his lordship tell me in so many words?" Maeve shook her head. "Not exactly."

Rayne's brow rose in surprise.

"Not from snooping," Maeve said indignantly. "Cleaning. As is my job."

Ciara snickered and brushed by Rayne on her way to the open door. "Way to go, princess. You're just making friends all over the place."

Rayne's cheeks heated. "I'm sorry, Maeve. Didn't mean to imply anything like that. Of course you would know. Did he take anything else, like vitamins? Supplements?"

Maeve's ruffled feathers settled. "No. The work around here kept him fit. I've got Garda Williams in the blue parlor downstairs. Oh, what's this?"

Maeve homed in like a missile to the torn letters that Rayne had put on the bed to decipher later.

"Just trash," Ciara said. "I'll take care of it."

Maeve frowned at the stack, turned around, and led the way out of the room, carefully closing the door once they were all in the corridor once more.

Rayne glanced at Ciara. Was she trying to protect her dad's memory by tossing the love letters herself?

Maybe she'd let Rayne read them first. It seemed strange to tear up correspondence from a lady friend, unless there were secrets in there Uncle Nevin didn't want anyone to read. Why keep them?

To quote *Alice in Wonderland*, it was "curiouser and curiouser."

Maeve urged them forward. "Should I invite the garda to stay for dinner? We're having roast lamb, and Neddy's made plenty."

"No!" Ciara barreled toward the stairs. "He needs to work on the case."

"A man must eat," Maeve murmured. "His lordship always extended an invitation to a meal."

"Dominic suspects everyone in this house of Da's murder, except for Rayne." Ciara paused at the top of the stairway.

"What?" Maeve put her hand to her chest as she and Rayne strode in step, finally reaching the grand staircase. "Even me?"

The housekeeper sounded so indignant that Rayne chuckled.

Ciara waited on the top stair, her hand on her slim hip. "Now how do you feel about having him stay to dinner?"

Maeve's chin tipped. "Not so keen."

"We're on the same page at last." Ciara skipped down the steps.

"I never," Maeve muttered. "Cormac and I have been in this house since before we married. I was seventeen and hired as a maid by the previous Lord and Lady McGrath, and Cormac trained the horses. We had a large stable back then."

Rayne thought that sounded interesting—except for the part about the horses. The large animals terrified her. She and Maeve reached the main floor and turned left. Ciara was ahead of them, her long legs making quick work down the hall.

"I can't believe I offered that man lace biscuits with his tea." Maeve stopped at the door to the parlor.

"His job is to suspect everyone. It's not personal," Rayne said.

Ciara breathed in. "You have the prescription bottle, Rayne?"

"I do." She patted her front jeans pocket.

"Ready?" Maeve asked. Her voice held the slightest quiver.

Rayne and Ciara nodded. Maeve opened the door for them, and Rayne entered right on Ciara's heels, stopping near the sofa.

Garda Williams sat in a straight-backed chair next to the tea table with a cup in his hand. He placed it down when they came in.

"Hello again," the officer said.

Rayne waved her fingers. Ciara crossed her arms and glared at the policeman. "Well?" she demanded.

"I just wanted to let you know that we've finished out by the tractor. My partner is typing the report when she gets back to the station."

"We didn't know about the heart medicine, so we went upstairs to Uncle Nevin's suite." Rayne offered the prescription bottle to Garda Williams. "This was in his private bath."

The officer accepted it and shook the bottle; the pills inside rattled. He read the dosage, then made several notes on his tablet.

Maeve waited quietly by the door, practically blending in, as if she didn't want the garda to send her from the room.

The officer glanced at Rayne. "May I keep this?"

Rayne looked at Ciara. Her cousin shrugged and said, "If it helps, then certainly."

"I'll return it once we're done with the investigation." Garda Williams pulled an evidence bag from his pants pocket and placed the pill bottle inside it.

"A side effect of the medication is dizziness," Rayne said. "There's a warning on the label not to operate heavy machinery."

The garda sighed. "That fact complicates matters. My partner is not as certain as she used to be. An accident would be far easier on the community."

"Except it wasn't," Ciara said sharply. "You have to promise that you won't give up!"

The policeman stiffly bobbed his head. The hat didn't slide at all. "I'll be going."

Maeve darted from her post by the door and stood in front of Garda Williams, her shoulders trembling as she stared him in the eye. "I loved working for Lord McGrath. My husband and daughter are loyal staff members. We would never hurt him. Ever!"

Garda Williams's boyish cheeks turned pink under Maeve's attack.

Rayne had respect for the officer as he stayed calm. "Ma'am, we are questioning everyone."

Maeve raised her chin, then narrowed her gaze. "Make sure to speak with Lourdes McNamara, his ex-girlfriend."

"His girlfriend?" Garda Williams reached for his pen and tablet.

From the way he asked, Rayne guessed he hadn't known about the relationship.

"*Ex*," Maeve said. "It wasn't a big deal."

Garda Willams turned to Ciara. "Did you know about this?"

"Unfortunately. Da and Lourdes!" Ciara sighed. "They'd argue to shake the roof, but that was just their way."

The housekeeper blew out a breath. "Our lordship wanted to break it off, and so he did. And now he's dead under suspicious circumstances? A woman scorned." Maeve *tsk*ed.

Rayne and Ciara exchanged nods. A newly broken relationship explained the torn letters.

"When was this?" Garda Williams asked.

"Wednesday evening, before he died on Thursday," Maeve said with certainty.

Rayne pursed her lips. Lourdes could have given him more medicine somehow. "But he didn't mow until the next day."

"Da had a schedule for mowing," Ciara said. "It was the only way he could keep up with the lawn. Lourdes knew that if she wanted to talk to him, he'd be in his office doing paperwork on Wednesdays."

"It was also the last Wednesday of the month," Maeve said. "He holds an open house to hear grievances."

"So anybody could have come in?" Garda Williams lowered his pen.

"It will be in his journal," Maeve said.

"Which is where?" Garda Williams asked, starting to sound a little stressed out.

"I don't know." The housekeeper hooked her thumb toward the door. "I haven't seen it. I can ask Cormac."

"I didn't find it in his office. Might be in the locked cabinet," Rayne said. "His keys would be helpful."

Garda Williams nodded. "Noted. Why did they break up?"

Maeve tucked a strand of light-red hair behind her ear. "I'll tell you. Lourdes wanted to be lady here, and Lord Nevin would have none of it."

Ciara winced, and Rayne assumed she was reacting to the idea of Lourdes as Lady McGrath.

Maeve rocked on her heels. "His lordship told me she was getting too full of herself and it was time to break things off. I heard shouting from his office, and a vase shattered."

"She threw a vase?" Garda Williams asked, making another note. "I will interview her."

Rayne preferred the idea of the ex-girlfriend being at fault much more than she liked thinking it was someone in the Lloyd family. The torn letters hinted at a less-than-amiable breakup. Ciara gave a little head shake when Rayne raised her brow in question.

Okay. Ciara must be curious as to what the letters said too.

Rayne considered who else the garda guy should question. "Do you know Richard Forrest?"

Garda Williams took his attention from Maeve to Rayne. "Of course. He operates the mill here . . . when it works."

"Yes. Well, I was at the pub today with Amos, and he flung some insults at me—nothing awful. I can hardly help being American." She smiled. The officer did not.

"And?" Garda Williams tightened his grip on the pen.

"Richard blames my uncle for not helping him with the broken paddle. Loudly. Amos said that Nevin had in the past but that he'd drawn a line. I guess Richard's got some horse betting problems."

The officer wrote something down.

"That he does, poor man," Ciara said, with surprising empathy. "Da offered to pay for counseling, but Richard refused to take him up on it."

"Did the arguments get violent?" the officer asked.

Ciara shrugged. "I doubt it would be physical. Da could be gruff, but he cared about his people."

"Richard is seeking guidance from the church," Maeve shared in a quiet voice. "We hope it helps him. Give your addiction and woes to the Lord."

Gamblers Anonymous was what he needed more than church, Rayne thought. Then again, prayer was very powerful. If the man was pushed during a confrontation with Nevin, could he have gone off?

And what?

Pushed the tractor over?

It didn't make sense.

"I will speak with Richard too," Garda Williams said.

"Speaking of violent, Freda punched Uncle Nevin on the arm," Rayne said.

"Councilwoman Freda Bevan?" Garda Williams asked, aghast.

"Yeah." Ciara nodded. "At the town meeting."

"Did you see it?"

"No. I heard about it, though. It was all over the pub the next day," Ciara said.

"I don't believe it." The garda frowned at Ciara as if she might be lying to him. Rayne sensed undercurrents between them.

"Da admitted it when I questioned him!" Ciara said.

The officer groaned. "Freda lives in my village. What did they fight about?"

"She wanted Da to sign her petition to join our villages. Da said he wasn't interested. It escalated."

Rayne laughed at the understatement. It boggled the mind to imagine shouts at a town meeting becoming punches.

"Well," Maeve said. "Aren't you going to write her name down on your list?"

Garda Williams shut his eyes but then opened them again. "I will ask the councilwoman about it." He added her name. "I'm sure it was a misunderstanding."

"We'll see about that," Ciara said. "You can't treat her special just because you both live in the same village."

"I would never," the officer said, offended.

"That's exactly how I felt, me lad." Maeve crossed her arms. "I would *never*."

"The important thing is to find out what happened the night of the accident with the tractor," Rayne said, bringing the conversation back to Uncle Nevin's demise.

"You inherited the castle," Garda William said. Statement. She'd already answered when he asked the question. Was he fishing for something?

"It's complicated." Rayne turned as a knock sounded.

Cormac opened the door. The buttons were done on his jacket, his hair combed. "Lady McGrath. Boxes have arrived for you, requiring your signature."

She arched a brow at the butler. What was this *lady* nonsense, after she'd asked him to call her Rayne? Was he trying to make a point to the officer?

"I'll be right there." Rayne excused herself with a nod to Garda Williams and followed Cormac out to the foyer, where a delivery person with three boxes from the United States waited patiently.

Scanning the contents, she read *sewing machine* and squealed. She'd forgotten all about the small Bernina she'd started on years ago that she'd stored at her apartment. She signed for it, patting her pockets for a tip.

"It's already been taken care of, Lady McGrath," the courier said. "Good afternoon."

"Thank you!" She whirled toward the three boxes, which had been stacked in the foyer near the round table. "My small sewing machine from the apartment! I forgot all about that. Just in time for me to make gowns. I have three July brides, and I'll be working my fingers to the bone." *Thank you, Lauren!*

Aine arrived with Neddy. Maeve and Cormac stood side by side. Ciara tapped her toe.

"Just wait until you guys see this—oh, I'm so excited. I can't stand it!" Rayne reached for the top box on her tiptoes, but it was heavy.

"Let me help!" Cormac moved to assist her with the top box, as did Garda Williams.

"Thank you." Her heart hammered at having something from home, even though she hadn't been gone a week. A year was a long time to be away. She picked at a loose corner of the packing tape.

Garda Williams offered her a pocketknife just as Amos and Blarney entered, probably to see what the heck was going on.

"What do you have there?" Amos asked, his sexy Viking hair settling around his shoulders.

"Lauren sent me my sewing machine—my first Bernina." Rayne wouldn't dwell on why she couldn't have her specialty machine just yet. It was still part of a crime scene. She banished Landon too.

"Lauren?" Garda Williams asked.

Ciara snorted. "She calls her mother that."

"Strange," he said.

She ignored their commentary and with her free hand patted Blarney, who sat eagerly at her side to see what was in the boxes.

Aine inched forward, her eyes sparkling.

Rayne sliced through the thick tape at the side of the box, and out tumbled her designer shoes. Jimmy Choos, Steve Maddens, Louboutins.

Ciara burst out laughing. "Figures."

Blarney got hold of a cubic zirconia high heel worth a few thousand dollars and ran with it outside, as Amos hadn't shut the door all the way.

Dafydd came in from the barn, his hands up, his look very confused. "Does Blarney have the crown jewels in his mouth?"

Aine scooted to the pile to help put the shoes back in the box. The maid's body was shaking with suppressed giggles.

Rayne wished the floor of the castle would open up and swallow her whole.

Chapter Sixteen

Rayne suffered insane mortification when the next two boxes turned out to be her lingerie and designer handbags. The lingerie had been packed around the small sewing machine, which was very out of date and didn't even have a computer chip. It was better than sewing by hand, but just barely. Naturally, her silk nighties were given lots of side-eye.

Her mom had dropped in a note with a check for five thousand to buy a new machine in Dublin, along with the fabrics for her July wedding gowns. Each dress would bring in between four thousand and six thousand.

While she greatly appreciated her mother's loan, the deluxe sewing machine she'd programmed with her signature stitches was unavailable while the case was open, and *that* Bernina had cost over fifteen thousand.

It was a blow.

Amos helped her carry the boxes to her dad's bedroom to be dealt with later. He hadn't bothered to hide his amusement. "I have to ask—why so many fancy slips and robes?"

"I make them as patterns for the brides. Once I don't require them anymore, I offer them for sale on the website."

"Ah, that makes sense. I'm glad I asked," Amos said. He put the boxes on the floor by her suitcase.

"All the accessories but none of the clothes!" Rayne said, closing the bedroom door.

"There's more?" Amos gave a robust laugh. "You'll need to take over the third-floor storage."

"Funny." She wondered if he was kidding but filed the information away for her subconscious to examine later. "My mother texted that the rest of my clothes will be here this week sometime. Two boxes."

"Ask Maeve where there is available space—she'll know better than anyone." Amos nudged her arm. "Your dad's room is stuffed already."

They reached the top of the stairs. The scent of mint and rosemary filled the air in the foyer. Blarney hadn't returned with her very expensive Jimmy Choo. "I hate to take up too much space."

"Rayne, you need to tour *inside* the manor. There are at least three unused chambers on the second floor and just as many on the main floor. It was built to hold a lot of people back then."

Her mind raced as they descended the stairs. "And the bungalows?"

"Four are habitable. Two should be demolished," Amos said. "The horses like them, though. If it's suddenly lashing rain, it's better than being in the open."

"You, Dafydd, and Richard all have one?"

"You want to move out of the big house?" he teased. "The fourth cottage is like camping with no services."

"I prefer hot water and a full kitchen. No thanks."

Amos touched her elbow and leaned down to whisper in her ear, "How did I know that?"

Her body warmed.

Cormac crossed the foyer from the kitchen, his brow furrowed. "What a disaster! The gardai are gone, but Owen and Daisy Hughes are here for dinner. Maeve said in all the upheaval, she forgot that his lordship had invited them. Sunday, June sixth, in her planner. Right there. What's the point of having it if she doesn't read it?"

"I heard that, Cormac Lloyd," Maeve said, joining them, her redhead temper a match for her husband's. "Aine is setting two extra places in the formal dining room."

"But, he's . . . gone," Rayne said.

"It's odd," Amos agreed. "Unless they just want to pay their respects? Normally in this situation, folks would come to the house, view the body, and share stories."

"Well, this isn't normal. Maeve told me that the garda said we were under suspicion! As if!" Cormac huffed and opened the door, a smooth smile on his face as he greeted the Hugheses. "Welcome!"

"Should we go?" Daisy asked behind a large bouquet. "Owen suggested calling to make sure, but I wanted to give our condolences in person. This must be a nightmare for you all."

Rayne knew good manners dictated that she welcome the couple, so she held out her hand. "Nice to see you both again."

Cormac accepted the bouquet and placed it on the round table in the foyer, moving the bog oak statue to a different table near the stairs. It brightened the room with yellows, blues, and whites.

"This is lovely." Rayne nodded at the flowers. It was obvious Daisy and Owen had been here before because it was just the right size.

"Thanks! From our garden." Daisy smiled.

"You grew these?" Rayne was amazed at the woman's talents.

"Aye. My da taught me how to put together raised beds with a hose system and natural fertilizer. You'll have to come back to tea again and let me bore you with the back garden."

"It's an organized jungle," Owen said, pride in his voice.

Owen shook her hand after Daisy did. The two were in what Rayne imagined would be their Sunday church clothes, Owen in a brown suit, Daisy in a summer print dress with cap sleeves and a shawl. They resembled father and daughter rather than husband and wife, but that was quite normal in Hollywood.

In fact, *nobody* appeared their age in Hollywood.

Amos said hello next, and they all followed Cormac to the dining room. Ciara was already seated next to Dafydd. She'd made the effort to dress for dinner in black slacks and a striped top. Her curls had been combed to waves with a barrette at the side. A gold claddagh ring was on her finger. Rayne's mom still wore the one Conor had given her at their engagement—two hands holding a heart.

To Rayne's surprise, Richard was also at the table, shaved and in a fresh shirt and slacks. Had her uncle always welcomed everyone for Sunday dinner? She didn't remember, having been eleven when she was last here.

"Hello again, Richard." Rayne braced herself for any snide "American" comments.

"Howareye." He didn't quite meet her gaze.

"Fine."

Ciara looked up at Rayne. "Da had a standing invitation on Sundays for the staff and boarders to eat together. Richard hasn't been around for a while, but he's welcome."

Richard's face flushed. He made no excuse, so Rayne was left to surmise that he had been so angry with Nevin that he hadn't wanted to share a meal.

"Sorry about earlier," Richard murmured.

Rayne nodded. "Let's try again."

The Hughes duo sat across from each other.

Rayne was put at the head of the table, which was very uncomfortable. She didn't like it but was stuck.

Amos was to one side, Ciara the other. Neddy brought in the roast lamb, and Rayne forgot all about her discomfort at the feast he placed in the center of the table. Mint sauce, gravy, and green beans. Cubed potatoes with scallions. The meat pie and curry fries had worn off with all the drama of the day.

"Shall I?" Cormac said, picking up the carving knife after Neddy and Maeve were both seated.

Ten people filled the room, which Rayne thought was much better than just her and Ciara a few nights ago.

"Yes, please."

Daisy and Owen made pleasant small talk over the meal. Neddy and Richard discussed a local football team that seemed to be on a losing streak. At this, sweat popped out on Richard's brow. A bet gone wrong?

Aine finished eating first and discussed the injured sheep with Amos.

Rayne felt as if she were part of a large and boisterous family, and she could easily envision her dad here, growing up on this property.

What would he think, to see her here right now?

She believed in life after death. Spirits. That there was more. They were all connected by energy somehow.

Had she ever seen a ghost?

She hadn't, but she acknowledged the possibility. After her dad had died, she and her mother had hired a medium to see if Conor was all right.

Padma, famous Hollywood medium, had shared messages that only her dad could have known, and it had given her mother peace to let him go, though Conor McGrath would always live in her heart.

"Don't you think so, Rayne?" Daisy asked.

Rayne blinked. "Sorreee! I was daydreaming."

Daisy laughed. "Happens to me all of the time. I was just saying that this property is so beautiful. Can't imagine the McGraths not living here."

"And you won't have to," Owen said to his fashionable wife.

"At church this morning, Father Patrick mentioned our lordship's accident. Do you know when the funeral services will be?" Daisy sipped water.

Her accent was different than Maeve and Cormac's. Dafydd, Welsh. Ciara, Irish-London. They were a mishmash. Rayne's mother was brilliant with accents and could do them all, sounding like a local.

"We don't know yet," Ciara said. "I told Father Patrick that I'd call him."

"What's the holdup?" Richard asked. He scraped the last of his lamb into the mint sauce, then popped it into his mouth.

"His death is under investigation," Maeve said. "Garda Williams was just here. Can ye believe it?"

Aine's eyes widened. "Might that affect the will?"

Owen patted his mouth with a cloth napkin. "I don't believe so." The lawyer turned to Rayne at the head of the table. "What a mess you've landed in! Poor dear. Is there anything we can do?"

"Speed the clock so that the year will pass?" Rayne suggested.

Amos laughed and eyed the ceiling.

"Did you know that Da was taking heart medication?" Ciara asked Owen. "For heart arr . . ."

"Arrhythmia," Rayne supplied, when Ciara was too choked up to finish the word.

"Oh no!" Owen said, concern in his gaze. "I hope he was going into Kilkenny or Dublin for a doctor. Dr. Ruebens is old as Methuselah, and God knows what he might have given Nevin."

Great, Rayne thought. Just to make things more muddled, an ancient doctor.

"We're going to call him tomorrow," Ciara said.

"It's awful," Richard said. His brown eyes welled. "Our last conversation, it was, it was." He put his fist to his mouth and bowed his head. "I'm ashamed."

Neddy gave Richard's shoulder a pat.

Maeve sniffed delicately. "It's never too late to mend your ways. I know his lordship believed in you."

"I will. I will!" Richard brushed his coppery hair back from his forehead.

"Aine, will you help me bring in the pudding?" Neddy asked.

Cormac and Maeve cleared the dishes, and the four were gone in an instant.

"They have this routine down," Rayne said.

"They should!" Amos smiled at Rayne, his blue eyes twinkling. "Every Sunday since I've known them."

"And me," Ciara said. "Though if it's just six of us, we use the other dining room."

"This is the prettiest room," Daisy said. "Always feels like I'm on holiday. And oh, that Neddy can cook. What's for dessert?"

"I'm too stuffed for dessert!" Rayne would be puffy as a marshmallow at the rate she'd been eating, with no workouts.

She changed her mind when Neddy arrived with apple crumble and custard in individual pie crusts. Aine, Maeve, and Cormac offered dessert plates and forks as the cook served.

One bite of the warm apples with custard, and Rayne was in for the whole thing.

They discussed everything but Uncle Nevin's death. It was too real. Too sad. This bonding was the break they all needed.

Once the meal was over, Aine gathered dishes with Neddy. "This won't take a minute," she said. "Coffee? Another whiskey?"

"I shouldn't," Owen said, his hand on his tummy. "I have an appointment with a client in the morning first thing."

He and Daisy got up to leave. Rayne and Ciara walked them out, with Cormac moving ahead to open the door as he'd been trained.

"I hope you two can put your differences aside," Owen said in a grandfatherly way. "That will be best for the whole village."

"We'll see," Rayne replied in a dry tone. "The weight of the village is a bit much, though. I'm trying to figure out the castle first."

Ciara snorted behind her.

Blarney waited on the front landing with the crystal Jimmy Choo. It was ruined beyond repair and had cost three times as much as Blarney. Could she wrestle it from his mouth? He wagged his tail at her, wanting to play. She couldn't be mad when she looked into those golden-brown eyes.

Daisy gave Blarney a wide berth. "What on earth does he have in his mouth?" The dog growled and shook his bottom half, begging her to try and take it.

"Oh, it's all right," Ciara declared. "One of Rayne's fancy shoes . . . a Jimmy something or other."

Daisy's eyes rounded, and she peered back at Rayne in horror. "Jimmy *Choo*?"

"Usin' it like a teething ring." Ciara snickered. "Rich people. Completely mental, but hey."

Rayne was tempted to give her cous a little shove down the last stair but didn't.

"Let us know if there's anything we can do for the funeral service." Owen rested his hand on Ciara's forearm. "Your dad was well respected."

"Thank you," Ciara said, standing next to Rayne. "We will."

"Good night!" Rayne called as the couple descended the wide stairs, Daisy helping Owen more than the other way around. Blarney darted in front of them, and then around the car, and then . . . off over the hill to who knows where. She caught a glint of crystal as her shoe hit the evening sunlight.

Richard left next, then Dafydd, then Amos. It seemed nobody wanted to go over Uncle Nevin's last day.

They'd lived with the man and had closer relationships with him than Rayne.

Rayne hoped to talk with Ciara about the letters upstairs in her dad's room. It might be nice to work together and decipher them. If it was important, then they could tell the garda right away. It just might be a clue to catching Lourdes.

"Ciara?" Rayne peeked into the downstairs rooms.

Her cousin had disappeared for the evening like a ghost.

Chapter Seventeen

Rayne chatted with her mother for an hour after Sunday's incredible meal, lounging on the bed with pillows. Since the castle didn't have internet, she was racing through her cell phone data.

She cracked the door of the bedroom open to see if Blarney would come in, or if she could catch her rattling-chains ghost in the act. "I hope Blarney knows I'm not mad at him."

"We should contact the pet psychic to see what's going on with that poor dog. He's got to be traumatized," Lauren said. "Finding Nevin like that. How smart to bark for Amos."

She could picture Ciara's reaction to that idea. Her cousin would probably hurt herself laughing. "I don't think that would fly. Then again, Ciara is going with her gut about something happening to Uncle Nevin, and then look—Garda Williams found too much medicine in his system."

"That's very spooky. We should never deny our intuition." Her mother snickered. "I'm sorry that the rest of the clothes didn't come yet. I never laughed so hard—the idea of your lingerie strewn over the foyer. Your shoes!" Lauren let out another peal of laughter.

Rayne smiled. Now that hours had passed, she could see the humor. "I wanted to die. Mom, thanks again for the loan."

"It's a gift, honey. I wish I could do more." Lauren sighed.

The sigh was new. "What's wrong?"

"I hate to burden you right now with this, but Paul is worried our sitcom might not be renewed for another season."

Rayne's stomach cramped and she felt sick. It had been on for almost twenty-five years, which was an incredible run. "Oh, Mom!"

"I know." Lauren expelled a breath. "I've been trying to keep it to myself, but we tell each other everything."

They were very close. Rayne knew she was lucky to have a mom that was also her friend. Not everybody had that kind of relationship.

"This is our twenty-fourth season. That's quite a long time for a sitcom." Lauren chuckled sadly. "I thought *Family Forever* meant forever."

"I hope that you're wrong. That Paul is mistaken."

"Oh, me too. Taxes have gone up so much on our house that I must keep working. I can't retire at fifty-three, for heaven's sake. I'll be the old-lady-character actress."

"First of all, you are not old. Second, Helen Mirren rocks her age, and so do other leading ladies over sixty. Third, no way could they just shut the show down. Not to mention the series will be optioned on other networks." Like *Happy Days* or *Friends*.

"But we're prime-time!"

After a few minutes of commiseration, her mom wanted to get off the phone. Rayne realized how much she missed her mother, and she'd been at the castle less than a week. Lauren must have spent a fortune in shipping costs to get Rayne her things.

She wasn't used to thinking in terms of thrift. Her entire business was based on luxury. That was okay—she'd started in her living room and could do it again.

Rayne set her alarm for six and lay back to doze. Noises woke her later. Her Jimmy Choo sandal, missing all but two crystals, was on the pillow next to her and Blarney was on the floor, inside by the door.

Protected, Rayne went back to sleep.

* * *

Six AM came early. She never had liked waking to an alarm, but mornings with her bedroom window facing the ocean had been her favorite way to greet a new day.

This was a chilly stone castle that was going to take some getting used to.

She patted Blarney behind the ears, praising him for protecting her against ghosts during the night. She picked up the sandal, already imagining how she might make earrings or sew the remainder onto a bodice.

"No more chewing my shoes, okay?"

Blarney lowered his muzzle toward the ground, ears down too.

"These cost more than you do, buster. And right now, my finances are on the downslide. Our secret."

He thumped his tail and cautiously lifted his head.

"Do you miss Uncle Nevin?"

Blarney woofed. His nose twitched, and he tilted his head as if listening to her.

"Well, I'm here now, all right?"

She got dressed, deciding to rock something stylish for her day of shopping in Dublin. Black cigarette pants, an orange silk sleeveless blouse, and black heels. She rolled her hair into a side bun and added orange earrings. Orange lipstick completed the look.

Blarney watched her the entire time with sad eyes.

"You're killing me, Blarney! I'll have Lauren contact the pet psychic. Maybe there's something she can do for you, so you understand what happened to Nevin. I won't let Dafydd sell you. 'Kay?"

Blarney whined and hurried out of the bedroom. She followed at a slower pace to the cozy kitchen.

Neddy was up making a breakfast of cinnamon rolls and sausage—patties, not links. "*Maidin!*"

Rayne nabbed a piece of sausage and tossed it to Blarney, who caught it in one bite. "Good morning to you too."

Aine opened the side cellar kitchen door, and Blarney slipped out—stealthy for a sixty-pound dog.

Another routine? Maybe with Nevin?

Before Rayne could ask, Maeve and Ciara entered the kitchen. Ciara, dressed like an adorable hillbilly in denim coveralls and a T-shirt, plonked her elbows on the table and gave a dramatic sigh.

"All that talk about ghosts yesterday made me think I was hearing things last night, Rayne." Ciara fluttered her fingers—still wearing the gold claddagh ring. "I blame my mood on you."

Neddy slid her a cup of tea. "Here you are." He handed the coffee to Rayne next. "In order of need," he chuckled. "Here's the honey, Ciara."

Rayne wouldn't argue and liked that Neddy was willing to overlook her lady status. It was nothing she'd ever wanted or could imagine getting used to.

"*Bainne* and *siúcra* for you," Aine said, passing the bowls of cream and sugar. "You look very fine!"

"Thank you. When should we go to Dublin?" Rayne doctored her coffee.

"I'll be finished with the upstairs dusting at eleven. After that?"

"All right." That gave her time to start moving furniture in the pink parlor. Rayne turned to Ciara. "What are you up to this morning?"

"I texted Dafydd that I'd catch him later in the field. He was upset and pressed the point that we need to know the finances so that we can get the fencing." Ciara stirred her tea. "So I thought I'd help you."

"He did?" Maeve raised a brow.

Ciara missed the expression, but Rayne didn't.

What was Dafydd's game? "You're sure there is no extra key to that cabinet?" Rayne asked the housekeeper.

"I don't have one. Pity." Maeve moved to the stove. "Can I help, Neddy?"

"Ah, sure—take the sweet rolls and I'll finish the sausage," the cook said. Maeve brought the iced cinnamon buns to the table.

Rayne flexed her fingers. "Ciara, how good are you at jimmying locks?"

"Break into Da's cabinet?" Ciara shook her head. "Oh no. No way."

"Who knows when we might hear from Garda Williams?" Sensing the way to Ciara's cooperation, Rayne said, "The sooner we know what we have and what we don't, the sooner we can get that fence."

Ciara slurped her tea like a truck driver on the road and scowled at Rayne over the rim of her mug. "I'll help you look."

"Okay. Let's do that before I go to Dublin."

"Dublin is a waste of time and petrol," Ciara declared.

"I beg to differ. I need that fabric and a bigger sewing machine." Rayne did her level best to keep the panic from her tone. They all thought she was a rocking success, and she couldn't blow her cover.

She'd carried her mom as a safety net in the back of her mind over the past week, but now that net might be gone. What would Lauren do without her show? It was her life in many ways.

"Your ring is sure pretty . . . engagement? How come you don't wear it all the time?"

"Manual labor. I don't want to lose it." Ciara smiled at the gold band. "Dafydd bought it for me, and it means the world."

Neddy put two black patties on a dish for Rayne. "Here you are. Blood pudding for you, Ciara?"

"Three, thank you." Ciara eyed Rayne. "Protein carries energy, so I'm not famished by lunch."

She swallowed. Blood pudding was sausage? "Does everyone eat lunch together?" How to ditch the patties without hurting anybody's feelings?

"Not really," Maeve said. "Neddy makes soup or meat pies, sandwiches. Easy and quick."

Aine watched her, her red brow raised in question.

"Who eats it?" She nudged her dish toward Aine, who nodded and stabbed a patty for her own plate, then dropped her cloth napkin over it. Rayne still had one.

Ciara curled her upper lip. "The folks that work here and live on the property. Trust me—food is not the place you want to trim the budget."

Neddy looked horrified as he delivered patties to Maeve's plate.

Maeve gasped. "Oh no. We don't waste a thing here. Sheep are used tip to tail," she said. "Cows too. We grow our vegetables in the back of the property. Have fruit trees. Our grain is wheat we've grown for our own flour—or it was, but the past few years we've had to buy grain because of bad crops. Anyway, McGrath Castle is self-sufficient. Any extra gets donated to Father Patrick at the church. He disperses it where he sees a need."

"It's a dream a lot of Americans have," Rayne said. It hadn't been her dream. No, she'd wanted silks, satins, and ballgowns— never a big farm.

Aine laughed. "America has so much land!"

"Not like this," Maeve said proudly. "Nowhere is as beautiful as Ireland."

Rayne smiled and cut the patty in half. Now what? The napkins were cloth and not thrown away. They didn't use paper towels. "My dad said so too."

"Why'd he leave, then?" Ciara asked.

Rayne tore off a roll and passed the basket. Maeve took one and then gave them to Aine. "He fell in love with my mother while visiting Hollywood."

Maeve dabbed her eyes. "A true love. It's what we all wish for in this short life." She reached for Ciara's hand, the one with the engagement ring. "And you will have with Dafydd."

Ciara smiled her thanks.

Rayne's cousin didn't seem the lovey-dovey type, but when it came to matters of the heart, well, all bets were off.

She had no room for an opinion, since her lover had robbed her blind. Rayne managed to clear her own plate and hide the sausage. She felt terrible about it, but blood pudding was not to her taste.

Rayne owned Aine big—not only for the sausage thing but for driving her to Dublin. She would buy her something special while they shopped.

After breakfast, Rayne and Ciara went to Uncle Nevin's office.

"What are you going to do with this space?" Ciara asked, her voice hesitant as she shut the heavy wood door behind them.

"What do you mean?" The decor was masculine manor and did not match any of Rayne's aesthetic.

"Well, you inherited," Ciara said. "You should use the office for what you want."

Rayne felt like this was a test and considered her options. Finally, she said, "Well, it's not really my place. It's the Grathton family, past and present. Is that what you mean?"

"Yes." Ciara nodded with a smile. "I wasn't sure if you'd understand. I had Da teaching me all about Grathton pride in a crash course, since I didn't grow up here. I guess, since you've always known this was a family home . . ."

"It's bigger than you and me," Rayne said. "Or our fathers."

"Exactly." Ciara went to the large desk, which had been made of solid wood to stand the test of time. She peered underneath it and ran her hands along the edges. "Looking for a hidden key."

Rayne left her to it and studied the lock on the cabinet. "Okay. You do you."

"Huh?"

"I've already done that, but you might have better luck." She'd never jimmied a lock in her life. She tried to Google it but couldn't get cell service. "I've searched everywhere, but I'm glad you are too, just in case I missed something."

Ciara had moved from the desk without luck to the shelves full of books and family photos.

"We need to have internet," Rayne said. She opened the drapes of the window and held her phone next to it with a prayer. Not even half a bar.

"There is broadband available to the villagers, but because we are in a rural area, the connection is slow. Freda is against mobile towers in the rolling fields." Ciara shrugged, lifting a vase and putting it down. "I agree with her. Da and I were opposed on that."

"Meaning?"

"Da wanted progress, and I didn't. You might think it's strange that I am not about the modern life, but I grew up in London—not a lot of green space."

"I hear what you're saying." Rayne opened the drawer of the desk and found a straight pin. She took it to the lock on the cabinet. "Since I can't be in LA with my business, I need to have high-speed internet access here. I'm giving up a lot, Ciara. I *will* find a way to pay for it if you don't approve it for the budget."

"You gave up a lot, all right." She glared at Rayne. "Da is dead."

"I'm very sorry." Couldn't trump the dead-dad card.

"But yours is gone too. I suppose we have that in common." Ciara opened the hidden cabinet with the whiskey. "A wee bit early, though you make me mental."

Rayne didn't take offense and joined her cousin. "That's so clever." This close, she could see an indent from years, centuries perhaps, of McGraths reaching for the whiskey.

"Da loved his after-dinner whiskey. Like clockwork, he'd have one with dinner, and one afterward." Ciara's smile faltered. "Sometimes two." She pressed her hand to her heart. "We need to call the doctor today."

Rayne blew out a breath. "Could you believe what Owen said? That Dr. Ruebens isn't the best around?"

"Aye, old as dirt, but Da would go to him anyway, just to support a local physician. I've never been sick a day since moving to the country."

"His office probably doesn't open just yet. It's only quarter to eight." Rayne returned to the chest of drawers by the window and placed the point of the pin in the lock, jiggling.

Nothing.

"What do you think of everything that's happening?" Ciara stood by the fireplace. "Since you haven't been here for a long time, you might see things differently."

"Maeve sure was upset about Garda Williams suspecting her. I don't think she had anything to do with your dad's accident. Cormac either." And Aine was a doll.

"No." Ciara picked up the picture of her dad, Amalie, and Padraig from the corner of the desk. "The Lloyds would have given their lives for his, I know it. Not just because of the feudal lord thing, but there was genuine love and respect there."

"I hear it when they talk, and totally agree." Rayne bit her lower lip and repositioned the pin. "Now, tell me about Dafydd. You seem protective of him. How long have you known him?" To her mind, he'd had an overreaction to the garda's questions yesterday. Had it only been yesterday?

Ciara hesitated, and Rayne wondered if her cousin would ignore her question. At last, she said, "Da hired him years ago to replace the shepherd who passed away." Ciara glanced toward Rayne. "Da gave him another chance."

Chills raced up her spine. "About?"

"Dafydd was in jail in Wales." Ciara put the picture back on the desk.

"Whoa." Rayne quit pretending about the lock and faced Ciara. The man had been in jail, in a different country, and he had the run of the castle grounds. Mechanic for the truck and the tractor. The tractor!

"What?" Ciara crossed her arms and dared Rayne to say a bad word.

Rayne cleared her throat. Did a few yoga breaths—then calmly asked, "What was he in jail for?"

"Not that it's your business," Ciara said, "but he was caught stealing bread from the market."

Not what she'd braced herself to hear. "Bread? Can they send folks to jail for that?"

"Aye. He was caught on security cam."

Rayne sighed, thinking of a good reason for a grown man to steal bread. "I'm assuming because he was hungry?"

"And his siblings. Dafydd was nineteen at the time and did three years." Ciara's gaze dared her to say anything judgy. When she didn't, Ciara continued, "His parents died in a car accident, and he was in charge of his two younger siblings."

How sad. "Why didn't they get help from the government?"

"What help is there when you're poor? When the town you live in is poor?" Ciara eyed Rayne like she was a simpleton.

"The church, like Maeve said—Father Patrick gives to those in need."

Ciara raised her palm. "I'm not defending his choices. I understand what happened. Dafydd paid for his crime, and his sisters are now both married with good jobs. Families."

"That's great, Ciara."

"Aye. Dafydd came here to start over when he was twenty-four. He's now twenty-nine. Anything else you want to know?"

"His birth sign?" Rayne joked.

Ciara didn't laugh. "Dafydd respected my da for giving him a second chance. Like the Lloyds, he would have given his life for him."

Somehow she didn't quite believe that. Ciara's love for the Welshman might provide rose-colored glasses. Rayne had worn some when it came to Landon.

"Besides, I think Lourdes is guilty." Ciara pulled the torn envelopes from her coveralls pocket. "I read these as best I could. She threatens him."

"A threat?" Rayne crossed the room in a rush. "Let me see!"

"Here."

Rayne accepted the stack of five letters taped together and scanned the scrawling cursive. It was mostly English with the occasional lapse into Irish.

"I see." Rayne raised her head after a few minutes and put them on the desk. "They were fighting because Lourdes wanted him to marry her, and he refused. Maeve was right on the money."

"We need to give these to Garda Williams when he drops off the keys. *If* he drops off the keys. Dominic is not always reliable. Any luck with your pin?"

"No."

"Didn't think so." Ciara sighed.

"Hey! Can we call a locksmith?" Back home, there'd been a list to choose from. "There's got to be somebody."

"Let's wait and see." Ciara stepped away from the shelves and gathered the letters from Lourdes.

"What's wrong? Don't you want to show them to the garda guy?"

"Definitely." Ciara's shoulders bowed. "I just feel like these are condemning. I know Da didn't love her like he did Amalie, just like he didn't love me the same as Padraig. I feel bad for her in a way. Lourdes gave him her heart, even if he didn't want it."

Rayne leaned her hip against the desk. In this matter, she was not as soft as Ciara. "If Lourdes tampered with his medicine and killed your dad, then she deserves to be punished."

"I never expected to feel sympathy for someone in this position. I think it's because Lourdes could be my mom. You know, in the same position. Not wanted." Ciara dared to look at her.

Rayne was glad and countered, "Not the same. Your mom chose to be a single mother to let Nevin be happy. Lourdes, if she killed Uncle Nevin, is not the same type of woman at all."

Ciara blinked moisture from her stormy eyes. "Really?"

"Really."

Rayne checked the time on her watch. Nine already?

"The cabinet is freaking locked." Rayne smacked the top, certain answers were inside.

"Now who needs to calm down?"

Frustrated, Rayne sat at the desk and dialed the doctor's office after finding the number in a phone book. She gritted her teeth through the recorded message. "Closed on Mondays. Our hands are tied!"

"Your temper is flaring, Rayne." Ciara stuck her thumbs in her pockets, giving the coveralls a stylish look. "I like it. I'm going to take one of the horses out to run. I need to burn some energy. Want to come for a ride?"

"No. Not a fan of horses. How about joining me and Aine for a girls' trip to Dublin?"

Ciara's eyes rounded and her mouth twisted. "I'd rather help Dafydd give the sheep an enema."

Chapter Eighteen

To say that Rayne was comfortable being a passenger in the driver's side of the Fiat would be a big fat lie. She flinched every time a vehicle came toward them.

Aine was so tiny that the car seemed large around her. The McGraths and staff used the Fiat for errands, and like the pickup, it wasn't anybody's personal vehicle. Rayne took her life in her hands on the LA freeways, but it was a breeze compared to the narrow roads leading to the motorway toward Dublin.

"M is for motorway," Aine instructed. "N is a wee bit smaller, and R is for an arterial road and usually narrow. Mum said your American driver's license is all right to use here. If you'd like, I'll take you to practice until you're comfortable."

"I can't be responsible for anybody dying—it's too danger-ous." Rayne gripped the interior passenger handle while trying to be cool.

"It's only scary at first—I love to drive," Aine said. They kept the windows rolled up as they sped along. "The only thing that makes me nervous are the traffic circles. Do you have those?"

Rayne nodded. "We do."

"Then it won't be a problem for you!" Aine turned on a radio station to pop music, reminding Rayne again of how young the maid was. She'd dressed for a day of shopping in cute jeans, leather half boots, and a green top that made her eye color pop. Her red hair was styled in a long braid, with a blue bow at the tip. Peace earrings dangled from her lobes.

"Thanks for bringing me."

"Oh, my pleasure to get away from the castle. No offense meant, but I can't wait to go to the city."

"Do you want to move away from the castle ever?"

"No. This is nice for a day, but I love the castle and nature more."

Rayne read her list on her phone. "Aine, I'm sure you've heard the gossip going around. What do you think happened to my uncle?"

After daring a quick peek at her, Aine said, "I don't know. Lord Nevin was always good to me. I just can't believe anybody would try to harm him on purpose."

"I understand completely."

Aine turned up the radio and sang along with the song, which seemed vaguely familiar to Rayne. "Do you like One Direction? They're broken up, but this song is classic. Niall Horan is Irish and a celebrity. I think he's the cutest. His solo stuff is brilliant."

"Yeah—they were signed on by Simon Cowell. Harry Styles." Rayne tilted her head and went along with the obvious subject change. "Zayn Malik messily dated Gigi Hadid. She's a gorgeous model."

"So beautiful!" Aine sighed. "Do you know her?"

"I don't. I wish. Can you imagine if she'd model one of my Modern Lace dresses?"

"Bangin'!" Aine tapped her thumb to the wheel. "You wouldn't be able to keep up with orders."

That would be an amazing problem to have. "So, I did some research. Grafton Street seems like it's high-end, which is fun, for ideas. There are several fabric shops. I was surprised at the selection."

Rayne eyed the small back of the Fiat. Would there be room for it all? She supposed she could have things delivered.

"Grafton Street is a dream. What do we need first?" Aine asked.

"A sewing machine. I called a few places, and the Singer Sewing Centre sells Janome machines. I've never used one. I've been Bernina all the way."

"What's that?"

"Oh, sewing machine brands. Sorry!"

"That's all right. Do you want to use the GPS on your phone for directions? The car doesn't have one." Aine giggled.

Rayne smacked her palm to her forehead, then plugged in the address and made a list of things she'd need for the dresses due next month. The women had paid half of the price for the gowns up front and been in for fittings. What to do about the final fittings?

The costume designer at her mom's studio might be able to help, for a fee. Rayne would have Lauren ask—she sent off a text before she forgot.

The first gown due had pearls, silk, satin. Chiffon. So many different fabrics to choose from. She prayed her hardest that she'd find a machine that worked, and fabric for at least the first dress.

Hopefully all three, but she didn't want to be greedy with her expectations.

They reached the outskirts of Dublin. Traffic zoomed along, and she quit flinching thinking she was going to die. Aine exuded positive energy.

"Do you do yoga?"

"No. I never learned," Aine said. "Is it hard?"

"Not really. I mean, the stretches help with toning and building core strength. I used to go with my best friend every Saturday, and we'd do yoga on the beach. It's good for your mind"—Rayne tapped her temple—"body, and soul."

"Sounds *craic*," Aine said. "You must miss your friends."

"And my mom." Rayne adjusted her sunglasses against the sun's glare. There were lovely blue skies today. "She's great. It hasn't even been a week since my birthday, but I feel like I'm a hundred instead of thirty."

"Thirty? You don't look it."

"Sweet of you." See, Aine was the kind of girl who would be interested in lotions and creams. Facials. Unlike Ciara. Rayne couldn't picture inviting her cousin to a spa day. What else could they do together for fun?

The phone beeped. "We need to take Bard Street." To exit the motorway, Aine had to get off on a traffic circle.

The Fiat was in the inner section but needed the outer one. "Hang on!" Aine zipped across the circle to the exit like a pro.

Rayne swallowed her stomach back down, as it had lodged in her throat, certain they were going to be crushed by a semi advertising dairy.

"That truck! I thought . . ." Rayne's pulse pounded.

"The lorry?" Aine chuckled. "Nah. We had plenty of room!"

There was no freaking way Rayne was ever going to drive on these roads.

Aine slowed and turned into a shopping center. Rayne would have to get used to the different spelling. *Centre.*

"This isn't the exciting part, but want to come in?"

"Aye," Aine said. "I want to know all the steps to be a designer too."

The pair entered the sewing machine shop, and everything in Rayne started to hum and sing. She enjoyed sewing magical creations. The right tool could make or break a gown. Lingerie. Stockings. The needle couldn't pull or snag.

Rayne had programmed her Bernina with her own stitch, which she'd have to recreate on the new machine.

"*Dia dhuit!*" a saleswoman said, walking to the front of the store.

"Hello," Aine echoed.

"Hi. I'm Rayne McGrath." Rayne lifted her hand. "I called earlier?"

"*Fáilte.* Welcome," the woman repeated in English for Rayne. "Let me show you what I have that might fit your needs."

An hour later, Rayne purchased her very first Janome sewing machine. The saleswoman promised that Rayne could return it if it didn't work out, so long as it wasn't broken.

Twenty-two hundred euro from Rayne's stash. They packed it carefully in what Aine referred to as the boot of the car.

"If the back is the boot, what is the hood?"

"That's the bonnet. Duh." Aine laughed, and they both got in. She started the car and turned to Rayne. "Was it too much money? Why didn't your mum send your favorite machine?"

"It's fine. It's just that . . ." Rayne couldn't tell Aine what had happened to her in the States. The theft hadn't made the news. Why would it? She was just another idiot who had trusted a guy who stole from her. Not even an original plot. "I'll only be here a year. I'd hate to take a chance that my Bernina would get ruined in transport."

And for Rayne to earn her hundred thousand euro, she and Ciara had to bring the castle to a profit. She was starting to realize that Uncle Nevin's concern for the people in the village was a responsibility that went back centuries.

"Oh." Aine pursed her lips as if not happy about that. "Where to?"

Rayne grinned to lighten the mood. "Oasis Fabric Store! Luxury silks—according to their website, anyway. It looks like a candy store for fabric lovers."

"You got it!"

Ten minutes later they were on Grafton Street, which was as busy as anything in LA. Buses and cabs, cars. Bicyclists. Walkers.

"This is crazy." Rayne leaned forward to see it all.

"I love it! There's a garage ahead—this is the posh end." Aine's braid bounced as she bobbed her head to the music.

"When did you decide to get into fashion?" Rayne asked.

"I've always liked to mix styles up. From the time I was fifteen, Mum gives me a yearly subscription to *Vogue* for Christmas." Aine glanced at Rayne. "I follow you on Twitter and Instagram. Well, Modern Lace Bridal Boutique. You don't have a personal page, or I would follow you there too."

Rayne sat back in shock. "You do?"

"Yeah."

"For that, I'm going to buy you a very fancy lunch. You pick." She wondered if Aine also followed Landon but didn't dare ask.

"Feckin awesome!"

Aine parked with more confidence than skill, but she'd be great in time. Rayne wasn't going to complain.

"Let's shop first."

"Just silk?"

"Oh, Aine. Wait and see. Silk, satin, taffeta, chiffon, tulle, organza, linen, damask, brocade, illusion, netting." She sighed, happy to share this part of her world with someone who loved it too. "Those are fabrics off the top of my head. There's more. And the trims on a gown." Her feet floated on air as they left the garage for the bustling Grafton Street.

"This way," Aine said, tugging on Rayne's elbow.

She'd been to Dublin as a kid, sure, but now as an adult, the cathedrals and brick, the cleanliness of the streets, wowed her. "There is so much to see!"

"We can come back another day to tour the Dublin Castle, if you'd like. Trinity Church, or St. Patrick's."

"We won't have time today," Rayne said with regret.

"Nah." Aine shrugged. "I don't mind coming back again."

"You're right. This is a different trip."

Aine dove into the crowd, and Rayne had a hard time following the smaller young woman. Her phone rang, and she glanced at the number, her stomach knotted. Officer Peters! She slowed and answered, "Hello!"

Rayne let the shoppers swirl around her, aware that Aine had moved ahead. She didn't want her to overhear the conversation.

"Rayne? Officer Peters here. Can you talk?"

"Not really. Is there progress? Have you found Landon?"

"We're following several leads," the officer said. "The insurance listed on the lease for the boutique was a fake."

"At this point, I expected that." Rayne bowed her head. She would get nothing from the theft of her gowns.

"I'm sorry. We'll keep looking. If you think of anyplace Landon might have gone, family he mentioned, give us a call."

"I will. Bye now."

Rayne shook off the frustration to smile at Aine, who stood on the stone stoop of Oasis Fabric Store.

"Come on!" Aine opened the door.

Rayne went inside, and it was like all the stars had opened in a night sky, only this was rows and rolls of fabric.

"Heaven!"

A salesman, tall, thin, but handsome, with dark-brown hair and eyes, said, "I feel the same." He scanned her orange sleeveless top and heels, her fitted black pants. "You're lovely. An actress?"

"No. A bridalwear designer."

"Rayne McGrath is the owner of Modern Lace Bridal Boutique, in America," Aine stated proudly.

"Ooh la la. American." The salesman's brow rose. "Well, darlings, I'm Nolan Rourke, manager of Oasis Fabric Store. If we don't have something, I can order it for you."

She exhaled. "Perfect."

"I love your accent," Nolan said.

"I love yours too."

They all laughed. Aine's eyes shone bright as she admired the fabrics and trims. If the young woman was serious about following a career in fashion, then Rayne could teach her as an apprentice.

She'd need another machine. Something inexpensive but good. As much as she adored her first Bernina, it didn't have a computer.

"Well, ladies?"

Now it was time to get the most bang for her euro. "I'm making three wedding dresses, due in July. I had to leave everything behind, from my machines to my trims to my needles."

Aine watched her avidly. Rayne wasn't going to say anything about the castle—understanding again why her dad would refer to it as a manor house with a turret. *Castle* was a smidge over-the-top.

Nolan must have been a theater major, for he fell back against the bolts of colorful satin and hung on. "Let me help you!"

Just the words Rayne was waiting to hear.

She had $2,700 left from her mother's check, which she'd been able to deposit closer to Dublin with her mobile banking app. Nolan realized right away that she knew her fabrics and was no dupe as far as what they should cost.

It was nice to have an ally in Aine, who had a discerning eye for the various shades of white and ivory.

"Is the pound used here?" she asked.

Nolan shivered and brought his slender fingers to his mouth. "Northern Ireland uses the pound. We in the Republic of Ireland use the euro."

"I see."

Rayne didn't but would ask Aine in the car to tell her the difference. Her father had downplayed any Irish politics, saying it wasn't good for the gullet, whatever that meant. She'd need someone to decipher that too.

"If you use a debit or credit card, the bank will do the exchange for you," Nolan said.

"Perfect!" She dove into the interior, mentally cataloging cloth type, weight, and quality. This place was a treasure trove.

"Can I help?" Aine asked.

Rayne held up a sheer fabric, then another not as sheer. "I'll need to make an underskirt. This, or this?"

"So, you want it to have more shape?"

"Exactly."

"Not so sheer." Aine spoke with confidence.

"Good choice." Rayne brought the bolt to the counter for Nolan to cut.

An hour later, there was a stack of fabrics. Silk, satin, illusion. "Now let's check out the selection of lace and trims." Rayne had a running tally in her head of how much she'd spent. "I need a lot of thread."

Somehow another hour passed. Aine was a huge asset in tracking what each bridal gown required for extras.

"I think that's everything," Aine said.

Buoyed by creative energy, Rayne hustled to the counter, ready to pay for her purchases. There was a small sewing machine on a shelf with a red tag on it. "Is this on sale?"

"Last year's model," Nolan said.

Rayne read the box. "I've never heard of this brand either."

"It's a good little machine, and the price is ridiculous," Nolan assured her. "Since you've bought so much, why don't I discount it a wee bit more?"

"Would you? Yes, please!"

Rayne held her breath as Nolan totaled everything for her. They had five large bags and the machine.

"Three thousand four hundred euro," Nolan said, his dark-brown eyes glittering. "I haven't had a sale like this since Christmas."

"Thank you, Nolan. You've been an immense help!" She put the remainder of the purchase on her credit card. She had five hundred left on it until she turned in the dresses. Panic much?

"Selfie? We can post it to your social media." Nolan held out his long arm for her cell phone after she put on the camera. Aine had to stand on her tiptoes, but all three of them made it into the shot.

"You looked me up?" Rayne said, surprised.

"Hashtag Modern Lace." Nolan winked. "Oasis Fabrics followed you. Come back and see me anytime. Bring our Aine. And I was serious—if you need something special, I have connections." He waggled his brows.

Laughing and staggering under the weight of their purchases, Rayne and Aine went back to the car, loading it all up.

"Lunch!" Rayne declared, realizing it was after four in the afternoon. "I'm famished."

"Really?" Aine asked. "That was a lot of money."

"I'm sure. You earned a treat." Rayne patted the box with the sewing machine. "How would you like to learn to sew? You can set up this machine in the studio, all right?"

"All right!" Aine grinned and closed the door, locking the car. "You're the best—so brilliant. Of course I want to learn from you! Pull out that Chanel wallet, Lady McGrath. We're going to the ritziest place on Grafton Street. It's on the roof with a grand view of Dublin Bay."

And so Rayne delivered on her promise of fun, and they had Irish coffees on the roof while sharing wild mushroom risotto and potato gnocchi with sage butter.

Rayne could see for miles. Dublin had lovely green spaces, unlike LA, which was basic palm tree decor and lots of buildings unless you were by the beach. "Is that a public park over there?"

"Aye. Phoenix Park. Kinda famous for the wild deer. You want to go?"

"I'm going to need a full year in order to see all that Dublin has to offer."

Rayne adored new experiences, and she'd forgotten what it was like to hear the lilt of the Irish accent all around her.

She missed her dad so much.

How to get her mother to come here too?

"Why do you look so sad?" Aine asked, putting down her fork. "Didn't we get everything on the list to start the gowns?"

"Yes. Thanks to the best assistant shopper ever." Rayne scrunched her nose. "I was thinking about my mom. She doesn't fly; can you believe it?" The great Lauren McGrath, aka Susan Carter on *Family Forever*, handled every situation with grace— and the help of her cast.

"I've never been on a plane," Aine said, smiling. "So, yeah."

Rayne sipped her drink, the whipped cream long gone, the coffee cooling. "But you would."

Aine nodded. "I would try it."

Tears stung Rayne's eyes. "I have to find a way for my mom to try, so she can visit where Conor was born and lived. My dad loved Ireland."

"It's a beautiful land. Lord Nevin never let us forget it. He's passed on the McGrath torch to you."

It was very heavy for a mystical torch. "I hope to make him proud. My dad too."

"I know you will. This has been a magical day, Rayne. And though I hate the reason you are here, I am very glad you are. Ta!"

"Thank you." They bumped their Irish coffees, the warmth in Rayne's heart not just from the whiskey in the drink. "*Sláinte!*"

Chapter Nineteen

Tuesday morning, thirty years and one week old, Rayne pried open her eyes at six when the alarm went off. Blarney once again had slept like a guardian on this side of her bedroom door. She'd made him a dog bed from one of her satin nightgowns.

Who did she have to impress here? Nobody. She pushed Amos and his Viking shoulders and blue eyes from her mind.

Last night she'd dreamed of her dad and what his life might have been like here at the castle. Two boys in saffron kilts, dogs, trees, a turret, knights in shining armor. Aunt Claire as a princess with a bow and arrow. Her ancestors had protected this land with their lives when necessary. A family history of heroes.

"I won't let you down, Dad. I'd love a hint on how to make Grathton Village thrive again."

Rayne pushed the comforter back, her muscles sore from the heavy lifting she and Aine had done yesterday to get the pink parlor into working shape as her sewing studio. Calendars had been hung, schedules sorted. Everything put away in its new place. The only thing she hadn't touched was Aunt Amalie's walk-in closet—a proper closet with a mirror and a vanity. She'd dropped into bed so exhausted that if there *had* been a haunting last night, she'd slept through it.

Ciara had been in a snit when they'd returned with bags of fluff, as she'd called it. They'd missed dinner with the family and gone straight upstairs to tackle the area. That fluff was going to bring in money Rayne desperately needed to start her business over.

Dressed for the day in her last outfit from her original suitcase, checked brown-and-ivory pants with a bright-yellow shirt and brown heels, Rayne and Blarney went down the grand staircase to the kitchen, drawn by the scent of coffee and ham. What delicious thing would Neddy be making now?

Aine smiled at them. "Morning. How was your sleep? I dreamed of bridal gowns." She twirled, arm extended.

"I dreamed of my dad and Uncle Nevin in kilts." She gave Blarney a piece of ham and ushered the setter out the side kitchen door. "Aunt Claire was in a princess gown with a bow and arrow. Padraig was a knight in shining armor."

"Brilliant. I was just a babe when you last visited, but I grew up on stories of Conor McGrath, poet and adventurer." Aine flipped her braid, again in her uniform of tan pants and white shirt.

"I like the sound of that."

Maeve and Neddy entered the kitchen from the cellar, arms laden with filled canning jars.

"Peaches," Maeve said, setting two on the counter.

"I'm going to make homemade peach ice cream." Neddy pulled a book from the shelf near the refrigerator. "This old cookbook has a million recipes."

"That would be fun to browse someday," Rayne said.

"Help yourself." Neddy opened it to a place he'd marked with twine.

Rayne stood by the table. "Where is Cormac?"

"In his lordship's room." Maeve lowered her voice. "He misses Lord Nevin. They were friends as well as employer and staff."

That tugged at Rayne's heartstrings. "Is there anything I can do?"

"Eventually we'll need to prepare for a funeral service. Once the body is released." Maeve brought her thumbnail to her lower lip. "It's been twelve days since the tragedy."

Rayne acted on impulse and hugged Maeve, as the housekeeper had once done for her as a child.

The older woman sniffed. "We're grieving, but the process is drawn out by not having the wake or church service and then burial. It's like we're in limbo and can't move on."

Neddy poured coffees. "Cream and sugar on the table." His voice was thick with emotion. Maeve already had hot tea.

Ciara strolled in. "Why the sad faces?" Then she held up her hand and averted her gaze. "If it's Da, then don't tell me. I'm feeling the weight of him being gone this morning too. Garda Williams couldn't be any bleedin' slower."

She accepted a mug of tea from Neddy and added honey before she sank onto a wooden chair.

"Let's go to the doctor this morning, Ciara," Rayne suggested. "Surprise him as soon as he opens."

Ciara considered this, then nodded. "I should be done feeding the animals by nine."

"Porridge today?" Neddy lifted the lid off a thick black pot. "Currants and cream to make it sweet. Ham on the side."

"Sounds delicious to me!" Rayne said. Despite her misgivings, her clothes still fit after she'd been eating things like gravy, oatmeal with butter, and thick toast.

"Rayne is going to teach me to sew, Mum." Aine got bowls for the porridge, Neddy ladled a hearty scoop into each of them, and the maid passed them out.

"You already do the mending." Maeve accepted a bowl.

"Like, on a special machine." Aine gave Rayne one, then Ciara. "She said I could make my own clothes."

"Oh!" Maeve blew on a spoonful of oats and currants.

"If she likes it, I'll pay her for piecework," Rayne said. "To help with the wedding dresses." There were simple things Aine could do that would speed the process.

"You don't have to pay her extra," Maeve said right away.

"I wouldn't feel right about it otherwise." Rayne held the housekeeper's gaze. It was important for Aine to have some independence and income. "It's not a fortune, but she'd also be learning a skill." In the event something happened and Rayne epically failed in her bid to save the castle.

Maeve gave a wise nod, as if reading Rayne's mind.

"What are you going to do while I feed the animals?" Ciara asked. "Nap?"

"Funny girl," Rayne said. "I'm going to pray for a strong signal on my phone so I can transfer the pattern for the dresses to the chip on my machine. Because I had to leave everything behind, I'm starting from scratch." Sweat slid down her back. No need to panic. "Might have mentioned that they'll bring in money?"

"How much can a wedding dress cost, anyway?"

"It's not just the single gown, but also the peignoirs for the honeymoon." She swallowed a bite of oatmeal. "A bride will put down half for a deposit. My first dress due is five thousand dollars. She paid a portion upfront and will pay the remainder on receipt."

The kitchen fell silent. Aine grinned at Rayne. Because she'd actually followed Modern Lace on social media, she knew what to expect.

"You have to be joking," Maeve said.

"No." Definitely not a joke. "You see why it's important I have space to create?"

Ciara nodded, bemused. "I had no idea. Take over Da's room too if you need to spread out. Lordy, lordy. And women have already bought dresses?"

"Yes. I can mail them to the States from here, but they're expecting me to be on Rodeo Drive at my boutique for fittings."

"What are you going to do?" Ciara sounded concerned. "You can't leave here, according to the will. That's awful, Rayne."

Empathy from her cousin? Huh. "Yeah. I may have a solution in that my mom's costume designer might do the fittings on the side. The perk is the bride will get an unexpected tour of the studio. Hoping to spin it right."

Ciara finished her breakfast and stood. "See you out front at nine."

She left, and Rayne and Aine exchanged a look. No snarky comment? Neddy said, "I have the best luck connecting on the tower when I need signal. So long as it isn't cloudy."

"Smart!" Rayne hadn't thought of that, but it made sense. Highest peak of the castle and no trees to interfere.

She thanked everyone for breakfast, stopped in her room for her laptop and sketchbook, and climbed the inner tower stairs. This space was the oldest in the castle. The walls stone, the steps worn by time but still sturdy.

She opened the door to the six-foot-wide landing that circled the tower. A stone railing surrounded that. If she brought a chair up, it could be comfortable. What a view! She saw the lake and recalled Amos next to her. It was his favorite place. She could see why. The sheep were in the hills, flowers bloomed, and all this nature was just what her soul needed.

Opening her laptop, Rayne connected to the outside world. Intermittently. By eight forty-five, she was more frustrated than anything but had managed to send the pattern to her computer on the sewing machine.

Small wins.

She put her laptop and sketchbook away, refreshed her lipstick, and met Ciara at nine. Her cousin was already in the car.

Ciara hadn't bothered to freshen up since her chores in the barn, and hay stuck in her short hair.

Rayne didn't mention it.

"We could walk, but I wasn't sure if you were up for it."

"Next time." She'd dressed in heels like she always did. "I'll wear wedges."

Ciara rolled her eyes.

Seven minutes later, Ciara parked on the side street in front of the lawyer's office and the doctor's. There was a pharmacy between the doctor's and a general store.

Rayne got out of the Fiat and smoothed her brown-and-ivory-checked slacks. Ciara—in jeans, of course, and boots—stomped toward the door. Daisy was outside the solicitor's office with a pink toolbox and a hammer, bracing the large flower boxes in front against the stone wall. Golden marigolds and daisies of all colors preened in the sun.

"Morning, ladies of the manor!" Daisy swiveled on a chunky heel, her short hair up in a clip, her sundress as pink as her lipstick.

"Hello," Rayne said. Ciara echoed the greeting.

"Feeling okay?" Daisy asked, her tone concerned.

"We're fine," Ciara said. "Just had some questions for the doctor."

"Oh?" Daisy's smile fell. "About your dear dad. I saw him around the end of March leaving the office. I was just planting the flowers, and he didn't answer when I said hello. Had something on his mind."

Rayne removed her sunglasses. He'd probably been in shock that he wasn't so healthy after all. "That was about the time he changed his will," she said.

"I suppose so! You'd have to ask Owen." Daisy gestured to the office door. "Want to come in?"

"That's okay," Ciara said, admiring the flower boxes. "Did you make these yourself? They're grand."

Daisy flushed, pleased. "I did. And the flowers I've grown from seed."

"That's incredible. I have a brown thumb." Rayne inched toward the doctor's office, eager to get answers.

"Everyone has different talents, for sure. I adore your style, Rayne. You let me know when you're set up for business. I'll place an order for your lingerie." Daisy winked. "Have to keep things exciting, if you know what I mean."

Ciara groaned and opened the door that read DR. RUEBENS, practically pulling Rayne inside. "I do not want to think of them in the bedroom. Ugh."

Rayne laughed as the door closed on Daisy's good-byes.

A brown-haired woman in her twenties greeted them with surprise. "Howareye, Ciara. I don't have you down for an appointment."

"No. Don't have one." Ciara put the keys in her pocket. "Didn't know you worked here!"

"I'm helping Granddad while I go to school online. Not sure what I want to be yet. Just turned twenty and feel like I should know. Got married, got divorced, and live at home." She whirled her finger and rolled her eyes.

"Rayne, this is Sorcha."

The young woman held out her hand. "Sorcha Ketchum for right now. Nice to meet you, milady."

"Just Rayne, please." They shook hands.

Sorcha smiled and sat back down behind the reception desk. "How can I help you? Ciara, I'm so sorry about your dad. I keep waiting for news of his service at church."

"Thanks," Ciara said glumly.

"We'd like to speak to the doctor," Rayne said. "If he's not busy?"

Sorcha gestured toward the empty waiting room. "He's not. I'll go get him. I keep telling him he needs to retire and enjoy his golden years with Mum and me pampering him, but he won't stand for it."

Rayne smiled, liking this young woman a lot.

An old, old man joined them from a back room, the door opening with a creak. "I heard that, Sorcha. I thought I asked you to be professional."

Sorcha batted her unnaturally long lashes. "Sorry."

He shrugged bowed shoulders in his white doctor's coat. "How can I help you? Ciara, we've met at church, but you're healthy as can be. Got that glow from a country life." He turned to Rayne. "And you upset the applecart by inheriting and stealing the castle from our Ciara here."

"Oh!" Did others in the village feel the same way?

Ciara studied her boots.

"I'm Rayne McGrath. No need for the lady title. Ciara and I are managing the castle together, for the good of the village."

Ciara lifted her head and glanced at Rayne with a raised brow. Rayne continued, "Uncle Nevin's death came as a shock."

"He was young, without a family history of heart problems," Dr. Ruebens said. "I prescribed diltiazem hydrochloride daily to try and even out the arrhythmia." He wagged an old finger. "I warned him not to drive and told him to skip his nightly whiskey."

"You knew about his drinking?" Ciara asked.

"I'm his doctor. You can't fool me."

Old, yes, but capable, unlike Owen's observation. Dr. Ruebens probably topped Owen by a decade.

"He didn't give it up." Ciara blew out a breath and rubbed her hair, knocking the hay from it. "Said he had whiskey in his bones. We didn't know about the heart medicine."

"I spoke with Garda Williams yesterday." The doctor put his hand in his coat pocket, which was unbuttoned.

"You were closed," Rayne said.

"Garda Williams is an officer of the law and knows where I live." Doctor Ruebens chuckled.

"True," Rayne said. "Is it possible the medicine and the whiskey could've made him dizzy and lose control of the tractor?"

"Could have. What concerns me is the amount of medicine the coroner found in his system." The doctor tugged his smooth-shaven wrinkled chin. "No way could it have been an *accidental* overdose, as sometimes happens when patients start something new. No, this was more than five times the amount."

Rayne drew in a breath. "Oh. And you told that to the officer too?"

"Of course!"

Garda Williams hadn't said anything to them. Did he still suspect the family and staff? Rayne was a little annoyed at the officer. "Thank you so much for your time, Doctor."

"What plans do you have?" Sorcha asked, hope in her gaze. "For the village? I love it here, but there are no jobs to keep me. Granddad feels sorry for me and lets me answer the phone."

Ciara jerked her thumb at Rayne. "She's running the show. Wedding dresses."

"*We* are." Rayne managed to keep a neutral expression. "That was the deal. Once I'm settled, I'd love to hear ideas, Sorcha, if you have any."

"Aye. I'll think on it. I sure love your shoes."

Waving at them, Ciara headed for the door. "I had to drive the princess because of those fancy heels. Let's go, Rayne."

Sorcha laughed, and the sound followed Rayne outside to the Fiat. Daisy was inside. Rayne got into the car, perturbed.

Ciara started the vehicle. "Don't pout. That was a good one."

Rayne did her best to not pout, and by the time Ciara parked in front of the manor, she'd pulled her lip back in. Ciara's teasing was an improvement over her being mad. "Come see what I'm doing."

"In the pink parlor?"

"It's now to be known as my sewing studio."

"Want a sign?"

"Hey!"

"I'm just slagging you—learn to take a joke."

"Maybe when I hear one." Slagging? What the heck?

Cormac opened the door for them. "Ladies. How did it go?" The foyer smelled wonderfully of roses from Daisy's bouquet.

"Good," Rayne said. "Dr. Ruebens confirmed that Uncle Nevin took that heart medicine and had too much in his system."

Cormac's brown eyes clouded with sorrow and anger. "How? Who?"

"We don't know—yet," Ciara said. "We won't stop asking questions until we do."

"Excuse me." Cormac blinked moisture from his gaze as he hurried toward the suite that he shared with Maeve.

"Poor man," Rayne said.

"It's a tragedy," Ciara agreed, her shoulders bowed.

Rayne and Ciara went up the main staircase and turned right to what used to be Rayne's aunt's parlor. Rayne opened the door and stood back.

Her cousin stepped inside, her mouth open in shock. Score! The woman was speechless. The pink had all been toned down with colorful throws of fabric. Aine's assistance had been invaluable. Two tables held sewing machines, and a third was ready to be used for cutting or measuring.

Rayne's computerized machine faced the window looking out over the barn and driveway toward the village. She had shelves of fabric. Containers of trims in baskets and boxes. The picture of her and her dad by the lake was on the window ledge.

"It's so neat," Ciara said, her tone impressed. "Tidy. Bleedin' organized down to the last safety pin."

"Thanks." At her boutique on Rodeo Drive, she'd had mannequins. Landon sometimes filled in as well when she needed another body to drape with cloth. Her cousin had tall, slender beauty. "You could model for the gowns."

"We don't need two divas in the same house." Ciara crossed her arms and regarded Rayne over her nose.

"Rude." That's what Rayne got for trying to be nice.

"It's grand of you to teach Aine how to sew and pay her a wee bit extra." Ciara gave her the side-eye. "Better not be with the castle funds, since we're broke."

"It's not. Besides, we don't know for sure. Strange that Garda Williams didn't call yesterday about the medicine, huh?"

"Aye." Ciara lowered her arms and went to the windows to peer out at the barn.

"I was thinking . . . your dad liked to mow on a certain schedule, right?"

"Tuesday, Thursday, and Saturday." Ciara turned to face Rayne. "Clockwork."

"He also liked his whiskey during dinner, and after." Rayne was thinking aloud, not judging. She'd grown up with both her parents enjoying evening cocktails.

"As he told the doctor," Ciara agreed, "and he wasn't going to give it up. Stubborn!"

Rayne stepped toward Ciara. "What if someone added the medicine to his whiskey at dinner, knowing that he would mow the lawn? If he fell dizzy, it would appear to be an accident."

"To the whole decanter?" Ciara frowned. "We all would have gotten sick. I mean, I didn't feel well, but I thought it was because my da was dead. We should ask the others how they felt."

"Dafydd and Amos. Who else?" Rayne mused. "Maeve and Cormac? Aine?"

"They are not guilty. I would stake my own life on it," Ciara said. "I have to have faith in something, and the Lloyd family loyalty is it."

Rayne nodded.

A knock sounded on the sewing studio door. "Come in," Rayne called.

Cormac stepped into the room. "Garda Williams is here to see you both. I've put him in the blue parlor."

Chapter Twenty

T he cousins walked side by side after the butler. Rayne was taller than Ciara, thanks to her heels. She wished she'd had time to refresh her lipstick, but it would have to do.

They couldn't have appeared more different if they'd tried out for an audition of city mouse, country mouse.

Garda Williams stood, hands behind his back, his blue hat covering pale strawberry-blond hair to his nape as he looked at a painting of the castle done in 1850. The outside hadn't changed a bit.

Cormac cleared his throat, and the garda turned to them.

The officer's smile was pinched. Not the greeting of a man with terrific news, like *Hey, caught the bad guy, you may all resume your lives.* Oh well.

"I've told Cormac I don't need tea. I'm here to drop off Lord McGrath's personal items." Garda Williams nodded to a clear bag containing the prescription bottle, keys on a shamrock chain, and a wallet.

"Thank you," Rayne said.

The garda waited. If he thought she was going to open the cabinet this instant, he was mistaken. She wanted to go over those things with Ciara, not the cops.

Just in case. What? She didn't know, but it seemed like something they should do together in private. As a team.

Ciara raised her brow. "Lourdes and my father broke up, and I found letters upstairs of her threatening him. Have you talked to her?"

Garda Williams adjusted the brim of his hat. "Aye. As a matter of fact, I spoke to her yesterday. Lourdes McNamara has an alibi for the day in question."

"Ha." Ciara crossed her arms low on her hips. "I bet. She was close enough to Da to know about the medicine. She could have slipped it to him when he broke up with her as revenge."

"I've spoken to multiple witnesses," the officer maintained. "Ms. McNamara was in London, on a conference with her company."

Not even in the country. Sugar snaps. Rayne had thought for sure Lourdes was a possibility.

"Oh." Ciara pinched her brow. "What about Richard?"

Rayne had seen the sincerity in the miller when he said he wanted to change, but addiction made people do things they normally wouldn't.

"Thursday around that time, Richard was at the Sheep's Head watching the game. Lots of witnesses," Garda Williams said. "Beetle vouches for him."

Rayne and Ciara both sighed.

"That leaves Freda," Ciara said, sounding somewhat desperate. "*Your* councilwoman."

Garda Williams flushed. "She is my councilwoman, since she lives in the same village as me. We are both civil servants, Ciara. I will question her in my own time. I thank you to stop behaving like I don't want to find out who is behind this."

"You didn't believe me at first." Ciara narrowed her eyes at the officer so heatedly that Rayne expected to smell smoke.

"It's not that I didn't believe you . . . I required proof before barging ahead." The police officer waved his hand.

Her cousin and the policeman just rubbed each other wrong, like when you petted a cat so its hair stood on end.

"And now you have proof. We talked to Dr. Ruebens this morning," Ciara said. "*You* didn't bother to tell us that he confirmed the amount of medicine in Da's system couldn't have been accidental."

The guard guy exploded, his face red. "You are under suspicion, Ciara. My fellow gardai at the station won't let me forget that point—that's why!"

The air between the pair sizzled. Suddenly Rayne realized a different reason that these two might be at each other's throats.

They'd hooked up.

Rayne looked from Garda Williams, who was attractive in a boy-next-door way, to Ciara, very attractive and the lord's daughter.

It made complete sense.

She kept her mouth closed about it and stepped between them, her arms to her sides. "I don't think Ciara is guilty," she told the officer.

"I need more than your opinion." Garda Williams gathered himself. "I need for Ciara to have a witness that isn't her fiancé, who has a checkered past."

"Dafydd did his time, and he had his reasons," Ciara shouted.

Garda Williams's jaw clenched. "How well do you know him, Ciara? Were you with him the whole afternoon?"

"He is a shepherd. A solitary job. I was working in the garden during the day, with Aine. I brought Dafydd lunch on horseback. Had a picnic by the lake. Amos saw us."

"And who will vouch for Amos, then?"

Did the garda truly believe Amos would be guilty? "He's the grounds manager here. Why would you suspect him? From what I gather, he was one of the few people who didn't argue with Uncle Nevin."

"Amos discovered him by the tractor. Could be he found him after messing with the tractor or getting him to take more medicine?" Garda Williams touched the brim of his hat. "Or both."

Rayne thought back to a typical murder plot. "Blarney alerted Amos. Besides, Amos has no motive. He has a job on the manor grounds, a bungalow. Food and company when he wants it."

"Perhaps," the garda said. "But Ciara does, and her fiancé, Dafydd. To inherit the castle. Maybe Ciara found out about the will change and went raging."

"That doesn't make sense," Rayne said, defending Ciara. "If my cousin knew she wouldn't inherit, she wouldn't want Uncle Nevin dead."

The garda frowned, seeing the logic. "So maybe she didn't know about the will change . . . it would have been a shock to discover after his death."

"I did not want my father dead. End of story, Dominic!" Ciara barged from the room, her body emanating such fury that even though she didn't touch the officer, he stepped back.

"Feck it," the garda murmured.

Rayne added that to her list of nonswear swear words. "Do you have concerns over Dafydd?"

"He's the bleedin' mechanic, but will she tell me so?" The garda pulled himself together after the door slammed. "I have to go. Please, stop interfering with this investigation. I don't know how you do things in America, but here, we abide by the law. We have rules."

"And community." Rayne tapped her temple. "I remember."

Garda Williams strode from the blue parlor. She heard Cormac wish the officer a good day.

She eyed the keys on her uncle's ring but didn't feel right opening the six-drawered cabinet without Ciara. The girl had serious issues with her temper. Like Rayne used to have until Mrs. Westinghouse.

Left to her own devices, Rayne changed her shoes, grabbed her sketchbook, and went outside to the landing. The police car was gone. In the distance, she made out a woman with short blonde curls on horseback riding to the hills. Blarney saw Rayne and bolted on gangly puppy legs down the path from the barn toward her.

"Let's go for a walk, boy."

Blarney wagged his tail, raced ahead, barked, and then hurried back to her.

The grounds were gorgeous and green. Needing a mow, since it had been almost two weeks, the grass cushioned her steps. It wasn't the beach, but nature still filled something inside her.

The sheep were out on the hills with Dafydd. Amos and the truck weren't around. It was the perfect summer day to daydream and let your inner wisdom shine. Since she wasn't doing yoga on the beach, she needed a different outlet for her meditation.

It was when you were very quiet that answers came.

She passed the ravine, the tractor on its side, and continued along the dirt path. Blarney barked and ran down to the tractor, then back to her.

"Come on, Blarney. I want to sketch you by the water." She could see creating a boudoir piece with the amber of Blarney's fur. The golden-brown of his eyes would be a rich accent. Perfect colors for fall.

Rayne reached the edge of the lake where a wooden picnic table invited her to rest and draw. Nothing was as powerful as letting her mind free to sketch what it would. The lake. The turret of the castle. Wedding bells. A gazebo. A gazebo? Happy couples. Her wedding dresses. Silk ties the color of Blarney's fur. In fall, the colors of the trees here would be stunning. She could create a leaf design . . .

Her concentration was interrupted when Blarney chased a duck into the water with a splash and a quack.

"Blarney!"

The dog ran back to her, his ears up and his tongue lolling.

Miracle of all miracles, her phone dinged with a text message. From her mom!

Can you talk?

Yes!

Her phone rang, and she put it on speaker. She was afraid to move from this magical outdoor spot with cellular. "Lauren! How are you? Is everything all right?"

"Yes, of course. Officer Peters said she tried to call you but couldn't reach you—she has an update about Landon."

Rayne had totally forgotten about Landon the Thief. She gasped when she saw the time. She'd been here three hours. "They found him?"

"No. He sold one of your gowns, though, and they're tracking him. What a numskull! Every good criminal knows to lay low for a while."

Rayne laughed at her spotless-record mother saying such a thing. "Which one? The ecru chiffon with crystals? The silk mermaid?"

"I don't know, honey. I can ask her."

"Okay. Thanks." Recalling the hours spent on those dresses, she sighed. "I'd love to get it back."

Blarney barked and put his paw on Rayne's knee, wagging his tail.

"Is that Blarney? Hello, pup!"

Blarney rumbled in his chest and winked.

"I think he's saying hello."

"He probably misses Nevin," her mom said.

Rayne agreed, one hundred percent. "He brought Amos to Nevin after the accident."

"Poor thing is traumatized. I have a call in to our neighbor to see if she can pick up on anything. She worked wonders with Paula Abdul's dogs."

"Like who killed Uncle Nevin?" Rayne asked.

"Wouldn't be surprised. She's got an amazing reputation. There's a waiting list to get in, but she said she'd see what she could do. Send me a picture of Blarney."

"Now? All right." Rayne took her mom off speakerphone and used the camera. "Smile, boy." Blarney tilted his head in a pose. "Thanks." She sent the image to her mother, then returned to the call. If the police could track down Landon, what would that mean for her? She had to be in Grathton for a full year. This was so hard, and she was out of her element.

"Got it!" her mom said. "Oh, he's so cute, Rayne. No wonder you're smitten."

She supposed she was at that. Blarney darted off after another duck brave enough to leave the lake and wander the shoreline. "So, they call police officers gardai here. Garda Williams is in charge of the case, and he brought Uncle Nevin's key ring back. When Ciara returns, I'll see if she wants to open the cabinet with me."

"Why wait?"

"It would seem odd, like I was doing it behind her back. It feels important, you know? This is her legacy too. I don't know what I'll do if we're broke. It's not like I can hang a closed sign on the castle. There's so much involved with the farm, and the sheep, and then the villagers. Church. What am I going to do about *church*? They're relentless!"

Lauren laughed softly. "When I'd go with your dad on the rare occasion he asked, I said my own prayers. The God I believe in doesn't care about semantics. Love and kindness are what matters."

"Same. That's a good idea. I think it's very important to them that I go, as a McGrath."

"You're very good at finding solutions. What were you doing when I called?"

"Sketching! I have an idea floating around the edges of my brain that needs some more cooking time." A gazebo by the lake. Happy couples. Her marketing mind was on fire, but this wasn't just about her. Ciara and the others all had a voice too.

"I'm here as a sounding board if you want, but it will come to you. I still remember how excited you were to start Modern Lace—and that was before Landon came onto the scene."

"True." She'd been working for five years with her dresses, but Landon had gotten them Rodeo Drive. He'd taken them to the next level. Why had he betrayed her?

It didn't matter.

"I'm going to give that psychic another call and show her Blarney's picture. How could she say no to that face?"

They hung up after loving good-byes.

Call a pet psychic—why not? Rayne laughed and continued sketching her gazebo. So very Hollywood.

Chapter
Twenty-One

Rayne walked back to the castle at a brisk pace, Blarney at her side. A lot had changed in the last week, and she could hardly remember her old life as she navigated this new one.

"Go to the barn, Blarney. Good boy."

The dog did as she asked. The truck and Fiat were both still gone, and there was no sign of Ciara.

Cormac wasn't around either as she entered the foyer. What did the butler do when he wasn't answering the door or overseeing meals? She imagined he'd cared for Lord Nevin as a valet, and now that her uncle was gone, he had to be at a loss.

She had a plan to go through the furniture in storage, and Cormac would be a huge help there. The lovely flowers from Daisy gave a hint of perfume. She'd inherited a freaking castle.

This was *hers*. Her blood, her history, her ancestors. Rayne walked the hall and studied the portraits of her uncle, her dad, her aunt Amalie, Ciara. Padraig.

Her great-grandfather, her grandpa, her dad, and her uncle individually posed in saffron kilts with three emerald shamrocks down the side. Dress kilts for parades, her dad had told her. The ladies of the family wore emerald green. There was a painting of her aunt Claire as a little girl on the property, before she'd died. Rayne wanted her picture on the wall too.

She followed the smell of lavender down the hall and heard Aine and Maeve laughing in the laundry room. It was very homey. Would they be willing to do the extra labor her idea would require? She didn't interrupt them but returned to the foyer, and then the blue parlor for the keys to open the cabinet in her uncle's office.

It was imperative that she face the music in order to move forward. The clear plastic bag with Nevin's things in it was still on the side table where the officer had placed it.

She picked it up as Ciara ran into the room. "Hey! I was looking for you. Where were you?"

"By the lake," Rayne said, her shoulders rising at Ciara's tone. "Sketching."

"I just don't get you." Ciara folded her arms and glared.

"What?"

"We have work to do. All the time. And you . . . *sketch*. How is that helping?"

"Ouch! Cous, you have got to find a hobby and learn to decompress before you keel over yourself." Rayne exhaled. "You're the one who took off after the blowout with the garda— on a horse."

Ciara suddenly found the area rug interesting. "I needed some air."

"Well, so did I." Rayne poked at the bruise. "So, you hooked up with the garda guy?"

An audible gulp sounded, and then Ciara said, "I don't know what you mean."

Could be a cultural slang thing. Rayne repeated, "Hooked up. Dated. Sex? Just kissing? A crush?"

Ciara's face turned bright red. "A very long time ago. It's history. Did Dominic tell you?" Her lip curled. "That eejit!"

"No, I guessed it. Since I have so much spare time—*not*—I understand body language." Rayne stood her ground.

"You are bloody impossible. How can we get along?"

"You can start by not judging me. By accepting me for who I am without all of your biases." Rayne shook the bag in her hand for emphasis. "I accept you." *Faults and all*, she said to herself.

"You don't either. You look at me like I need a haircut."

Did she? "I don't mean to. How about we call a truce?"

Ciara rubbed the back of her hair, her attention on her dad's things. She smelled of outdoors and sunshine. "Whatever. You ready to open the cabinet?"

"I was waiting for you."

"Thanks." Through gritted teeth, Ciara said, "Sorry about taking off like that."

"It's okay. I'm sorry too. This is a lot to process."

They left the blue parlor and walked down the corridor to Uncle Nevin's office on the other side of the stairs. Ciara held up the key. "Got it from Maeve."

"Smart."

Inside, Rayne went directly for the cabinet, which was the only thing she hadn't searched for the banking information. It was about five feet tall, with six drawers, and solid wood. She took out the shamrock key ring and put the bag with the wallet and pill bottle on the desk.

"Fingers crossed that what we need is in here." Rayne found the right key on the third try. "Yes!" The lock tumbled, and she twisted the key.

Her uncle was very neat, and all the papers were in labeled folders. Ciara read over her shoulder. "*Bank of Ireland* is the green folder. Brilliant," she said.

"Here's one with household accounts. *Budget*. Let's get this one out too."

Rayne pulled both folders, and she and Ciara went to the desk. Ciara sat in her dad's chair, and Rayne dragged a hard-backed chair next to Ciara's.

"Banks with Bank of Ireland." Rayne tapped a checkbook.

"I do too. Debit and credit cards." Ciara toyed with a curl over her ear. "Not that there's much in there."

"Did you receive a salary or hourly wage?"

"No." Her nose wrinkled. "I got to live here. Roof and meals."

"How'd you get money for yourself?"

"Gifts." Ciara shrugged. "We all get a percentage of the wool when it's sold, or of the harvest, after costs are paid. At least, that's how it is with me and the Lloyds. Dafydd. I don't know about Amos or Richard."

Rayne couldn't believe it. "And that was okay with you?"

"Yeah." Ciara looked at Rayne with sad eyes. "I never thought I'd move from here again. I have everything I need. And then Da died. The whole thing's bollocks. How could he name me as manager when I'm not even on his bank account? He didn't have much faith in what he'd taught me, which was precious little in the scheme of things, to give the whole thing to you."

"This is a mess, no lie. But Ciara, he's been teaching you all he knows of the castle's history, the way the manor works, inside and out. That's hands-on value."

Ciara pursed her lips, and Rayne could see she wasn't on board. Could Rayne blame her? Not a bit.

"Ciara, he trusted you could manage it. Uncle Nevin left it to me but knew I would have zero chance of success on my own. Listen, if at the end of this year you want to take your money and go, I understand."

Ciara briefly closed her eyes. "Can we just look at the bank statements?"

"Yep." In other words, back off.

The bank balance was almost twelve thousand euro. That wasn't so bad, right? Savings, only three hundred. *Budget* was written on one side, with the monthly cost of keeping the manor afloat totaling seven thousand euros. There were lots of line items crossed out in red. Uncle Nevin's scrawl on the notebook read *Just the basics.*

"Holy macaroons," Rayne said. "We only have one and a half month's expenses." The castle had been built in 1723, and now, almost three hundred years later, she was at the helm of a sinking ship. What would her dad say?

Ciara turned to Rayne in panic. "This doesn't look good."

Rayne pressed her fingers to her thrumming jugular. "My financial adviser said that six months of savings for living expenses is crucial before expanding on risky ventures."

Ciara's nose scrunched. "Your financial adviser? Rayne, you sound so ridiculous sometimes. We need cash, not advice. Unless you're going to take your personal money and put it into the castle?"

"It's . . . tied up."

Gone, stolen, who knew where. And she'd been a Grade A fool to trust Landon and put everything into their joint account, just to impress potential investors in Modern Lace.

Rayne did sound ridiculous, giving advice. She bowed her head. "I'm only trying to help."

"I know." Ciara glanced at her and tapped the folders. "Don't suppose you could give the manor a loan?"

She'd started her successful company with a sewing machine and her sketchbook, then grown it with Landon, who could sell ice cream to Eskimos.

"I wish I could, but I can't. I don't have a lot of cash right now."

"What about your wedding dresses? They bring in a lot of money, you said. Why not do more?"

"I have to get settled here first. The profit from the July gowns will buy more fabric for the August gowns."

Ciara exhaled with a look of disappointment. "Not a lot in the bank, then? Kinda like us."

"I'm building, Ciara. It takes time." Rayne reached for the previous year's notebook, where things were a little better. Her uncle had books going five years back, and things had gotten progressively got worse. "How does money come into the estate?"

Ciara sat back, her elbow on the desk. "The castle is self-sustaining. Anything left, we offer at a discount to the villagers. After that, Freda's village. Sheep are food and wool. We have the orchard; we have grain to make flour, but the past two years the crops have been bad, so we've had to buy it. Then the paddle broke, and it's been a nightmare with Richard gambling on anything that runs from horses to rabbits."

An unhappy man for many reasons, Rayne figured. He had no purpose. "We could get Richard busy with a paintbrush on the barn. Get this place looking sharp." Now that she'd seen the figures, she could plan.

"We need a fence for the sheep," Ciara said. "More important than appearances. The back wall of the barn isn't stable and could use a post to prop it."

"We need internet. Wi-Fi. Without it, we aren't connected to the rest of the world."

The cousins stared at one another. Rayne's head spun.

Rayne traced her finger along the accounts, seeing big deposits and then larger deductions. "When would the next income be expected?"

"Summer is slow as things are growing." Ciara cupped her chin. "The lambs for meat are slaughtered at around nine months to twelve months, for the sweetest flavor."

Rayne swallowed. This was something difficult for her Hollywood sensibilities. "Okay. When will that be?"

"These sheep just gave birth in February. So November, December."

"And how much will they bring in?"

"About five hundred per sheep."

Nodding, Rayne jotted down the figure on a scrap of paper. "So that will bring in fifty grand. That's a nice chunk to have in the bank."

"Aye, but you have to pay extra for labor."

Rayne divided the amount into twelve months. "About four grand a month average if we were to split it up. The budget is seven grand." *Not enough.* "What else do we have?"

"Wool."

"I'm beginning to see the importance of these sheep."

Ciara relaxed. "Thank goodness for that, Rayne. It varies, depending on the quality of the wool, but we bring in another seven thousand."

Rayne pinched her brows as she did the math. Still not enough to cover the basic expenses. "How was Uncle Nevin making it?"

"We sold fruit from the trees, we sold vegetables. The businesses all pay rent to Da, but if they weren't making a profit, Da would forgive it."

"This is a very bleak picture, Ciara."

Ciara closed the budget and bowed her head. "I didn't realize how bad. No wonder he didn't want to give up his whiskey."

"Can't blame him." Rayne leaned back and eyed the secret panel. "Shall we?"

Ciara rose without argument and went to the wall, pressing the button. Her cousin poured them each two inches into glasses.

Rayne joined her. They clinked and drank.

Two sips of the pungent spirit cleared Rayne's head, and she set the tumbler aside for her pad and pen. "All right, cousin. Help me make a list of what needs to be done first. I know you think the sheep need a fence, but we have got to get reliable internet so that I can have email and contact my clients, who all live in LA."

Ciara swallowed and nodded. "Bet you're sorry you chose to stay."

It was strange that this catastrophe had trumped her personal tragedy. Rayne leaned her hip to the desk. "I don't do regrets. Let's make the best of this situation. I'll call the cable company and see what we can do."

"We have the money for June and part of July," Ciara said. "We can check with Amos, but July and August are good for veggies. He'll know how many workers we will need for that. September and October we'll have apples to sell."

"I have my wedding gowns, but like I mentioned, I need to buy more fabric with the money." She thought of how to trim her expenses and made a note to call Nolan, the manager at Oasis Fabric Store. "I can maybe come up with two thousand euro to put toward the running of the house. But I won't get it until July."

Ciara held the tumbler to her chest. "That will help. I suppose I can gather scraps around the property to make a fence. Not pretty, but functional."

"Will that work?"

Ciara shrugged. "Dafydd won't like it."

"I will have more in August and September. I can advertise that I'm taking orders for wedding dresses again."

"Daisy wants lingerie. Sell it to her," Ciara suggested.

"I have satin and lace for it." Her heart sped. "This was not the life I ordered," Rayne joked.

Ciara refused to get sidetracked. "We need to patch the roof. I don't know if Richard can handle that. We can Google how from the Coco Bean—Sinead's got Wi-Fi. Ask around at the church for advice. Maybe he can take over mowing?"

"Okay." Rayne sipped the amber liquid. "So. Internet. Fence. Roof patch on the manor. Paint. Brace the wall."

Ciara's phone dinged. She read the message and then tossed the whiskey back like a sailor on leave.

"What's wrong?" Rayne's stomach clenched.

"Drink up."

Rayne did. Her body was tight with apprehension. "What?"

"The barn wall collapsed." Ciara took both their empty glasses and put them on the tray.

Rayne clapped her hand to her chest. "We have to save the sheep!"

"The sheep are out with Dafydd; they're fine. But we need to have a watertight space, which means that the wall just moved to the top of the list." Ciara pulled at the back of her hair. "How did Da do this? No wonder he had heart palpitations."

Rayne stayed on Ciara's heels as her cousin hurtled out of her dad's office. Cormac met them at the front door. "I heard a crash," the butler said. His jacket was gone, his white shirt tucked into black pants.

Rayne dashed in front of him to the door and yanked it open.

"Amos texted the barn wall collapsed," Ciara explained, her voice shaking.

"Oh no! Any of the animals hurt?" Cormac bumped into Rayne on the landing. They all looked toward the barn.

Where was Blarney? Was he okay? Rayne squinted to bring the barn into sharper focus.

"I don't think so. The lamb rejoined the flock yesterday." Ciara ran as if her heels were on fire. Rayne hadn't realized Ciara could move that fast but kept up with her cousin. Cormac was with them the whole way.

Blarney barked at the barn door, alerting them to the problem. She was so relieved that he was fine. Dusty, but fine. The pickup truck was parked next to the horse paddock, a motorcycle on the other side.

Dust billowed into the air, reminding Rayne of smoke.

Amos blocked them from going in, arms wide. Dirt smudged his face. "It's too dangerous. Wait here."

Chapter Twenty-Two

"What's going on?" Maeve shouted as she ran toward the barn. She was going so fast her apron flapped at her side.

Aine followed behind her mother, her hand on a kerchief she'd used to cover her hair. "It was so loud! Is the barn on fire?"

The Lloyd women stopped to catch their breath in the patch of gravel.

"Dirt is all," Amos explained, his blue eyes hard. "I'd just come out of the barn after putting the tools away. Boom!"

"You could have been hurt," Rayne said.

"I'm fine. I hope I didn't cause it!" Amos whirled and dug both hands in his hair, concern and worry pulsing from him.

Blarney danced between them as if to make sure Amos was all right.

Cormac peered into the sooty barn. "It's a disaster."

"The horses are okay in the paddock," Ciara stated. She stayed close to the gray one and patted its long nose from over the fence. "It's summer, so they don't need shelter unless it lashes rain."

They all looked up at the blue skies. Rayne said a little prayer that the weather would continue to hold.

"There's the shed, if we need to put them there," Cormac said. "Or that sorry excuse for a bungalow in the field."

Rayne remembered that Maeve had mentioned he'd started off at the manor as a young man in charge of the horses.

Dafydd arrived over the crest of a green hill, one of the sheep-dogs with him, the other probably with the remaining sheep. A few sheep followed him, but most were out of sight.

"What happened?" Dafydd called in a worried voice. "I saw a plume of smoke!"

"Dirt," Amos corrected. "A section of the wall collapsed."

"This place can't catch a break. What's going on?" Dafydd stared at Rayne, his expression hard to read. "You need to help the property with all your wedding dress money."

She wasn't going to explain her life to Dafydd, of all people. Rayne crossed her arms. Blarney paced before her.

Ciara said, "Dafydd, we found the budget. There's no money for a fence. Especially now that we need to build a wall. Is the entire barn ruined?" She stomped to the side of the building.

"We have to wait for the timber and rock to settle. We can make a better judgment then," Amos said. He backed up and eyed the barn door, which was open. "I'm afraid to touch it."

"You were lucky, Amos," Rayne said. "What happened?"

"I heard a rumble, like a whisper in the stone. I looked and didn't see any living thing, so I bolted." His expression was sheepish.

Any living thing? Was he suggesting a ghost?

Ciara shook her head. "Don't tell me you think the barn is haunted."

"I can leave my options open, lass," Amos said without apology. "This property is old, and who knows what's happened on it."

"Padraig, drowned. Nevin, in a tractor accident," Aine whispered.

"You stop that right now, Amos," Maeve declared. "If we have any ghosts around here, they're the friendly type."

Blarney barked and wagged his tail.

"Where's Neddy?" Cormac asked.

"He's down at the pub for a bite with Richard," Maeve said. "He'll be upset he missed the excitement."

"Can we afford to buy lumber?" Amos asked.

Rayne and Ciara exchanged a look. It was a necessity. Did they dare tell folks how bad things were?

Ciara gave a firm nod. "How handy are you, though?"

Amos shrugged and patted his biceps. "I'm more muscle than knowledge."

"I can help," Cormac said. "I did my share with the bungalows. The ones we remodeled."

"I know what to buy for a simple shelter," Dafydd said. "I'll make a list."

"Of course you do," Amos said. "Why am I not surprised? Thanks, mate."

Dafydd actually blushed. "Used to work construction is all. I didn't do university, so it was manual labor to pay the bills."

Rayne imagined getting any job after jail time would be difficult. She didn't let her empathy for his situation cloud the facts. Someone in this village had killed Uncle Nevin.

"All right." Ciara checked the time on her watch. "It's one in the afternoon. How about Amos and I drive into Kilkenny for lumber. We'll work late if we need to. It'll be light till half past nine at least."

"How can I help while you're out getting supplies?" Rayne asked.

Amos gestured for her to follow him around to the side. The barn was made of stones piled between timber posts, then spackled. It was a two-story building, and most of the rocks had slid free like spilled sugar. "It's not too complicated."

"We can sort the rocks for when the timber posts are up again. We'll need cement." Cormac showed her the crumbled pieces. "See? They used hay to hold the clay together. Cement will be easier."

"All right." Rayne brushed her hands together. "I'm ready."

"You should probably change your clothes first," Ciara said, her brow lifted. "Unless you don't mind another ruined outfit?"

Rayne glanced down at her checked linen slacks. She'd changed into ivory Converse for her walk to the lake. Since she happened to really like these pants, she nodded.

"All right." She gestured toward her cousin as Maeve spoke quietly to Cormac. Aine was at the paddock with the horses. "Ciara, will you come with me for a sec?"

Ciara fell into step beside her, her boots and jeans much more practical in this situation. "What?"

"I think you should write a check on your dad's account or use your dad's credit card," she said in a murmur. "I know you'll be frugal but get what you need. We'll figure out how to manage."

"Jaysus wept," Ciara exclaimed. "How are we supposed to access the accounts? I never even thought about that."

Cormac called behind them, "Excuse me, ladies?"

They stopped and waited for the butler. Maeve folded her hands in front of her as she watched them.

"Yes?" Rayne asked.

"Maeve just mentioned the budget. I didn't have an extra key to the cabinet, but I'm on the household account. Lord Nevin thought it a good idea."

Why hadn't he said so? Rayne pulled Cormac with them toward the house. "Do you know what a mess we're in? We have enough for *six weeks*, Cormac. That's not allowing for emergencies like this wall collapse."

The butler patted their shoulders as they walked. "I understand. We will be all right. It's the McGrath way to persist. I apologize for not speaking up sooner, but I've been out of sorts. Nevin was my friend too."

They climbed the stairs to the foyer. Blarney slipped in behind her as if nobody would notice her furry red shadow.

"No worries," Rayne said, heading to Uncle Nevin's office. "Starting now, we need a plan. We have to work together. I'm going to call the cable company and get decent internet so I can open Modern Lace for orders online. But it costs money to make money at the beginning."

Cormac nodded. "I can do that for you, milady."

"Rayne."

He shrugged.

Ciara picked up her father's keys and his wallet. The prescription bottle. "You didn't know about his heart medication?"

"He never told me in words. But I saw it. It was only six weeks ago that he started with it. I wondered if he'd had a heart attack while on the tractor."

"Why didn't you say something?" Ciara asked, her tone hurt.

"It wasn't my place. But it's why I didn't support your idea that there was foul play . . . I thought the garda would tell you about his heart. What difference did it make, in the end, if it was a heart attack? My loyalty was to his lordship."

"Commendable. Moving forward, just to be clear," Rayne said, "I don't like secrets. 'Kay?"

The butler nodded. "Maeve told me what you two learned at Dr. Rueben's. I'm very sorry that I didn't support you, Ciara."

"That means a lot," Ciara said. "I agree. No more secrets."

"Your father was a friend," Cormac repeated. "I'd like to string up whoever did this by their toes. Garda Williams said they're narrowing down suspects. Including us, of all the nerve."

Rayne crossed her arms. "Did the officer tell you when we'll be able to use the tractor again?"

"No. If it's broken, it will need to be fixed. Dafydd will do his best with it, but supplies cost." Cormac scowled down at his shoes.

Ciara pocketed her dad's wallet. "You should come with me, Cormac. So there isn't a delay with the banking situation. We'll need to get that sorted as soon as things are . . ." Her voice caught.

"Next week," Rayne suggested, hoping Garda Williams wouldn't give up even if he was being pressured by his colleagues. "We should have more answers then."

"You mean, my father's killer should be found." Ciara's chin jutted.

"Yeah. I sure hope so." Rayne nodded toward Ciara in empathy.

"I'll go," Cormac agreed. "Will you let Maeve know, Rayne? We'll be back in a couple of hours. That old truck doesn't go past thirty."

"I will." Cormac and Ciara left, and Blarney looked up at her with big trusting eyes. "If only you could talk," she said. "Let's go change."

Rayne chose denim capris with a cotton T-shirt from Chanel. Black leather boots that were more style than comfort, but she'd make it work. She hurried out to the barn, Blarney at her heels. Dafydd watched her from the far side of the building, where he'd dragged a bag of powdered cement and a long stick that reminded her of a shillelagh.

Aine had changed into jeans as well. "Dafydd said we need to brush all the loose dirt off the stones and put them in a pile."

"Okay." Rayne adjusted the brim of her floral baseball cap.

Aine leaned close to Rayne's ear. "I also heard him tell Ciara he didn't think you'd come back out to work."

"Hey!" She and the shepherd were going to have a serious chat.

"He's wrong about you," Aine said. She dusted off a rock and dropped it in a bucket.

"What do you mean?"

"Dafydd thinks you're a spoiled American with all of the riches and toys. Clothes. *Shoes*." She giggled. "Can't blame him there. What happened with Blarney is the talk of the village."

"Great." Rayne kept an eye on the driveway in case her clothes arrived. No way would her reputation survive another mishap like that one. "Where is your mom?"

"She called Neddy, who's on his way back from his lunch break with Richard. She's going to make sandwiches for everyone."

"All right. Who?" It was just the three of them.

"If I know the villagers of Grathton, they'll all show up to help once the wood is here."

Rayne picked up a rock and brushed the debris free. "Do you think so?"

"Yes, of course." Aine sounded very certain. "We live in a place where you can count on your neighbor. We may not have a lot of cash, but we're always willing to lend a hand."

As it turned out, Aine was right. Neddy and Richard had told Beetle, and the barkeep had spread the word. Like in the old days, the pub was the center for news and gossip.

The pickup arrived, the back end weighted down with lumber, followed by a wave of able-bodied people with hammers, buckets, and gloves.

Rayne watched in admiration as Maeve organized everyone according to skill level. The most experienced were sent with Dafydd, Cormac, and Amos to assess the damage to the barn. Ciara headed up another group to assist.

Aine introduced Rayne to everyone, and they all greeted her with a bob of the head and a *milady*.

Rayne checked them out just as they checked her out. She kept a smile plastered on her face. She felt the weight of their regard and didn't want to fall short as their lady. These were her people. Well, hers and Ciara's. The connection to them and the land was deep-rooted.

She swayed at this new awareness.

The villagers knew how to rebuild with old stone, timber, and thatch. Beetle brought two kegs of ale and suggested tossing some dry hay into the cement mix, like in the old days.

"Are you settling in?" Sinead asked. "I brought day-old choc-olate biscuits. Gave them to Maeve to hand out."

"Yes, thanks. We sure enjoyed the toffee squares. Aine told me you have the best place to connect for Wi-Fi. How do you feel about modernization?"

"My hubby and I are all for it. Nevin used to spend a lot of time in our café discussing the future."

Sinead moved on, and Sorcha greeted Rayne with a grin. "Howareye," she said.

"I'm fine, thanks. You?"

Aine snickered at Rayne's confused expression when Sorcha walked on. "It's a greeting, that's all. Not a real question."

"Oh! Sinead had greeted me the same way at the bakery—and I answered." Rayne adjusted her cap. "I feel silly."

"Don't worry." Aine touched Rayne's elbow. "They all just want to get to know you."

That made her feel very vulnerable, and she immediately raised both hands. "I'm not that interesting. Sheesh, Aine, I'm making more mistakes than anything. And I can't understand half of what y'all say!"

"You're a boutique wedding designer. That's grand enough. We should be snapping pictures," Aine said. "To show your thousands of followers that you're not afraid to get your hands dirty." She whipped her cell phone from her back pocket and shot a few photos of Rayne and Blarney, the barn crew behind them. "You've gained hundreds more since Oasis Fabrics tagged you."

God bless Nolan. "Really? That's so great! Thank you, Aine."

Ciara waved at them, soot on her forehead along with a wide, satisfied smile. "Come see!" The side of the wall that had fallen in now had fresh wood planks.

Amos was shirtless, and that was an especially nice sight as he heaved timber into place, his muscles flexing.

Rayne and Aine helped Maeve and Neddy hand out chicken fillet sandwiches, which were battered sliced chicken tenderloin on rolls with packets of Tayto crisps. It was the favorite brand of potato chip in Ireland, according to Aine. Fresh chilled lemonade. She didn't miss the ice.

At the end of the night, flasks of whiskey were passed around as the wall was completed. There was a lot of talking going on at a pleasant murmur. Dafydd lit a small bonfire in a barrel.

Amos wiped his forehead with a towel and sadly put his shirt back on, then drank deep from a hip flask. "It's done."

"I can't believe it!" Rayne said, her body warm from the whiskey, Amos, and the moonlight. "Great job."

"You made some admirers today," Amos said. "Me you already had."

She nudged him.

Ciara and Dafydd joined them. "Did you tell her, Amos?"

"No. Been busy, Ciara lass."

Ciara gave a begrudging nod, followed by a smile. "You'll never guess who we ran into while we were in Kilkenny, Rayne. Freda Bevan."

"The councilwoman? At the lumber store?"

"Aye. Picking up flowers for her garden, she said. Anyway, I took it upon myself to invite her to lunch tomorrow here at the castle," Ciara said. "She loves to visit and is always angling for an invitation."

Rayne, feeling mellow, raised her gaze to Ciara's. "Did she accept?"

"Aye." Ciara grinned.

Laughing, Rayne asked, "What's the plan?"

Ciara raised her flask. "We get her excited about dining with the new lady of the castle, then trap her into revealing whether or not she poisoned my dad."

Rayne was sober in an instant. "Buzzkill."

Blarney leaned his head back and howled at the moon.

Chapter Twenty-Three

Midweek, two boxes arrived special delivery for Rayne from the United States. She'd been upstairs working on a wedding dress. Getting up so early allowed her to get a lot done.

"My clothes!" she said. The delivery man put them in the foyer, next to the beautiful bouquet, which was still going strong. She signed for them, and he left.

Ciara, Aine, Maeve, Cormac, and Neddy all watched her. Blarney had come inside following the boxes. Amos and Dafydd were out working, thank heaven.

"There won't be another show," Rayne promised. Her lingerie was packed away in her room. "I have no space left in my dad's wardrobe for clothes."

"Can we see?" Aine asked, her eyes shining. The girl had been bitten hard by the fashion bug.

"All right."

Cormac offered her a box cutter. Blarney circled the boxes with a wagging tail and eager eyes. "We had a talk about eating my shoes, right?"

Blarney lowered his head.

"Ah, poor pup," Aine said.

"My behind," Ciara scoffed. "How much was that Choo shoe?"

Thousands. "I don't want to talk about it. It's in the past."

Rayne opened the box and pulled out jeans, brand-new with tags on. Flannel shirts, work boots, and thick socks.

"What the heck?" Rayne frowned. "My size, but not my clothes." She shook her head. "I bet Lauren bought them for me once she realized my things are really not meant for outdoorsy stuff, like repairing a wall."

"Nice mum," Aine said.

"She is!"

Examining the contents of the other box, Rayne sighed with relief. "Finally!" She removed linen flared pants with a matching crop jacket in giant polka dots.

Ciara snorted.

Aine clasped her hands.

"I don't see you gardening in that," Cormac said, trying to keep a straight face.

"Probably not."

Next were her sundresses. Silk, linen, satin. Leather ballet flats with no sole to speak of. Last were her power pantsuits. Checked and plaid, solid black with satin pinstripes.

"You could wear that to church," Maeve said.

"Or to meet the queen," Neddy teased.

Rayne wasn't willing to tackle the church conversation just yet—although she liked her mom's idea. "Which one should I wear for the lunch today with Freda?"

"Ooh, the most obnoxious one you have," Ciara said. "She's a bit of a snob, and Da didn't like her at all. Puts her at the top of our suspect list. Anyway, I'm outa here to gather things for a fence with the sheep. I was talking to Sinead last night, and she mentioned that her cat had kittens, so if we want, we can pick two for the castle."

"Kittens!" Rayne saw Blarney's ears perk and raised a brow at the dog.

"Good idea," Maeve said. "I've noticed wee little tracks."

Could mice be what caused the noises outside her door? "I'm all for it," Rayne said. "Any thoughts on where to stash things while I figure out what I have?"

Cormac stepped forward. "The lounge next to the library."

Her cousin took off, snickering to herself, and Aine tapped the box with the new clothes. "I'll bring this one upstairs for you."

"Thanks." Rayne followed Cormac to a small sitting room that didn't seem to be used, ever.

"Here all right?"

"Yes, thank you. I'll put getting organized to the top of the list." She studied the room with interest. "This is terrific furniture."

"Period pieces," Cormac agreed. "We have a lot of rooms in this castle. Amos suggested I should take you on a tour."

"That would be great. Can we set it up for later this week? I have ideas for refurbishing some of the rooms." Possibly the third floor as well, but she didn't want to jump too far ahead.

"Of course, milady."

They returned to the foyer. Aine had taken the biggest box. "Let's catch up later." She raced up the stairs and into her room.

"You have clothes everywhere," Aine said. The maid put her hands on her hips as Rayne had seen Maeve do more than once. "Maybe you should bring some to the pink . . . er, sewing studio? You have hangers and a large closet that Lady Amalie used to fill. There might still be clothes in there." She pointed to a box. "You empty that into a pile, and I'll repack it with things you don't need in here so we can put it in storage and give you more space."

"Great idea." The two worked so well together that within an hour, Conor's wardrobe was filled with the clothes Rayne would use, a makeshift hat tree also held her belts and scarves, and the nightstands had been turned into lingerie drawers. A few of her stylish jackets were on another makeshift line, but everything was neat and easy to reach.

"I love all of your clothes," Aine said, once they were hung up. "Everything's done but that last box."

"I'll do it. You're welcome to borrow anything you like," Rayne said.

"And where would I wear it?" Aine sighed forlornly. "I don't even have a boyfriend."

Rayne laughed at the pretty and dramatic young lady. "Is there anyone you like?"

Aine scrunched her nose, and her freckles wrinkled. "Not really. They're so . . . well. They don't care about fashion at all. I want to be a designer like you someday."

Rayne hugged Aine. "You have a good eye for color." She checked the time on her phone. "I've got to get to the studio and sew. Will you help me dress at noon for the lunch with Freda?"

"Sure!"

They left the room. Aine went downstairs, and Rayne strode to the sewing studio with the box of fancy clothes. Blarney had disappeared. Once inside the studio, she set the box aside and lasered her focus on the pattern and materials. There was nothing she loved more than creating gowns for a bride's special day.

This bride was twenty-six, and her fiancé was in real estate in LA. He did very well, and she was into dressing houses, which meant staging a home for sale to look its best. They were a great match.

She and Landon . . . no. There was no Landon anymore.

The pattern was pinned to the fabric, and next it was time to cut. Her sharp shears were expensive but worth every penny. Silk snagged easily, which would ruin the piece.

Rayne lost herself in her creations. A knock sounded, and her heart hammered. She read the time on her phone. Noon already? "Come in."

Aine entered and took in the mess, but also the pinned cut-outs. "Oh, well done!"

"I have to work fast if I'm going to open Modern Lace for sales again." She got up and looked through the box. Outrageous and stylish. Hmm.

"I will help however I can," Aine said.

"You can start by zipping me into these pants." She showed Aine the chic pants and jacket with a peplum in lime green and black flowers. The pants were black, and she chose lime-green heels.

"So grand!" Aine assisted her into the tight pants and zipped. "How are you going to sit down?"

"There's a panel in the seam of the pants that gives to stretch," Rayne said with a wink. "Also, this fabric has five percent spandex in it."

"Freda will be very impressed," Aine said.

Rayne dug inside her purse for her makeup bag and applied red lip liner for full red lips.

"We want her to tell me all about Grathton Village and why she was angry with Uncle Nevin. I will be obnoxiously American."

"I wish I could see you," Aine said.

"Then I'd be nervous." Rayne checked the time. "One o'clock! Showtime!"

"Let's go!"

Rayne, followed by Aine, walked down the hall and descended the grand staircase, every inch of her body conveying wealth, status, and a smidge of snobbery. She channeled Rosalind Russell in *Auntie Mame*.

Ciara, in slacks and a cute floral-print shirt, had her mouth open slightly until Maeve discreetly elbowed her.

Cormac jumped into action as Rayne stepped from the staircase to the carpet on the slate foyer floor.

"Lady McGrath! Freda Bevan, councilwoman for Cotter Village." The butler held out his hand.

Freda was in her midfifties. Plump, with dyed brown hair and garish makeup.

Rayne adored her makeup, but an adept hand was key.

"The formal dining room, as you requested, milady," Cormac continued.

Neddy peeked out from the kitchen, and his eyes widened.

"Just perfect." Rayne looked over her nose at Freda. "I've been dying to get some culture since I landed. What do you do for the arts around this place? Not a theater to be found."

"Oh, well, Dublin, of course," Freda said. The woman gave a hesitant smile.

"Dublin! That little backwater that I flew into? First class and still exhausting."

"Well. Uh." Freda swallowed and touched a beringed finger to her throat. "There's Cork. It's known for their artists more so than Dublin."

"Cork. Hmm. I wish I could snap my fingers and be back in Hollywood. But as we both know, Freda, it's simply not possible." They reached the dining room, and Cormac ushered them in.

"Quite," Freda said. "Ciara mentioned that your mother is an actress?"

"*Family Forever.* A long-running sitcom. I'm sure you've heard of it? Lauren McGrath plays Susan Carter, the matriarch."

Freda blinked with stars in her eyes. "I haven't. I'll be sure to look for it."

Maeve served a fantastic lunch of shrimp and risotto, with lightly dressed greens on the side. Wine was offered rather than whiskey.

"Where have you been hiding the good stuff?" Rayne laughed as she sipped the delicate white wine. "I would've killed for this." She glanced over the rim at the councilwoman. "They've only brought out the rotgut whiskey."

"Whiskey is in our blood." Freda shrugged, uncertain.

"It's in mine!" Ciara drank from her tumbler.

It was in Rayne's as well, but this was a show for the councilwoman.

"Tell me," Rayne said, after a few bites of their meal. "Did you and my uncle see eye to eye on modernization?"

Freda swallowed, still bedazzled by everything. It was clear that she wanted to agree with Rayne. Perhaps she imagined many girls' lunches with the new lady at Grathton.

Maeve, hands folded, waited at the edge of the room in case she was needed. Rayne was aware that she also just wanted to know what was going on.

"Well." Freda scooped risotto onto her fork. "I adored Nevin McGrath."

Ciara dropped her knife to her plate with a clang. "*Adored* might be the wrong word, Freda."

Rayne fluttered her lashes at the crimson-cheeked woman.

"But he could be a bit . . . stubborn." Freda nodded, a rabbit sensing a trap but not seeing the danger.

"How so?"

Freda sipped, probably thinking how best to answer.

Rayne waved her hand airily. "I heard about the disagreement over combining villages."

Freda paled, making her lipstick and eye makeup even more cartoonish. "Events of that evening were wildly exaggerated."

Ciara cleared her throat. "Da told me what happened, Freda."

Freda reached for her wine and then folded her hands in her lap instead. Wishing she'd gone for the whiskey, no doubt.

"I was thinking of tearing down the pub and replacing it with an internet café," Rayne said. "And harnessing wind energy! Imagine the money that would bring in."

Ciara turned toward her with a neutral expression that had to be causing her all kinds of indigestion.

"Lady McGrath," Freda said. "We must keep the integrity of rolling hills and sheep. Fresh water for our animals and families. I don't believe we need wind towers in our vista, but what else can our poor kinsmen do if the villages fail?"

"Is Cotter Village failing? I'm sorry to hear that," Rayne said, deliberately misunderstanding.

Ciara covered a laugh with a cough.

"I didn't say that," Freda corrected.

Rayne crossed her fingers beneath the table. "Well, Grathton Village isn't either. We have plans to revitalize the area. Think satellite dishes the size of UFOs. Modernization."

Freda's cheeks turned purple. "That goes against the old ways. If we work together, combine our villages, we can have more say in how things are run."

Rayne worried for Freda's health but still played the idiot. "If you'd be willing to become Grathton Village and give up Cotter, then I might consider the alliance."

"Absolutely not!"

Neddy and Aine entered and whisked away the lunch plates, bringing dessert—baked meringue and lemon shortbread. Aine wasn't on the schedule to serve, but Rayne couldn't blame the lass for being curious.

"This looks delish," Rayne said. "You're the best."

Neddy and Aine melted back, but Maeve stayed put.

Freda regained control of herself and chose a shortbread. "I'd hate for any misunderstanding," the councilwoman said. "Cotter Village would remain the same, and we would welcome your villagers."

"Absorb us?"

Freda blinked. "Beg pardon?"

"You would absorb us into your village, and we would be nothing." Rayne hardened her tone. "I don't think Uncle Nevin would like that. I can see why you two would have butted heads."

Freda narrowed her eyes. "Butted heads . . ."

Rayne leaned forward as if inviting a confidence. "Is that why you punched him in the arm?"

"I!"

Rayne straightened, not daring to glance at Ciara or she'd risk letting Freda off the hook. "You see, like Uncle Nevin, I also think that modernizing would keep our youth here. If they had relevant jobs to the rest of the world."

"You don't know what you're talking about, young lady. You haven't been here that long." Freda's voice rose, and her skin resembled an eggplant.

"I have an idea." Rayne was on a roll, so she decided to spring it on both Ciara and Freda and let the chips fall. "It would offer employment."

"What is it?" Freda asked, desperate to make a connection. "I would support jobs, of course. Too many of our folk lose their way in drinking or gambling."

It sounded like Freda might be reasonable. Ciara glared at Rayne with suspicion.

"I would like to modernize the castle. Build a gazebo out by the lake. Renovate the bungalows and rent them out." Rayne pounded the table, on fire. "Let's make McGrath Castle a wedding venue. I know it can bring in loads of cash. Just think of the job opportunities!"

Ciara stood and dropped her napkin over her plate. "You are crazy, Rayne McGrath." Once again, she stormed out, but Rayne was getting used to it.

Freda waited until Ciara was gone, then leaned across the table toward Rayne. Her gaze was firm and unwavering. There was a teensy bit of victory in her overmade eyes. "You are going to lose this castle. I heard about the will. Ludicrous, but that was Nevin through and through. Opinionated and stubborn, with a temper. No way will you make this heap profitable, and I will be here to pick up the pieces." Freda tapped the table. "You are just like your uncle."

It gave Freda motivation. If the castle sold at a pittance, Freda could buy it. Or if there were no buyers, the councilwoman might somehow absorb the Grathton villagers into Cotter Village.

Rayne remained calm. "I happen to like my uncle. Tell me why the idea won't work."

"Grathton Village is an hour and a half away from Dublin. Who wants to travel that far?" Freda shook in her chair from her emotional outburst. "This is rural backwoods, good for farming and sheep."

"We have sheep. We *will* keep the sheep." If Rayne had learned anything, it was that the stinky cotton balls were very important. "It's not illegal for me to do this, right? Hold fantasy weddings on the property?"

Freda's nostrils flared. "You are a fool."

"No. I'm not." Rayne discarded all the theater and met Freda head-on. "I'm a business entrepreneur with a successful bridal boutique. I specialize in designer wedding gowns." She didn't raise her voice or look away from the older woman. "I know the industry inside and out."

"You make lingerie," Freda said, her mouth pursed.

Rayne spread her arm to the side and rolled her eyes. "What is it you people have against silk underwear?"

At that, Freda stormed from the room, spluttering. Just like Ciara.

Rayne reached for her shortbread and bit into it, savoring her sweet victory.

Chapter
Twenty-Four

Rayne remembered that Maeve was still in the room and turned, but the housekeeper was gone.

What would they all think of her idea? Freda and Ciara were against it, obviously. Before she deflated, she decided to call her mom.

Rayne left the formal dining room, not wanting this conversation heard until after she'd talked it over with Lauren. She headed up the stairs to the turret and the privacy of the tower roof.

All around her were those emerald-green rolling hills Freda wanted to preserve. Ciara same. Rayne didn't blame them. She did too—but there had to be compromise so they could find their way forward in the future.

It was six AM in Hollywood, and her mother was just waking up. "Good morning, Lauren!"

"Morning, darling. You sound very happy."

"Can you tell? I think I found a way to save the castle."

"Let me grab my coffee! All right, shoot."

Rayne touched the stone wall, running her fingers over the rough texture. "People love castles, right?"

"They do," Lauren agreed cautiously.

"If I don't create improvements for the manor and the village, it will be sold off at the end of twelve months. Freda, the councilwoman, wants it in order to make her village bigger and combine Grathton with Cotter. She might have killed Uncle Nevin. She's got a temper, and a motive."

"That's important." Her mom sipped. "I hope you didn't make her mad?"

"I did. But listen to this: everyone loves knights gallant and maidens fair. They love a fairy tale. Castles are *romantic*." Rayne clutched her fist to her heart. "I grew up with those fantasies. Love them still. So why not offer that to wedding couples for a very sweet price? I know the wedding industry. My sketch with the gazebo, the maze and gardens, the couples, and wedding rings was my subconscious nudging me toward this idea. What do you think?"

Her mom considered for all of ten seconds. "It's splendid! You could hire that Coco Bean café to do pastries; you said she was very talented. How much cash do you have?"

Her shoulders sank. "Mom, the castle is broke. We need money right away. Like, within six weeks."

"Oh. Honey, I don't know. That changes things. Is a new business practical?"

Rayne's stomach clenched tight. "Practical isn't an option. The castle and property, the village, it's all at stake."

She'd met the villagers and knew they loved Grathton, but Grathton was run-down and needed a jolt of energy. That energy would spread to the village.

"Well. The tarot reading said you would have a great opportunity. You've got to face the risk. You are fearless, Rayne."

"Terrified, you mean. But high-end weddings will bring in tourists with cash. We have private bungalows to rent. A gazebo to build. Just imagine the magic moments a wedding here will bring." Rayne surveyed the landscape and knew she was onto something big. "It will totally work."

"I love hearing you sound so happy, hon."

Rayne went on, the plans erupting from her mouth. "We can update the tower and rent it out for a premium cost. We'd need to add a bathroom to the suite, but that won't be too much money."

"Darling, it has to come from somewhere. I'm afraid I sent you what I have to spare."

"Don't worry, Lauren. There is furniture in storage here that we can put in the suites for rent. I can Google . . . ugh. I need Wi-Fi." She sank back against the stone wall of the tower. "Nobody will come if we don't have that basic luxury."

"These days, internet is a necessity," her mom agreed. "I know you can make this happen, and your dad and uncle will be so proud."

Were they watching her now? Rayne hoped she didn't fail. "Ciara hates the idea. I'm not sure what the others will think."

"You know, I don't think Conor or Nevin would haunt you to scare you. There is too much love there. How have you been sleeping?"

"Better since Blarney is in my room with me. It's our secret." She had two secrets that Ciara didn't know, between Landon and the dog. Rayne had told both Cormac and Ciara she didn't like secrets. Guilt twinged like a lower-back pain—sharp and insistent. "Aine helps me out. I like her a lot. I think she'll be on board with modernizing but keeping the castle aesthetic, which people will want and pay for."

"Good luck."

"Thanks! I've got to go. Love you, Mom. Hi to Paul!"

They ended the call, and Rayne studied the terrain visible from the tower. If it was done right, she could ask ten thousand euro a weekend to start.

She knew the wedding business and destination weddings were something people craved. They wanted romance, to be swept away.

McGrath Castle offered that.

She skipped down the interior steps, reached the foyer, and headed for the kitchen.

Nobody was there.

Fine. She had work to do on her wedding dress. "You can't avoid me forever, guys. Calling a family-staff meeting at dinner tonight!"

No answer.

She found a piece of paper by the landline and wrote a note that she placed on the center of the kitchen table. Rayne had work to do to bring in money and couldn't afford to pretend the castle wasn't falling down around her.

Aine knocked on the sewing studio door at five thirty. Rayne looked up from her sewing machine, clouds of fabric around her.

"You've been swallowed by satin," Aine laughed. She used her cell phone to snap a picture. "For your followers. Dinner is ready."

"I wish I could work through, but since I demanded a meeting, I'd better be there, huh? How'd that go, anyway?"

"Everyone is there. Everyone has opinions." Aine shrugged. "At the end of the day, according to the will, it's your decision as lady of the castle."

"It's worse that way. I want to be fair." Rayne shifted on the chair.

"I've only known you a short while, but I know you will be. See you there." Aine closed the door behind her.

Rayne eyed the picture of her and her dad at the lake when she was eleven, which she'd brought to the room with her. He'd died the next year. She wanted to make him proud and always had that in her heart.

"I'm going to do my best, Conor. Dad."

She disentangled herself from the fabric without snagging or tearing the skirt. It would be fit for a Disney princess when she was through. She wanted her brides to feel special and beautiful. Just imagining offering the entire wedding experience thrilled her, and she knew she was on the right track.

Rayne entered the less formal dining room. The whole crew was there: Cormac, Maeve, Aine, Neddy, Amos, Dafydd, Ciara, Richard.

Her stomach was a jumble of nerves. Dafydd and Ciara had dark expressions. Maeve and Cormac looked neutral, Aine and Neddy all smiles. Richard seemed scared.

What for? It wasn't like his castle was on the line.

Then she realized he probably felt that it was. Her uncle had certainly considered all of the villagers his responsibility.

"I can see that you've heard my idea about making McGrath Castle a high-end wedding venue."

She sat down at the head of the table, at Cormac's insistence.

Nobody talked. Cormac dished out a casserole with beef and vegetables. Neddy passed a basket of rolls.

They were giving her a chance to explain. Probably had been told to do so by Cormac. Bless the man.

Rayne cleared her throat and scanned each person's face. "So. To be blunt—we are solvent for the next month."

"Six weeks," Ciara said, then clamped her hand to her mouth. "Sorry. Didn't mean to interrupt."

Rayne folded her cloth napkin over her lap. "I have an idea about that, but we need to discuss it in private, cousin."

"There are no bloody secrets in this castle," Ciara said. "Besides, you just blurted your idea earlier with Freda, without discussing it with me."

Ciara had a point. "I was winging it."

"Beg pardon?" Aine asked.

"I hadn't planned to say it," Rayne clarified.

"Eat," Cormac said. "Before the food gets cold."

Rayne took a bite of savory beef and carrot in a rich gravy. Thick egg noodles. Neddy was a wonder. "This is great."

"I've been using recipes from the old castle cookbook." Neddy broke his roll in half. "It's been fun."

Fun. It was what Grathton required a hefty dose of. She swallowed a noodle. "We must have a plan to revitalize not only the castle but the village. We need jobs for people so they don't move away. So they stay in the family homes."

"A plan to do what exactly?" Richard asked.

"I'd like to have a wedding venue on the McGrath property. It is incredibly beautiful. With the right spin, we can be booked solid." She took another bite, famished.

"You're dreaming," Ciara said. "It's not practical to think of weddings on the manor grounds when we need a bleedin' fence. A roof."

"It's time for fresh ideas before McGrath Castle fades into obscurity," Amos said, coming to Rayne's side.

She smiled at him in thanks. "We need to change and grow, to reach the full potential here. Once we open for business, we could have plenty of money for a fence. The roof."

"According to the will, we only have a year," Ciara said.

"It's impossible to see a profit so fast!" Dafydd dunked his roll in the gravy.

"We have to move forward," Rayne said. She looked at Cormac. "Did you get ahold of the internet folks?"

"Aye." Cormac sipped from his tumbler of whiskey. "The cable company will be here tomorrow for an estimate."

"Cable?" Dafydd protested.

"Wonderful!" Rayne nodded her thanks at the butler. "We need Wi-Fi in order to compete with other venues. People want an authentic castle experience but with amenities. My dad had the bathroom installed for a reason."

"His lordship enjoyed his private bath," Cormac seconded.

"It isn't a necessity," Ciara argued.

Amos speared a pea onto his fork. "The rooms in the castle are solid stone. They were made to last the test of time."

"We'd have people in the house?" Maeve asked. Her faded red brow rose in concern.

"This is a conversation only," Rayne said. "If we opened it like an Airbnb, we would keep the private rooms locked and separate. I'd like to concentrate on the tower. I know we could get ten thousand euro for a weekend stay."

Dafydd choked on a noodle. "Ten thousand euro? Who has that kind of money?"

"Hollywood people," Ciara said, patting him on the back. "How will you reach them?"

Rayne was happy to answer that. "We live in a great time where things are global. Instagram and other social media outlets connect us."

Aine nodded excitedly. "Modern Lace is up to twenty-three thousand followers, and your partner has fifteen thousand."

Rayne felt as if the breath had been knocked out of her. Landon Short had his own page? Was it active? Holy moly. Why hadn't she thought about that?

"That's a lot of people," Maeve said.

She continued and hoped nobody noticed her lapse. "We need to focus on what's special about Ireland, as Amos mentioned—there are castles and ruins everywhere. I grew up believing in fairy tales. In knights and damsels. Other people love the romance of olden days, and we have it right here." She gestured toward the foyer. "The McGrath shield in the hall is museum quality."

"We have all sorts of things in the storerooms we could clean up and showcase," Maeve said. "Lots of local history."

"It's more work." Ciara shook her head. "You don't want to take that on."

"Our villagers *need* work. They came to our aid last night and showed me that they still feel tied to the manor," Rayne said. "Uncle Nevin felt responsible for them. What if we could give them an opportunity to thrive?"

"The bungalows wouldn't take much effort," Amos said. "The horses are fat because nobody but Ciara rides them. We could offer a horse and carriage for the weddings. Show folks the sheep and the farm. We can start with two of the cottages, and that way the inside rooms could be kept private, for family."

Rayne nodded, listening, banishing Landon. "The tower could be made to stand alone with its own entrance as well." She turned to Dafydd, who had proved his skills with carpentry just yesterday. "Could you build a gazebo, by the lake?"

Dafydd scowled and reluctantly nodded. "I think so. If I had a plan for it."

"I can sketch something for you." She turned to Amos. "Would you mind sharing your favorite place? It's lovely."

"No." Amos faced the others. "Not for twenty or thirty euro per head for day trips."

Richard laughed nervously.

"We could have a café with meat pies and Guinness," Rayne said, looking at Neddy and Maeve. "Whiskey. I don't know what the laws are or licenses, but maybe Freda could help us."

"You think Freda will help you after what happened at lunch today?" Maeve asked in disbelief.

"I never thought I'd be on Freda's side." Ciara stood and put her hands on her hips. "Da wouldn't have wanted this."

Cormac also rose. "Ciara, you're wrong, *leanbh*. Lord Nevin was willing to do whatever it took to save the castle, and the village, for this generation and beyond. For him, they are one unit." He twisted his pointer and middle fingers together like a braid. "The McGraths were given a responsibility in 1723. He never lost sight of that."

Ciara appeared stricken by Cormac's rebuff. Dafydd touched her elbow with support and concern.

Rayne motioned for everyone to sit. "Please. We all have to work together on this project. We need to be a team with the same goals."

Ciara and Cormac sat. Rayne said a silent thank-you for that particular miracle and hoped her cousin would stick around.

"I am going on record," Ciara said, "that I don't like it."

Blarney slunk into the dining room with a crystal in his mouth. She'd thought she'd found them all. Poor Jimmy Choo had never had this in mind when he'd designed those fabulous sandals.

Dafydd whistled. "Out, dog!"

Blarney paused but then continued toward Rayne.

The shepherd's cheeks flushed at being ignored.

265

What else did Blarney have? Was that a flower in his mouth? So sweet.

"It's okay, Dafydd. He can stay," Rayne said. The dog settled behind her chair.

"You've ruined him," Dafydd announced. "You've turned him into a pet. I'll put him up for sale tomorrow."

Blarney whined.

Rayne felt the stirrings of her own Celtic temper but tamped it down. "Is this not my castle?"

Silence descended as everyone stared at her in amazement.

"Aye," Aine said. Maeve shot her daughter a butt-out glare.

"I will pay for him."

Dafydd clumsily got to his feet, anger in his eyes. He tugged at Ciara, who also stood, torn on where her loyalty should be.

Rayne placed her hand on Blarney's head. "He's my dog now."

"Dafydd, you know Nevin spoiled him," Amos said, to diffuse the situation. "It's not Rayne's fault."

The couple left, arm in arm, ending further discussion for the castle's future.

Chapter
Twenty-Five

"Well, that could have gone better," Rayne said to the rest of the people at the table.

Neddy gave a nervous laugh.

"Amos is right," Cormac agreed. "Blarney is a pet. His lordship tried to take him duck hunting, and Blarney could track them, but the pup preferred playing instead. Lord Nevin told me that the dog's nature wasn't a killer."

Uncle Nevin had understood Blarney perfectly. Rayne glanced at the dog, who had the flower and crystal between his paws. "He's into beautiful things."

"Like you," Amos said with a wink.

Was he complimenting her beauty or saying that she and the dog were similar? Her cheeks heated.

Rayne changed the subject to deliberately lighten the mood. She didn't want to continue the conversation about the castle without her cousin there. "So, what's up with *slagging*?"

"It's insults between friends," Neddy said. "Beetle is a master!"

Aine got into the spirit. "Winging it," the maid said.

"Just playing it by ear," Rayne returned with a grin. "Crack?" She sipped her whiskey.

Aine frowned, then giggled. "*Craic*? It means fun!"

"This is totally *craic*," Rayne said, not getting the accent at all right.

Aine burst out laughing. "*Cula bula!*"

"Cool?" Rayne guessed.

"Exactly." Aine gave her a thumbs-up.

"We should do this more often, so I don't make a fool of myself, like I did yesterday with Sinead and Sorcha."

"What happened?" Maeve asked.

Aine grinned. "It was nothing. Rayne didn't understand that howareye wasn't a question that required an answer, so when Sorcha greeted her that way, you know, Rayne told her she was just fine."

They all laughed, but in a nice way.

"You'll get it with time," Amos said, his hand over Rayne's on the table.

"You all are being very sweet." She freed her hand and pushed her plate away from her, full. "I think I'm ready for bed. All of this crack-of-dawn stuff is catching up with me."

"It's been two weeks tomorrow," Cormac said softly. "Since his lordship's accident. We're ready for answers and closure. I know he would give your idea backing. I believe Ciara will come around."

"I hope so."

A few minutes later, Rayne took a tumbler of whiskey with her and Blarney to bed, no longer needing to hide his actions. Amos had reassured her that the pup had cost less than fifteen hundred euro. With no further word about Landon or her gowns, Rayne was quite aware of her low balance in her bank account.

In the bedroom, she got out her phone. One freaking bar. For the first time since Landon's betrayal, she went to his social media. His last post was from her birthday—he'd shared a picture of them both in sombreros from Cinco de Mayo. He'd wished her all the best. Jerk. Probably laughed while doing it.

She exchanged her phone for her sketchbook and drew the gazebo, then the bungalows, and the tower with the spectacular view. Once Ciara agreed, then they could move forward, but Rayne wouldn't do it until her cousin was on board.

Uncle Nevin's will had meant for them to work together.

"What do I have of value?" Her gaze scanned her dad's childhood room that she'd taken over with designer clothes, scarves, shoes, purses . . . shoes. She'd spent good money on her collection because she liked it. She doubted the shoes would go up in value. What about her handbags?

Rayne reached for her phone and tried to search collectibles, but there was no signal at all. "Blarney, this is baloney." The dog wagged his tail at her from his bed made from her satin nightie.

Tomorrow the cable company would arrive with news on whether they could get high-speed Wi-Fi and how much it would cost.

She'd have internet! She could sell her shoes and handbags online. Just a few to start. Maybe nobody would want them. She didn't like other people's shoes, but these were designer.

Blarney jumped up on the bed next to her and gave her adoring eyes. How could she say no?

"Just for a little while." Maybe there was a no-dogs-on-the-bed rule. She'd ask Aine. Then again, this was her castle.

She fell asleep, dreaming that her sheep were all wearing Jimmy Choos, Louboutin, Prada. Sombreros.

Rattles outside her door woke her time and again. It was downright annoying. She flipped on the light. Blarney sniffed at the closed door, tail wagging. Did he know the ghost? Was it her uncle Nevin?

She sucked in a breath and opened the door. Blarney darted out but came right back. Nobody was there.

Rayne sniffed deep, catching the cologne Dafydd had worn at dinner.

"*Rat*. Come on, Blarney."

When her alarm went off the next morning at six, Rayne was ready for war. She and Blarney went to the kitchen, the dog at her side, making it a point that the rules had changed.

Dafydd was at breakfast, sitting next to Ciara. Had he spent the night with Ciara? Not that Rayne cared—they were adults, for heaven's sake. She wished her cousin would agree to a bigger bedroom. Luxury.

Rayne let Blarney out the kitchen door. Neddy served everyone eggs, bacon, and toast.

"How'd you sleep?" Rayne asked Ciara. She fixed her coffee with cream and sugar. Aine and Maeve each had their breakfasts and beverages already.

"Fine." Her cousin gave a terse answer.

"Oh? I didn't sleep fine. That haunting I've been telling you about was really intense last night."

Her cousin stirred honey into her tea. "Sorry?" As in, not.

Rayne brought her coffee to her mouth and sipped. "Funny thing? The ghost was totally wearing Dafydd's cologne."

Ciara rolled her eyes. "You're imagining things."

Rayne shifted to gaze right at the bully. "Am I, Dafydd?"

Dafydd shrugged. He ate his breakfast in a hurry without answering. Neddy wisely changed the subject to the weather. Aine and Maeve jumped on the change in an attempt to keep the peace. Blue skies, another soft bonny day. No rain for a while. None in the forecast either.

Dafydd thanked Neddy for breakfast and scooted from the kitchen, Ciara hot on the heels of her fiancé. They argued very loudly in the hall, then he left with a door slam and Ciara returned to the kitchen.

She sat and picked up her tea. "Sorry. I mean it this time."

"Did you know?" Rayne asked.

"Course not. I wouldn't okay him acting the maggot. Since I'm apologizing, I'll add a third to the pile. Last night. I should have stayed and listened to your ideas."

"Oh?" Rayne's eggs caught in her throat, and she quickly swallowed. Yes! Ciara's support could make or break their future.

"You're right, about the castle. There is a reason that Da didn't leave it to me." Ciara's gray eyes welled with tears. "It's two weeks today since his accident. And we still don't know who killed him."

"Poor *mhuirnín*," Maeve said. Neddy dropped a dish into the sink. Aine sniffed, and Rayne's heart ached for her cousin.

"Means darling," Aine said to Rayne's questioning look.

She would need to buy a notebook for it all. Or better yet— Google translate, once they had internet.

"I'm fine," Ciara groused. "What's the plan for the day?"

"I could use your help in Uncle Nevin's office this morning," Rayne said.

"All right. I don't want to be around Dafydd for a while. He can manage the sheep without me."

Aine got up and refilled Ciara's tea.

"It will be easier together, for sure." Rayne reached for an apple in the bowl and polished it on her cloth napkin.

After a sip, Ciara said, "You have my support. Where should we begin? The castle is huge, and the bungalows, and a gazebo . . . the village! I don't understand how you can see it all together."

"It's overwhelming all at once, but if we parcel it out, it's doable. Like, a wedding gown has hundreds of pieces, but I can't think of it that way. I break it into parts. Bodice, skirt, underskirt. Sleeves."

"The cost is a big deal," Ciara said. "We both know there isn't much to work with."

Rayne bit into the crunchy apple and tilted her head. Would Ciara go along with her idea even though it put the castle at a potential risk?

Maeve opened her day planner. "As Cormac said yesterday, the cable people will be here at eleven for an estimate of price."

"Thanks, Maeve." Rayne turned to Ciara. "Next week, you and I should go to the bank together and manage that. I'm sure there will be paperwork to fill out. For now, Cormac can sign bills for us, since he's on the account."

Ciara nodded, her mouth unsmiling. "You said you had an idea about the six weeks' timeline?"

"Yeah. I was thinking that we can keep the funds for the month intact for June but use the two weeks earmarked for July for building supplies and paint. We can ask for help from the villagers, as a percentage from our first big tower rental."

Ciara wore an uncertain expression. Not that Rayne was surprised by her reaction.

"Work for free?" Maeve said.

"Not free, but money on the back end—like you already do for the wool shearing and harvest. It's not ideal, but we'd love to be ready for our first tower rental over July Fourth—it's a big U.S. holiday, probably not so much here." She felt her cheeks heat. Pointing to Maeve's kitchen calendar, she said, "There are four weekends in July. I will wager with Aine's help marketing, we will have it booked, at least once, and that's ten thousand euro."

"You have wedding dresses to make," Aine said. "I've been posting pictures to your social media. A lady this morning asked where she could buy a Modern Lace dress. You're getting a lot of hits on the pictures of you by the barn with Blarney, working at your own castle."

"You said that?" Rayne wanted to duck her head. In Hollywood, this kind of thing might happen, but in real life?

"It's true!"

"You're an angel, Aine. Get the woman's information. I'll need a quick redesign of my Modern Lace site. Thank heaven we're getting internet!"

"Will you show me how to do a website?" Aine asked.

"Yes, of course." Rayne thought of something even more empowering. "Later on, when we're settled, I could offer to teach anybody in the village who wants to learn. Keep folks relevant."

"I do," Maeve said, green eyes bright. "I want to be relevant."

Ciara snorted. "You are, without the internet." She raised her hand. "I'd also be interested in getting up to speed. But not at the cost of the garden, or the farm, or the sheep."

"Agreed! Knowledge is power, that's all."

"Even Father Patrick has a tablet." Maeve shook her head.

Rayne laughed and stood up. "Come on, Ciara. Let's bite the bullet and get this over with. Everyone else, keep brainstorming ideas! Maeve, you're so good with the planner; do you mind running out a timeline for the next month or two and what could be done? How many folks we'd need?"

"Aye, sure, and I'll be happy to do it."

The cousins left the busy kitchen. Rayne wanted to stay and be part of the creating process, but they had to figure out the ledger.

Rayne sat down in the same chair as before, leaving Uncle Nevin's for Ciara.

"I know this is hard and tedious, but promise me that you won't storm off anywhere until we get answers. Okay?"

Her cousin hefted her chin defensively. "I don't storm off."

Rayne raised her brow.

Ciara blushed and lowered it. "I've already told you that I have a wee bit of a temper."

"I used to. Someday I will amuse you with the tortures of deportment school." Old Mrs. Westinghouse. "My mom called it my wild Celtic blood and said we needed to water it down."

Her face scrunched. "Deportment classes? That's why you're so cold."

"I am not cold!"

It was Ciara's turn to raise a brow.

Rayne got up and unlocked the cabinet, retrieving the ledgers. "I hope that taking a break will allow me to see things clearer here. It was such a mess last time that my eyes crossed." She pressed a thumb between her brows.

"Same." Ciara leaned her elbow on the desk and shoved her fingers into her short hair. "Ready."

"Okay." Rayne dropped the stack to the desk, and one of the ledgers slipped off the edge onto the floor.

"Show me what this all means for us." Ciara frowned as she opened the folder on the desk.

Rayne picked up the ledger, and a half-folded piece of paper fluttered to the side. Her nape tickled. "What's this?"

"Ooh. What do you have there?" Ciara narrowed her gaze on the paper.

"I don't know. It was tucked loose in the ledger." Rayne placed the accounting notebook right by the one Ciara had.

Ciara wore a very confused expression.

Rayne perched on the edge of her seat and unfolded the paper, setting it next to the open ledger. "We have two lists here. One with initials and that little squiggly, the one that had been tucked away. One with just initials."

"That's the euro sign," Ciara explained.

"Instead of a dollar sign." Excitement that this could be important raced through her body.

Ciara read off the ledger. "OH. RF. LM. DN, FB, AL, CS. That's probably me," she said. She compared the list to the paper that Rayne had found. "But euro signs? Da never loaned me money. I mean, I never asked. He made it clear everything went into the property."

Rayne tapped the initials. "OH. Owen Hughes?"

"Probably. RF. Richard Forrest." Ciara looked at Rayne, then the ledger. "LM. Lourdes McNamara."

"DN . . . who is that?"

"Dafydd Norman." Ciara swallowed and touched her throat. "FB. Freda Bevan. AL. Amos Lowell."

"These are all people that he worked with. But the euro signs! Did he owe money to these guys?"

"No." Ciara spoke with absolute certainty. "Da never borrowed. He paid his debts."

"Ciara." Rayne sank down to her knees and looked right into her cousin's eyes. Her stomach clenched. "Girlfriend. We need to figure this list out. It's a clue for sure. He never borrowed. He never loaned. What else could the euro sign stand for?"

"I don't know! I was never good at reading his mind." Ciara strummed the desktop. "I asked Cormac if Da kept a personal journal, like Maeve had suggested, but he didn't. Da was private with his thoughts. Just the business ledgers that we're looking at here."

Rayne rose and paced the room, her brain spinning with possibilities. If he hadn't loaned money to people, then why the euro sign? Why the separate set of figures with initials? It was a puzzle, and they just had to figure out the solution.

Oh yeah. Easy-peasy.

The two sets of numbers made her wonder if he'd been figuring out something on his own. Were they following his train of thought? "I feel like we're following breadcrumbs."

"I don't understand."

"Hansel? Gretel? Never mind." Rayne crossed the room, wishing it weren't too early for whiskey. "Your dad had a reason for putting down the euro signs. He had that folded and tucked away as if he was also trying to figure something out. I bet that will lead us to who killed him."

"All right. Let's go over the initials." Ciara chewed her lower lip. "FB. Freda Bevan. She was angry at him, but she didn't hate Da—they were more like two worthy opponents lining up to fight."

"Okay. I can see that." Rayne immediately pictured Freda in boxing gloves. The councilwoman had wanted to make her point and had kept her temper, in the end, though Rayne had deliberately pushed her buttons.

"RF. Richard has a lot of other stuff going on, with his gambling habit. I think he wants to get well. Da would support that. At the end of the day, they were friends as well as tenant and landlord."

Rayne nodded. "I don't get the bad-guy vibe from Richard."

Ciara tilted her head and quirked a brow. She read another set of initials. "We know it wasn't Lourdes. Garda Williams said she had an alibi, but her initials are right here."

Rayne read the next set. "AL. What about Amos?" As much as she wanted him to be innocent, his initials were there, with the euro sign.

"Amos doesn't have an alibi. I mean, Dafydd and I saw him at the lake, but that was way before the tractor accident."

"And Amos found him." With Blarney. "A cover-up?"

Ciara shrugged. "I hate this. I hate you for making me look at my friends as if they could be murderers."

"It's not my fault!" Rayne stared at her cousin. "Hate is a little strong."

Ciara smacked her hand to the ledger. "Sorry." But from her tone, Rayne could tell that she wasn't.

"You and Dafydd. How sure are you that your fiancé is innocent? He was haunting my rooms, Ciara. He's been to jail."

"He played a bad joke to make you want to quit," her cousin said, defending Dafydd. "He wouldn't hurt my da."

"If I quit, then you lose everything."

Ciara bowed her head. "I know. He knows. I couldn't make it clearer to him. We've been trying to find footing in all of this, as a couple. As two individuals who worked for my dad. He understands now that you not being here would make things worse."

"Dafydd tried to scare me, but Blarney recognized him and wasn't alarmed." Rayne figured that had to count for something. "And while the dog might not like your future husband, he doesn't growl at him either."

Ciara's chin jutted. "Dafydd would never hurt the dog. You undermined his authority last night. It embarrassed him."

"Yeah. He tried to scare me out of the castle. Not going to apologize."

Ciara exhaled. Loudly.

"Who does that leave us with?" Rayne didn't move.

Ciara glowered at Rayne, not happy.

Rayne returned to the ledger and picked it up. "What if your dad suspected someone was after him?"

"I don't understand." Ciara sat back in the office chair and looked at Rayne. "Da would argue over the shade of green on a blade of grass, but people liked him."

She'd heard the same from the villagers who'd come to assist when the barn needed fixing. "This could be a list of suspects."

"Well, take me off that list." Ciara shoved the sheet of paper across the desk. "I wouldn't hurt my dad."

Rayne brought the ledger to her chest, a figurative light bulb suddenly shining over her head. "You know who isn't on this list?"

"Nope." Ciara kicked her boot heel against the chair of the leg.

"The Lloyds. Neddy."

"I'm so confused!" Instead of walking out, Ciara pulled the paper back to her and read it through again. Rayne was very proud of her cousin.

"Maybe it wasn't personal danger," Rayne mused aloud. "Because of the euro thing, could it be related to his bank at all?"

"I banked where Da did because it was easier. We'd go into Kilkenny together and make a day of it with lunch and shopping. He always paid for whatever we needed. If I wanted something. There is nothing suspicious about it."

Rayne's skin tingled as if they were headed in the right direction. "All right. In my mom's show, she sometimes has to solve crimes. You start with what you know. Facts. What do we know is *fact* from this list?"

"We know that Da worked with these people," Ciara said. "Me included. That's something in common."

"Right." Rayne rummaged in the desk for a blank paper—nothing. She tore a piece from the back of the ledger, then handed it to Ciara. "You write that down—*work related*."

Ciara did. "What else?" She tapped the page impatiently.

Rayne pondered the names. "You all live in the same community."

"*Live*," Ciara said as she wrote. "That's good. Two things in common." She looked at Rayne, the pen to her lower lip. "Next?"

"*Why* would someone want him dead?"

Ciara's eyes filled. She shook her head. "Nobody had a reason to want to kill him. He wasn't an easy man to be around. That doesn't mean he had enemies in the village."

"Not to be blunt, Ciara, but if he had no enemies, he wouldn't have been poisoned with his own heart medication."

Ciara gasped. "You're cruel."

"I don't mean to be." Rayne placed the ledger on the desk. "I'm trying to help you find answers."

"I don't need any."

"Answers, or help?" Rayne crossed the room with exasperation and turned back, her arms folded at her waist. Her heart ached for Ciara. "Calling baloney."

Her cousin shredded the bottom of the page into little paper curls. "I don't know who would hate him enough to kill him."

Rayne returned to the desk, opened the ledger, and pressed her finger to the initials, then the page combining initials with the euro signs. "What else do they have in common?"

Ciara gave an angry shrug. "We aren't all from here. We aren't related. We don't have money." She rolled the paper into a ball in frustration and tossed it at Rayne. "This is stupid. I think I'd rather go make up with Dafydd."

The ball dropped to the floor. "You said you would stay and help me."

"Rayne, I want to know who killed my da. It's been two weeks. I want to have a funeral for him to make him proud. Nobody on this list would hurt him. Don't you understand that?" Ciara glared at her in utter agony.

"I am trying to find answers." Rayne retrieved the paper ball with the euro signs and initials.

"You're on the wrong track."

"How so?" Rayne unfolded the piece of paper and flattened it on the desk.

"I don't know." Ciara stared across the room, her gaze focused on nothing, her body emanating pain. Hurt. "I want to leave."

"Fine. Go."

Ciara did, letting the door slam closed.

Rayne swiped tears from her cheeks. Somebody had killed Uncle Nevin, and until Ciara stopped telling her who it *couldn't* be, how could they find answers?

Chapter
Twenty-Six

Rayne sat at her uncle's desk. On the corner was Garda Williams's business card. She reached for the landline and dialed. The black phone was practically an antique.

"Garda Williams," the police officer answered.

"Hi!" Rayne said enthusiastically. Totally fake, as her heart and spirit were crushed. "It's Rayne McGrath."

"Oh. Yes."

"*Yes?*"

"Hello. May I help you?" His voice hinted at irritation.

"Well, sure." Rayne waited, wondering how to approach the subject. She'd be direct. She was American, after all. "Anything new regarding Uncle Nevin's death?"

"I said I would ring you if there was anything to report."

Rayne shifted on the chair. "So, about that. It's been two weeks since my uncle Nevin's accident, and Ciara would like closure. A funeral is important to her, and to the community."

After almost a minute, Garda Williams said, "I'll call the coroner and ask when the body can be released."

She looked at the phone in surprise. "You will?"

"Aye."

"Thank you!" She couldn't wait to share that with Ciara. Or maybe she should wait until the officer got back with an answer. Her cousin was an emotional wreck.

"Anything else?"

She sat forward, the phone to her ear. "Well, I know that you were able to cross Lourdes McNamara off your list, but what about Freda Bevan? She was over for lunch yesterday."

"What?"

"Just a neighborly kind of thing," Rayne said with assurance. "Anyway, she seems very short-tempered. I was wondering if you'd questioned her at all?"

"As a matter of fact, I did. She was with her daughter and her grandchildren all day Thursday. Not that it's any of your concern."

"Oh." Disappointment weighted her shoulders. It was beyond stressful to find a killer. "She wants to combine the villages, you know."

"I do know."

"It's a good motive." One of the top, especially if her uncle hadn't been willing to join the villages.

"Ms. Bevan didn't do it." The officer's tone was very clipped. "If that will be all?"

"Yes." Rayne didn't want to press the man any further and risk alienating him. "That's it."

"Stop interfering in this investigation, Ms. McGrath. I have things under control. You don't know the villagers like I do."

Ciara had said the same. And yet . . .

"Oh! When can we move the tractor? It's been two weeks. The grounds need to be mowed."

"You've said that already. I am quite aware of how long it has been. Give me until tomorrow for a definitive answer regarding the tractor. It will need to be fixed before you can use it—the hydraulic line was cut very skillfully, which is why it took so long to find the problem."

"The line was cut?" Dafydd had worked on the tractor. Did the garda guy know that, or did he think the Welshman was just a shepherd? Rayne was about to tell him about the folded paper in the ledger and question the euro signs, but he hung up.

"Rude!"

Her mother called on her cell phone, and Rayne picked up, glad for the distraction. Was her cousin's fiancé a murderer? She went to the window and stood by it for the best reception.

"Hello!"

"I'll make this quick, in case we lose signal," Lauren said. "It's important!"

"Hang on—I'll call you on the landline." Rayne hung up on the cell and dialed her mother from the black phone at the desk.

"Darling, I finally spoke with the pet psychic," her mom said. "The picture you sent told her all she needed to connect with Blarney. Blarney saw everything that evening when the tractor tipped. He's so upset. He's trying to tell you, to communicate, but you don't understand."

"That would be true. Not fluent in dog." Rayne walked around the desk with the receiver to her ear and studied the painting of McGrath Castle. The beautiful grounds. They had to save the property for her uncle, and for her dad. For the village. For future generations.

"Well, it's got something to do with flowers."

"This whole place is covered in flowers! Roses to lavender for the laundry. It's a floral paradise. I have news too, about the tractor—the police officer told me that it had been tampered with so well that it was hard to detect. Dafydd is the tractor mechanic."

"Oh—that doesn't sound good. Poor Ciara! The psychic couldn't get more specific. Blarney loves you, though; she said that."

Rayne's heart warmed. "I offended Dafydd and Ciara yesterday, so Blarney is my pet now. Might have to sell my shoes to pay for him."

"Juicy fruit. I wish I could help. Well, we got word that we aren't being renewed." Her mom caught a sob in her throat.

"Mom! Are you all right?" The show was Lauren's everything and had been for as long as Rayne could remember. Rayne had learned her own work ethic from watching her mom's dedication to her craft.

"I've been crying all night, but it will be okay. What will I do with myself? I've been on the show for over half my life."

"You deserve to take a break." Rayne leaned back against the desk. "How's Paul?"

"Devastated. Oh, the whole crew is a mess. We need to finish filming, but that will be done in August." Her mom's voice grew thick. "Who am I when I'm not Susan Carter? Devout Christian, family matriarch, entrepreneur. Susan is so brave."

"So are you. Lauren McGrath is a rock star actress."

"I'm too old."

"You are not!" Rayne blinked back her own tears. "I wish I was there for you. I'd give you so many hugs."

"It's strange to not have you here." Her mother drew in a breath. "But it's okay too. You need to do this."

"I need to find Landon and my money. My wedding gowns. I saw a post that he'd done on my birthday. We were in sombreros, drinking margaritas."

"He's a . . . horse's behind."

"Come to Ireland, Mom. See the castle. Ciara promised to support the whole wedding venue, and I could use an ally around here."

"I don't fly. Don't be silly."

Rayne shook her head—a wasted action her mom couldn't see. "You haven't flown, which doesn't mean that you don't. These days they have really good medicine for anxiety to get you through the flight. You could sleep the whole way."

"No, thanks," her mother singsonged. "I have to run."

"Chicken! Lauren McGrath, think about it."

"You are the adventurer and the bold one. Love you!"

Her mom hung up, leaving Rayne with a dial tone. That woman. Maybe Lauren could channel her Susan Carter character to hop on the plane.

Margaritas, margaritas . . . Rayne dialed Officer Peters from her cell phone, since the number was stored there. No signal. She stood by the window. On the third try it connected but went to voice mail. Frustrated, Rayne left a message about Landon's social media post and how he liked to show off his Spanish-speaking skills. LA was less than 150 miles to the Mexican border. What if the BMW he'd left at the airport was a ruse and he'd driven to Mexico? With her dresses?

A knock sounded on the office door, interrupting her message. She quickly ended the call. "Come in!" Rayne left her lucky spot by the window and reached the desk as Cormac entered, followed by a man in a hard hat and a clipboard.

She checked the time on her phone, though she'd taken to wearing a watch as well, just in case her phone didn't work. Eleven thirty.

"Lady McGrath, I've escorted this gentleman around the grounds," Cormac said.

"Have a seat—both of you." Rayne gestured to two wooden chairs while she stood behind the desk.

"Nice to meet you. I'm Anders Carvel. You're a bit out in the fields here, so I understand why your signal isn't strong." He tapped the brim of his hard hat.

"I must have internet," Rayne said. She heard the sheer panic in her words and exhaled. Inhaled. "The calls drop. I can't get my laptop running for long. It's unacceptable for my business to not have access to the world."

Anders raised a hand. "We can get you set up with satellite."

"Yay!" Rayne clapped in relief.

Cormac looked dour. "Wait a minute, milady."

"What?" She pressed her fingertips together.

"They need to put a pole up in the field," Cormac said. "We have a beautiful landscape, and it will be ruined by technology. Not good for the new business idea we were discussing."

"A pole, sir. Not metal or anything unsightly," Anders told Cormac. "You can paint it or camouflage it." He turned to Rayne. "You'll hardly notice."

"Can't it be out"—she waved—"there, somewhere?"

"It needs to be close to give you signal," Anders said. "The walls of the castle are solid stone. Thick."

Rayne nodded. "It's a miracle whenever my cell phone works. I stand by the window in this room and have already gone through my high-speed data with my plan. It's now slow as a traffic jam during rush hour."

Anders peered over his clipboard at her. "Depending on the package you get, you can offer Wi-Fi extenders to folks in the village to improve their internet experience. Cormac said that everyone at the castle has a phone plan with data. You all will be able to connect to the satellite."

That sealed the deal for her. "We need to move ahead. Cormac, thank you for tackling this. Now, let's decide the least conspicuous place for it."

They went outside. Blarney joined her on the bottom step, and she gave her dog a pat.

Cormac's posture was perfect, but she could tell he was not a happy man. "He suggested the hilltop overlooking the lake. It's a bad idea."

"I agree," Rayne said. She turned to Anders. "We plan to create a wedding venue here on the castle grounds. We will be selling romance and maidens, history. Knights gallant, that kind of thing. Modern tech will definitely ruin the look we're going for."

"Ah," Anders said. "I understand."

Cormac relaxed a little.

"Good," Rayne said.

"My daughter just got engaged, so I'll have to let her know. We're in Kilkenny." Anders rubbed his chin, then turned around. "What about behind the barn?"

"That could work." Hidden from view of the house, anyway. "Cormac?"

"Aye. If we painted it to blend with the landscape," Cormac decided. "Let's check it out."

The trio—and Blarney—walked toward the barn and around the back. Rayne was quite proud of the new timber and stone.

She explained what had happened and how the villagers had pulled together.

"It's communal living at its best. This newness will fade with time," Anders said. "Or you could give everything a paint job, so it matches. There's rustic, and then there's maintained to appear rustic."

Rayne laughed at that. "I like that idea. You know anybody?"

Anders pulled a business card from his wallet. "I used this construction crew to help with a lake house."

Seemed the satellite business was a good one. "Thanks. So, what's the next step?"

"If you want to move forward, I can send out someone on Monday."

Rayne and Cormac exchanged a look, and he nodded, then she nodded. "See you Monday." Yeehaw!

Anders left, leaving her with Cormac. Amos drove by in the pickup, then parked in front of the barn. Something primal in her responded to his Viking shoulders and shaggy hair as he got out of the truck.

"Well? Will we be connected with the rest of the world?" Amos asked teasingly.

"We will, we will."

"That's great, Rayne. It's progress." Amos patted Blarney's head. "What is in your fur?" He plucked a flower bud from where it had gotten stuck in his collar. "Blarney wants to be fancy, like you."

She smiled. "This ol' thing?" It was one of her favorite outfits—wide-legged linen capris and a bright-pink top. She'd chosen her chunky heels in deference to all the walking.

"How's it going? I saw Ciara leave in a huff earlier."

"Money is a tough subject, on top of it being two weeks since . . . the tractor accident."

Cormac nodded. "Can I help?"

It was on the tip of her tongue to say no, but then she shrugged. "You might be the perfect person to help, actually. Do you use an accountant?"

With a proud smile, Cormac said, "I do our family's taxes. Simple enough. No need to pay out extra."

"I work for myself," Amos said. "Makes the accounts a wee bit more complicated."

"I learned to do my own accounts—Uncle Nevin's are a mess. He has a yearly budget, but I didn't see taxes."

Amos tucked a hand behind his back. "Nevin used the same woman I did."

"Who?"

"Daisy Hughes," Cormac replied. "Owen's wife."

Her heart thundered in her chest. Daisy's initials hadn't been on the paper. Owen's had. Made sense, if she was his accountant too—as she'd said that first day at his office. "Is Daisy from here?"

"No," Cormac said. "She's from Northern Ireland. They met online. You might have noticed the age difference."

"Not a big deal where I come from." She hurried toward the house with urgency. "Come with me, Cormac. You knew Uncle Nevin the best. The numbers might make sense to you."

Amos followed as well, and they entered the manor out of breath.

Neddy popped out from the kitchen, wiping his hands on a dish towel. "What's going on?"

"Did you use Daisy Hughes for an accountant?" Amos asked.

"No. Why?" He slung the towel over his shoulder.

"We're not sure yet," Rayne said. She didn't want to point fingers until she was positive. She'd been wrong about Lourdes and Freda. Blaming Dafydd was wishful thinking.

They raced down the hall to the office, and Amos shut the door behind them. Blarney watched them with big golden-brown eyes. The flower he'd brought and set at her feet suddenly made sense.

Not Freda—not even close. Rayne recalled Daisy with her pink toolbox, Daisy whose dad had wanted her to be a boy. She was handy at fixing things. Could she have tampered with the tractor's hydraulics somehow? Daisy had seen Nevin at Dr. Ruebens, so she had known something was up with his health.

Rayne's fingers shook as she tapped the ledger and the creased slip of paper that she'd unfolded. "Look here. Your initials weren't on them because you didn't use her for an accountant. Not Maeve, or Aine. Or Neddy."

She opened all five ledgers and used her phone as a calculator. After fifteen minutes, Rayne had a sick feeling. "The losses for the castle each year for the past five years are seven percent exactly. That's too precise to be a coincidence. Not a huge amount to take off the top, but consistent."

Blarney barked and raced around the trio as if to tell them it was about time they'd cracked the code.

Cormac's face paled and his body swayed. "Lord Nevin was very specific about inviting the Hugheses to dinner on June sixth. Sunday. He wouldn't say why, only that he hoped for it to be all right. What if he'd discovered that Daisy was skimming money?"

"It would be just like Nevin to confront the problem head-on," Amos said, a frown heavy on his brow. "I've never noticed a problem with my books. I'll have to go through them again."

Rayne studied Cormac, hoping for understanding. "Wouldn't he call the garda dude?"

"Nevin McGrath was the kind of man to offer her a way out. To make things right. What if Owen was in on it too?" Cormac's shoulders bowed.

The door banged open, and Rayne's pulse raced.

Ciara stood there, her hand on her hip. "What's going on? Neddy tore out of here in the pickup!"

Rayne shook her head. "Neddy? I don't know." He didn't use Daisy and wasn't on the list.

"What are you all doing with Da's accounts?" Ciara asked curiously. "I hope Cormac can help make sense of them."

"Did you use Daisy Hughes as an accountant?" Rayne asked.

"To file my taxes, aye." Ciara stepped into the office. "Why?"

Cormac sighed. "We think Daisy Hughes was possibly skimming from the accounts. Maybe Lord Nevin found out." He gestured to the ledger on the desk. "That's what these initials mean on the paper. He must have found out who else used her. That would be the euro symbol."

"No way." Ciara stumbled backward in shock.

Rayne caught her cousin, steadying her. "I think it's time to call the police."

"No feckin way!" Ciara shouted.

Chapter
Twenty-Seven

Rayne tried to calm her cousin down, but Ciara had no intention of calling the police and said so in colorful terms. "Garda Williams has been no help in this investigation. If anything, he's dragged things out! Why would he step up now?"

"He has rules and protocol to follow," Rayne said. "He told me that the hydraulic line was cut on the tractor."

"And what?" Ciara glared at Rayne. "You wanted to accuse Dafydd?"

"No!" A little. "What do you think we should do?"

"No thinking needed. I'm going to Daisy's right now." Ciara pushed away from Rayne, but Rayne held on to her cousin's shoulder.

"What about Neddy?" Amos asked. "Why would he leave in a hurry? Does he even know Daisy?"

"Neddy wasn't here that Thursday evening. His mum was sick," Cormac said.

"I'm going to confront Daisy," Ciara said. "About the accounts. If she's really stealing, she has to make things right. She might have been stealing from all of us!"

Ciara was headed out the door, and Rayne couldn't let her go alone. "You two call the police—I'm riding with Ciara." This was shouted, as her cousin was already out of the house and down the steps to the Fiat.

She wasn't surprised when Blarney jumped into the car with her. Her cousin stepped on the gas, dirt spinning behind them until the wheel caught traction.

The little car leaped forward.

Rayne braced her hand on the dash. Blarney whined, but his golden-brown eyes twinkled as if he was enjoying every minute. "What are we doing, cous?"

"Confronting Daisy to see if she was stealing from us. Or worse!"

They reached the end of the driveway and saw the pickup. It was banged against a tree, the engine smoking. Neddy was slumped over the wheel. "Should we stop?" Rayne said.

"No! Amos can help him. He shouldn't have been speeding in the first place. Why would Daisy steal?" Ciara's lower lip jutted. "She's got a cute house, a husband she will probably outlive, and a place in the community."

"*If* she did, I don't know why. We can ask her. Calmly."

"It was on that slip of paper that you figured out!"

It did seem plausible. "We thought other people were guilty, and they ended up being innocent. I'm just saying—we need to be calm about this. If you go in and demand answers, Daisy might shut you down."

"You need to stop being so damn California chill—this is our family we are talking about. Family!" Ciara shouted.

An older man crossed the street after they turned onto the main road, hand up in a two-finger greeting, and Ciara slammed on the brakes to avoid hitting him.

He cursed them out, the two-finger greeting now a V shape that Rayne understood meant something quite different. Another thing to add to her list.

"Sorry, Joe!" Ciara called. She slowed as they took the corner, narrowly avoiding two sheep.

"Slow down!" Rayne said, her stomach clenched. "Before you hurt someone!"

Ciara honked the horn and raced around the woolly beasts, hanging on to the steering wheel like a life preserver. "What if Daisy killed my da because he found out what she'd done? A few thousand euro skimmed from the budget was no reason for him to die."

"Agreed!" Rayne could totally understand wanting answers. Even the need to act. Her uncle murdered by a woman with a pink toolbox was hard to grasp. "Ciara, that's why we need to be calm and relaxed." She imagined Ciara physically threatening Daisy and the cops being called for harassment. "We don't have bail money!"

Ciara screeched the Fiat on two wheels around the block of the lawyer's office to the cute cottage and into the driveway. She parked, leaving the keys in the ignition.

"Wait! We need a plan!"

"Be quiet, Rayne. I want answers."

They got out of the car, Blarney at Rayne's heels. The cousins took a second to study the door. It was slightly ajar. How odd.

"I'm going in," Ciara said.

"No! Wait—see, it's already open!"

Too late. Ciara barged into Daisy and Owen's cottage. "Daisy?" Ciara called. "Get out here, now!"

Ciara went left to the kitchen. Blarney went right. Rayne kept her hand on his collar and stayed with the dog.

She heard a noise in the parlor and went inside the crowded room. Owen Hughes was tied to a dining room chair, the cuckoo from the clock in his mouth.

"Owen?"

He spit the cuckoo out and struggled against the restraints at his wrists. His legs were free. Tears flowed down his cheeks. "Hurry!"

Ciara came up behind her in a tornado of frenetic energy. "Where is your wife? Did you know? Did you?"

Blarney sniffed the cuckoo and dragged Rayne as he snuffled around the floor like a Roomba. She didn't release his collar.

"No." The older lawyer bowed his head. "Daisy was stealing. She wasn't supposed to hurt Nevin. He was my friend."

It was hard to feel sorry for the old geezer. He'd been duped just like many men by a pretty face. She'd hurt Nevin? Anger flamed hot and quick. "How?" Rayne pulled Blarney to her, and they backpedaled to the door.

"She disabled the tractor," Owen said. "Her da taught her everything. She's getting away!"

Fury simmered in Rayne. No more doubts about what had happened. Daisy had killed Uncle Nevin. "Where?"

"Out back," Owen cried. "She's hired a private plane to take her to London. I wanted to stop her from leaving. She attacked me when I tried to get out the front door to call for help."

That was the last match to the fire for Rayne, and she rushed out the back to the gorgeous garden just as Daisy was tossing her suitcase into the trunk of their sedan, focused on her escape. Rayne held Blarney's collar tight as the dog lunged forward.

She imagined Landon taking all of her money and escaping to a new life, just like Daisy wanted to do. As if the old one was so awful! No way could she let Daisy do the same thing.

"Stop!" Rayne shouted. She raised her voice and shouted again when Daisy ignored her. Blarney barked and strained against Rayne's hold.

"Last warning!" Rayne released all of the good-girl rules and channeled her inner wild child, slipping off one of her chunky pink heels.

Daisy turned with a *Screw you* grin.

Rayne imagined the shoe was a short shillelagh. The club was a weapon if used with that intent. She and Padraig had played with them as children at the castle. The heel hit Daisy square in the forehead.

The woman collapsed by the sedan as if boneless. Rayne freed Blarney, who sniffed Daisy's body and then stood guard with a bark of approval.

No pet psychic needed to interpret that.

Ciara, who was holding Owen with his arms behind his back, called, "Nice shot, princess." The pair joined her in watching Daisy.

"I don't understand," Rayne said, dragging in a breath. "How did she know we were onto her?"

"Daisy saw you talking to Doctor Ruebens and knew it was a matter of time," Owen said. "She was planning on leaving tomorrow, already packed, but Neddy overheard you and Ciara this morning getting close with the money. He warned her."

Neddy. Neddy would have been able to add the medicine to the whiskey. Traitor!

Ciara elbowed Owen. "They're together?"

Owen cried and nodded. "I didn't know. She's spent the morning crowing over all the ways she's made me a fool. Buying things we didn't have the money for. Nevin called me, and we were going to make it right."

Garda Williams came around the house, his baton at the ready. "Stand back." He made his way to Daisy. "Cormac brought me up to speed. Neddy is in custody, confessing to adding the heart medicine to Nevin's whiskey. He was supposed to meet up with Daisy at the plane, but she double-crossed him when he called to warn her."

Daisy groaned.

Owen collapsed to his knees and sobbed. "I'm so sorry for it all. Daisy, Daisy."

Another garda arrived.

"Can we go?" Ciara asked, stepping away from Owen.

"Straight to the castle," Garda Williams instructed. "I'll be by later to get your statement."

"It's over now," Rayne said, as they got into the Fiat.

"Aye, praise Jaysus and all the bleedin' saints." On the way home, Ciara patted Blarney and told Rayne, "Consider the dog a gift of the house."

Chapter
Twenty-Eight

Rayne dragged herself from bed when the alarm blared at six Friday morning. This was going to take some getting used to. Maybe they could trade the occasional weekend to sleep in.

Surely not *everybody* had to be up at the crack of dawn. It was no *craic*.

Blarney wagged his tail at her from his spot on the bed. They'd gotten a full night's sleep with Dafydd the not-ghost banished from the hall.

Would Ciara and Dafydd actually make it to the finish line for their wedding? "If it's true love, great. If not, well, Ciara could always make a move on Garda Williams," Rayne told her dog. The officer had been very informative last night.

Blarney barked.

"Is that a yes bark or a no?" Rayne didn't pursue the one-sided conversation and chose comfy yoga pants and a long-sleeved tee to wear for sewing in, as she needed to spend some time in her studio or there would be no progress. Progress equaled money.

She and Blarney hurried down the stairs. Ciara was already up, and there was no sign of Dafydd or Amos. Maeve was at the stove, manning the fry pan, and sausages sizzled. Aine let the dog out, and Cormac poured tea and coffee.

"We'll have to hire a cook," Cormac said. "Maeve can fill in, but once we have guests on the grounds, we'll need someone full time."

"Agreed." Rayne, still standing, added cream and sugar to her coffee.

"I'm in shock," Aine said, her voice tired. "Neddy worked here for four years. He was part of our family, I thought."

"I'm sorry." Rayne gave the younger woman a side hug and then sat at the table.

"He never had a mum to visit. Garda Williams said he just went to Cork to get away for a few days." Cormac's mouth pursed in disapproval. "He's from the coast. Not here." The butler slurped tea. "Neddy had access to the whiskey. As cook, he had the run of the kitchen and often poured his lordship's drink. It would be simple to add the heart medication. I thought about it all night—it must have been in the decanter in the dining room, and he would have done it that morning before he left."

"I was a little nauseous and tired, but I thought it was a reaction to Da's tractor accident," Ciara said. "You?"

Cormac pressed a hand to his belly. "I was tired, sure, but like you, I attributed it to the emotion at the time. I had to refill the decanter of whiskey that night, so it was all gone."

"Well, it's over now," Rayne said. "According to the garda, Daisy will go to jail for attempted murder. Poisoning Nevin was her plan, and she cut the line on the tractor so skillfully that it took a while to see the damage. She admitted to sneaking onto the property Wednesday night. She didn't want to give up her extra money from all of the accounts she had here in Grathton."

"What about Owen?" Aine asked.

"Owen's actions are being investigated as to what he knew and when. Neddy will also be put behind bars for murder, Garda Williams said. He planned to live the high life with Daisy in Costa Rica," Rayne explained. "It was a diabolical plan."

"Owen Hughes is a fool, but he didn't know what was going on until Lord Nevin called him and told him that Daisy was skimming from the accounts. Owen wanted to make things right, but Daisy had an exit strategy in mind—to take the cash and start over in Costa Rica," Cormac said. "With Neddy, but then at the end, she cut Neddy loose too."

Rayne hoped they would both be punished to the full extent of the law. Uncle Nevin was gone because of their actions. She sent a sad smile to Ciara. Her cousin had circles under her eyes.

"A cucumber compress might feel nice," Rayne said. And it would take away the puffiness.

"What do I care about compresses?" Ciara stirred honey into her tea. "Two people I trusted killed my father. The only positive thing about the tragedy is that now Da can be put to rest."

Maeve turned from the stove, spatula in hand. "I'll call Father Patrick today. Also, it's probably not a good idea to spread the word about Lord Nevin dying on the grass. And our chef being a poisoner."

Rayne reached for an apple in the fruit bowl, her tummy rumbling for breakfast. "It's not like we're selling the property, where we would have to disclose that kind of thing."

"Can you imagine?" Ciara shook her head. "Nobody would come to stay at the castle, and there goes our ten thousand euro a weekend."

"Actually," Rayne said, her mind spinning to make lemonade out of lemons, "a hint of a ghost might be just the thing.

We could charge more with the right story." She winked at her cousin. "Maybe we can hire Dafydd."

"Ha! He owes me for that one," Ciara said. She twirled her claddagh ring. "If you're serious, let me know."

"Can we talk about the wedding venue?" Aine asked. She tossed a red braid over her shoulder. "I want to think of happy things, not sad things."

"Sure!" Rayne wanted to encourage the young woman's enthusiasm. "What ideas do you have?"

"A horse-and-carriage ride through town." Aine sighed dreamily. "And swans. We need to get swans for the lake. It would be very romantic."

"Those things sound great to me." Rayne could sketch swans for an ad. Aine was right that they were romantic, though very disagreeable if someone got too close to them.

Ciara nabbed an apple and bit into it with a crunch. "Dafydd thinks the gazebo will take a week or so."

"I'll get my drawing to him today. Maeve, did you come up with a schedule so that we can reach our goal?"

The housekeeper turned from the stove and grinned, showing her gapped teeth. "One moment." Maeve opened the pantry door like Vanna White revealing a letter on *Wheel of Fortune*. Inside was a giant calendar with the next three months marked out.

"Wow!" Rayne rose from the table to study the calendar. To the right was a key with names color-coded to the job, date, and time. Each person had castle things to do in addition to farm property things.

"I've been running this place for decades," Maeve said, returning to the stove. She removed the patties to a towel to drain. Rayne was very glad it was the regular sausage. "We can have Father Patrick make an announcement at church on Sunday, explaining what we want to do. We should have a big meal here at the manor afterward. Whiskey for everyone, in Lord Nevin's honor."

"Excellent idea," Ciara said. "Rayne can meet Father Patrick then."

Sly, cousin, sly.

Cormac sliced the soda bread, and Ciara made room on the tabletop for the food. Eggs, sausage, bread, and fruit. Despite her changed eating habits, her clothes fit the same, and she attributed it to the stairs and walking the corridors. Aine topped off everyone's hot drinks, and Rayne retrieved the plates.

"Perfect. You've got it under control, Maeve. Point me in the right direction and I'll do my part. I also need to sew those wedding dresses. I would love it if Aine could be my assistant, but I hate to take her away from the plan."

"I want to help you! I'll ask Sorcha if she can fill in here at the castle for my duties while I learn to sew. If I can make it so you can put dresses together faster, then we can bring in more money." Aine raised her phone. "I was on the turret for your social media already this morning to share hints of a new big thing you're doing."

"Thank you!" Rayne thrived on creative energy. Just as she'd done with Modern Lace, before Landon had betrayed her.

"As of Monday, we won't need to climb the tower," Cormac said with a laugh. "Modernization, here we come."

Dafydd walked in through the side kitchen door, Blarney at his heels.

"Morning," he said. "Can I get a cup of coffee?"

"Sausage and eggs too," Maeve said. "You any good in the kitchen?"

"No. Not really." Dafydd shrugged and washed up at the sink. "My little sisters did the cooking. Richard might be decent.

I heard him talking with Beetle about some weird curry thing. Sounded like a foodie."

"That would certainly solve the Richard problem," Rayne said. "If he can step in as chef."

"He's a problem?" Aine asked.

"Not a problem." Rayne verbally backed up a step. "I'm just trying to find something he'd like to do here on the property in addition to the mill, which isn't needed all that often."

"Yeah. That's true." Aine narrowed her eyes. "We can ask him at dinner tonight, but I heard him tell his lordship that he could burn water."

Dafydd accepted the coffee from Cormac. "Ta. Well, it was a thought. Amos is on his way in the pickup. I worked on the engine this morning and got it running. That old truck is going to outlast all of us." He paused. "I was thinking that we could sell the tractor and get something smaller. More manageable."

Ciara rose and hugged him. How thoughtful to get rid of the tractor that had played a part in Uncle Nevin's demise. Maybe Dafydd would grow on her, Rayne thought.

Rayne smiled as Amos walked in, his broad shoulders filling the doorway. "Morning." She scooted over to make room for him to drag a chair from near the wall.

He sat.

"Coffee?" Cormac asked.

"Aye," Amos said. "So. I know a lady, around forty, newly widowed, that might be a decent candidate for a chef."

"To live in?" Cormac asked. "The room is small. Fine for a single man, but I'm not sure that a woman would find it spacious enough."

Ciara and Dafydd brought their chairs closer together. Blarney scooted around to her side.

"Could be," Amos said. "I was out at her neighbor's farm yesterday. He told me about her sad situation."

"Who?" Maeve asked, as if she knew everyone.

"In Cotter Village."

"Oh." Maeve served eggs and passed the plate of sausage.

"Frances Coplan." Amos looked around the table at them all, then stopped at Rayne. "Should I ask her to apply to be chef? I love Maeve here, but she has a limited repertoire."

Maeve laughed, as did Cormac and Aine. "I use the same cookbook, but the food doesn't taste quite as posh."

"Lord Nevin was smart to hire a chef. Neddy . . ." Amos shrugged. "Well, he didn't know how good he had it."

There was a murmur of agreement around the table.

Rayne's phone rang and she saw that it was her mother. Worry filled her. "It's eleven at night there—I have to take this."

She answered and walked out of the kitchen to the foyer. Someone had thrown away the flowers from Daisy and replaced them with pink roses that she recognized from the raised beds around the house.

"Mom? Are you all right?" Her mother's bedtime was never later than ten.

"I am! Honey—they found Landon."

The call dropped. Of course it did.

Rayne ran outside, Blarney with her, and called her mom back as soon as she had signal. "Could you repeat that?"

She hadn't told her new friends about Landon and being duped. She hoped to *never* share the news.

". . . Mexico. He's in custody. Officer Peters said you'd left a message? Well, it helped narrow the search. They got the rat! It's all over the news here in LA. It's not pretty, how he was found."

She sank to the landing's top stair. Sugar bear. Cinnamon sticks. Dang it. "What do you mean, Lauren?"

"There was an elaborate scheme, sweetheart. He never had an investor. You were a mark for him, and he's done it before. Twice that they know of for sure."

Rayne couldn't focus on just one thought, as her mind was a flurry of them. "I hope he goes to jail for a long time."

"You might need to come for court, the officer said."

"I can't leave Ireland." Rayne studied the blue skies.

"Your lawyer might be guilty of accessory to murder. I think you can find some wiggle room. Who would fight it, anyway? They're all on your side, hon."

"You have excellent points." It was nice to think she had an entire castle crew at her back.

"Landon hadn't sold all of the gowns yet—there are five left. I'm going to bring the dresses to you," her mom said. "Me and Jenn. September, okay? Right after filming ends."

Her mom, flying here? With Jenn? "Yes! That's really great. So proud of you!"

"To be honest, I asked the psychic about it, and she told me I'd died in a wreck in a past life and that I had to let go of my fears in this."

"Still, really brave."

"Have you told them, about Landon and what happened?"

"No." But Rayne had proved herself with her ideas for bringing in money to the castle. "If you can be brave, then I can too. I'm going back inside to confess that I'm not all that and a bag of Tayto chips." Er, crisps.

"You are! Keep your phone close—Officer Peters will call soon, I know. Love you!"

She loved her mother, who was facing her fears to help Rayne.

Rayne brushed her hands together. "All right, Blarney. Back inside to tell them I'm a fraud."

The dog nudged her fingers with his warm nose, wagging his tail with all his might.

She went into the kitchen. Dafydd and Ciara stole sweet looks and kisses. Amos smiled at her with his Viking grin.

Cormac and Maeve looked at her proudly, and Aine with stars in her eyes.

She cleared her throat and stood at the threshold, hands folded before her. "So. Full disclosure about my birthday."

They all swiveled to stare at her, perhaps sensing the change of mood.

"I thought I was going to get a new line for my gowns. That I'd impress investors with the hundred and fifty grand I had saved in the bank, all from my sales. I thought I was going to get engaged."

Amos's eye twitched. Ciara and Dafydd faced her full-on. Aine nodded encouragingly. Maeve and Cormac held hands.

"Instead, I woke up to find that Landon Short had taken me to the cleaners. My mom just called to tell me that they found him in Mexico, trying to sell my gowns."

"That's awful!" Maeve declared.

"Terrible!" Cormac seconded. "What a louse."

"I saw it on Instagram this morning," Aine confessed. "It was bleedin' brilliant. Landon tried to run but he was caught, wearing one of the wedding gowns and sling-back heels."

Rayne's mouth dropped. He'd never minded being her mannequin. She wore a women's size ten shoe, and he was a man's nine. It would be cramped but not impossible. "Landon? In my heels?"

"Not a winner, then?" Amos asked. His full lips twitched. Nobody seemed to be too angry with her.

"Not especially." Rayne sat back down. "No."

She braced for judgment or condemnation. She got empathy. "I didn't want to tell you because you all didn't know me. I was the American who stole Ciara's inheritance from her. Trust me, when I arrived, I thought I was going to get a painting as a bequest, not the whole castle."

"The dresses were found . . . what about the money?" Ciara asked. "It could help about now."

Rayne's cheeks heated with mortification. "The money is gone." Her stomach clenched. "I'm sure if Uncle Nevin knew what an idiot I'd been, he wouldn't have chosen me to head the castle."

"Oh no. Don't even think about backing out now. You agreed!" Ciara said. "No take-backs. You said you wanted to make a go of this *glorified manor with a turret*."

Rayne's skin dotted with goose bumps, and Blarney wagged his tail as he looked at her. It was like her dad was right there with them. "I'm not going anywhere. McGrath Castle will be the number one wedding venue in Ireland by this time next year."

Her heart was full, and she sat at the table, enjoying her breakfast. This was where she was supposed to be, and she couldn't wait to see what else being thirty would turn out to be.

Epilogue

O ver the next few days, Rayne learned the Irish folks loved a good funeral. They thrived on tragedy and spun the best stories. She knew more about her uncle than she'd ever wanted to know.

She wished her dad had been sent off in such a glorious way. As for Nevin, he wanted to be buried not in a church suit but in his saffron kilt. He and Cormac had discussed his funeral arrangements as something to be taken care of in the far, far future.

"Not so soon," Cormac said, his demeanor filled with sorrow. He'd brought the clothes from a cedar trunk in the storage upstairs and had laid the shirt and kilt on the bed. Blarney curled up on the floor on Nevin's side of the bed.

"This is what Da wanted?" Ciara traced the saffron kilt with the three green shamrocks down the side. Socks, brogues, a white shirt, and a green jacket. "You're sure? He'll look like a bleedin' leprechaun."

The suit would be a safer choice, but Rayne was a total fan of Uncle Nevin going out in style. "I love it."

"Aye. Here's the sporran." Cormac handed it to Rayne.

"What's this?" Rayne shook the leather pouch thing with a metal clasp. "A purse?"

"It's a pocket," Cormac said.

"Look inside!" Ciara urged. "Could be money."

Rayne felt a tiny bit strange opening the pocket that was totally a man purse. She peered inside and pulled out a manila envelope folded in thirds with *Ciara* written across it in neat penmanship. She smelled her uncle's spice cologne, and her skin prickled. The hair on her nape stood on end.

They were not alone in this room. "It has your name on it, Ciara."

Ciara stepped back and shook her head.

Rayne pressed it into her cousin's hand. Ciara accepted it as if it weighed fifty pounds, though it was just a regular envelope.

She walked next to her cousin to catch her if she tried to bolt. With Ciara, you never knew.

Ciara opened the flap.

Pulled out the documents.

Unfolded it.

She couldn't have gone any slower.

"What is it?" Rayne asked, her tone impatient. Blarney raised his ears and gave a *woof*.

"Adoption papers." Ciara fell back to the mattress with a whoosh, next to the kilt. Her gray eyes were as wide as nickels. "Signed. Da signed them."

"Ciara, that's wonderful."

"I'm a McGrath now."

Rayne hugged her tight. "You always were, cousin."

Uncle Nevin had given more than just the adoption papers— he'd gifted Ciara with family, and Rayne with her heritage.

Acknowledgments

Thank you, Tara Gavin, for seeing the potential in this story! Always thanks to Evan Marshall, best agent ever. And wow, first time I get to write a heartfelt thank-you to my husband, Christopher. ♥To my mother, Judi, and to Sheryl McGavin. Many, many thanks to the team at Crooked Lane.